CLIFF WALK

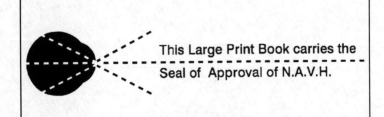

This Large Print Book carries the
Seal of Approval of N.A.V.H.

CLIFF WALK

BRUCE DESILVA

THORNDIKE PRESS
A part of Gale, Cengage Learning

GALE
CENGAGE Learning·

Detroit • New York • San Francisco • New Haven, Conn • Waterville, Maine • London

GALE
CENGAGE Learning·

Copyright © 2012 by Bruce DeSilva.
A Liam Mulligan Novel.
Thorndike Press, a part of Gale, Cengage Learning.

Thorndike Press® Large Print Crime Scene.
The text of this Large Print edition is unabridged.
Other aspects of the book may vary from the original edition.
Set in 16 pt. Plantin.

LIBRARY OF CONGRESS CATALOGING-IN-PUBLICATION DATA

DeSilva, Bruce.
    Cliff walk / by Bruce DeSilva.
       pages ; cm. — (Thorndike Press large print crime scene) (A Liam Mulligan novel)
       ISBN 978-1-4104-5066-1 (hardcover) — ISBN 1-4104-5066-X (hardcover)
    1. Journalists—Fiction. 2. Providence (R.I.)—Fiction. 3. Large type books.
    I. Title.
    PS3604.E7575C56 2012b
    813'.6—dc23   2012019215

Published in 2012 by arrangement with Tom Doherty Associates, LLC.

Printed in Mexico
1 2 3 4 5 6 7 16 15 14 13 12

For Patricia.
My lone regret is that
I didn't find you sooner.

AUTHOR'S NOTE

This is a work of fiction. Although some of the characters are named after old friends, they bear no resemblance to them. For example, the real Stephen Parisi is a Providence contractor, not a Rhode Island State Police captain. A handful of real people are mentioned; but only one of them — the poet Patricia Smith — has a speaking part, and she is permitted only a few words of dialogue. I also borrowed the colorful nickname of a former Rhode Island attorney general, but the fictional and real Attila the Nun are nothing alike and the character's actions and dialogue are entirely imaginary. References to Rhode Island history and geography are as accurate as I can make them, but I have played around a bit with time and space. For example, both the Newport Jumping Derby and Hopes, the newspaper bar where I drank decades ago when I reported the news for the *Providence*

Journal, are long gone, but I enjoyed resurrecting them for this story. Legal prostitution, a major plot element in this book, was in fact part of life in Rhode Island until 2010; but my depiction of how and why it was finally outlawed is entirely made-up.

1

Cosmo Scalici hollered over the grunts and squeals of three thousand hogs rooting in his muddy outdoor pens. "Right here's where I found it, poking outta this pile of garbage. Gave me the creeps, the way the fingers curled like it wanted me to come closer."

"What did you do?" I hollered back.

"Jumped the fence and tried to snatch it, but one of the sows beat me to it."

"Couldn't get it away from her?"

"You shittin' me? Ever try to wrestle lunch from a six-hundred-pound hog? I whacked her on the snout with a shovel my guys use to muck the pens. She didn't even blink."

To mask the stink, we puffed on cigars, his a Royal Jamaica, mine a Cohiba.

"Jesus, Mary, and Joseph," he said. "The nails were painted pink, and it was so small. The little girl that arm came from couldn'ta been more than nine years old. The sow just wolfed it down. You could hear the bones crunch in her teeth."

"Where's the hog now, Cosmo?"

"State cops shot her in the head, loaded her in a van, and took off. Said they was gonna open her stomach, see what's left of the evidence. I told 'em, that's two hundred and fifty bucks' worth of chops and bacon wholesale, so you damn well better send me a check 'less you want me to sue your ass."

"Any other body parts turn up?"

"The cops spent a couple hours raking through the garbage. Didn't find nothin'. If there was any more, it's all pig shit by now."

We kept smoking as we slopped across his twelve acres to the sprawling white farm house with green shutters where I'd left my car. Once this was woodland and meadow, typical of the countryside in the little town of Pascoag in Rhode Island's sleepy northwest corner. But Cosmo had bulldozed his whole place into an ugly mess of stumps, mud, and stones.

"How do you suppose the arm got here?" I asked.

"The staties kept asking the same question, like I'm supposed to fuckin' know."

He scowled as I scrawled the quote in my reporter's notebook.

"Look, Mulligan," he said. "My company?

10

Scalici Recycling? It's a three-mil-a-year operation. My twelve trucks collect garbage from schools, jails, and restaurants all over Rhode Island. That arm coulda been tossed in a Dumpster anywhere between Woonsocket and Westerly."

I knew it was true. Scalici Recycling was a fancy name for a company that picked up garbage so pigs could reprocess it into bacon, but there was big money in it. I'd written about the operation five years ago when the Mafia tried to muscle in. Cosmo drilled one hired thug through the temple with a bolt gun used to slaughter livestock and put another in a coma with his ham-size fists. He called it trash removal. The cops called it self-defense.

I'd parked my heap beside his new Ford pickup. Mine had a New England Patriots decal on the rear window. His had a bumper sticker that said: "If You Don't Like Manure, Move to the City."

"Getting along any better with the folks around here?" I asked as I jerked open my car door.

"Nah. They're still whining about the smell. Still complaining about the noise from the garbage trucks. That guy over there?" he said, pointing at a raised ranch across the road. "He's a real asshole. That

11

one down there? Total jerk. This whole area's zoned agricultural. They build their houses out here and want to pretend they're in fuckin' Newport? Fuck them and the minivans they rode in on."

2

A prowl car slipped behind me on America's Cup Avenue, and when I swung onto Thames Street, it hugged my bumper. A left turn onto Prospect Hill didn't shake it, so when I reached the red octagonal sign at the corner of Bellevue Avenue, I broke with local custom and came to a complete stop. Then I turned right, and the red flashers lit me up.

I rolled down the window and watched in the side mirror as a Newport city cop unfolded himself from the cruiser and swaggered toward me, the heels of his boots clicking on the pavement, his leather gun belt creaking. I shoved the paperwork at him before he asked for it. He snatched it without a word, walked back to the cruiser, and ran my license and registration. I listened in on my police scanner and was relieved to learn that my Rhode Island driver's license was valid and that the heap

I'd been driving for years had not been reported stolen.

I heard the gun belt creak again, and the cop, whose name tag identified him as Officer Phelps, was back, handing my paperwork through the window.

"May I ask what business you have in this neighborhood tonight, Mr. Mulligan?"

"No."

Ordinarily, I don't pick fights with lawmen packing high-powered sidearms. Anyone who'd covered cops and robbers as long as I had could recognize the .357 SIG Sauer on Officer Phelps's hip. But he'd had no legitimate reason to pull me over.

"Have you been drinking tonight, sir?"

"Not yet."

"May I have permission to search your vehicle?"

"Hell, no."

Officer Phelps dropped his right hand to the butt of his pistol and gave me a hard look.

"Please step out of the car, sir."

I did, affording him the opportunity to admire how fine I looked in a black Ralph Lauren tuxedo. He hesitated a moment, wondering if I might actually be somebody; but tuxedos can be rented, and a somebody would have had better wheels. I put my palms against the side of the car and as-sumed the position. He patted me down, sighing when he failed to turn up a crack pipe, lock picks, or a gravity knife.

When he was done, he wrote me up for running the sign I'd stopped at and admon-ished me to drive carefully. I was lucky he didn't shoot me. In this part of Newport, driving a car worth less than eighty thou-sand dollars was a capital offense.

I fired the ignition and rolled past the marble-and-terra-cotta dreams of nineteenth-century robber barons: The Breakers, Marble House, Rosecliff, King-scote, The Elms, Hunter House, Beech-wood, Ochre Court, Chepstow, Chateau-sur-Mer. And my favorite, Clarendon Court, where Claus von Bülow either did or did not try to murder his heiress wife by injecting her with insulin, depending on whether you believe the first jury or the second. Here, sculpted cherubs frolic in formal gardens. Greek gods cling to gilded cornices and peer across the Atlantic Ocean. Massive oak doors open at a touch, and vast dining rooms rise to frescoed ceilings. A few of these shrines to hubris and bad taste have been turned into museums, but the rest remain among the most exclusive addresses in the world, just as they have been for more than a hundred years.

Men who ripped fortunes from the grasps of competitors built the Newport mansions. Cornelius Vanderbilt, who stitched the face of America with rails and ties. Big Jim Fair, who dug silver out of Nevada's Comstock Lode. Edward J. Berwind, who fueled American industry with Appalachian coal. They were doers, and they built these forty-, sixty-, and eighty-room monstrosities as retreats, playgrounds, and monuments to themselves.

But that was generations ago. Today, those who live in the mansions are scions of the doers, living on somebody else's money in somebody else's dream. They try to keep the Gilded Age alive in a blaze of crystal chandeliers, the scent of lilies drifting over elegantly attired dinner guests. And they keep the likes of me out with ivy-covered walls, hand-wrought iron gates, and a vigilant local constabulary.

Except tonight. Tonight, I had an invitation.

Just past Beechwood, the Astors' Italianate summer cottage, I slid behind a shimmering silver Porsche in a line of cars drifting toward the gilded iron gate to the grounds of Belcourt Castle. One by one, they turned into the torch-lit, crushed-stone drive: a Maserati, a Bentley, a Ferrari, a Lamborghini, a Maybach, another Bentley, and something sleek that may have been a Bugatti, although I'd never seen one before. Trailing them was a poverty-stricken sad sack in a mere Mercedes-Benz. I wondered if Officer Phelps had hassled him, too.

Up ahead, liveried valets opened car doors, grasped bejeweled hands to help ladies from their fairy-tale carriages, climbed in, and floated away to distant parking lots. Then a nine-year-old Bronco with rust pocks on the hood, a crushed passenger-side fender, and a diseased muffler rumbled up, and I got out.

"Be careful with it this time," I said as I flipped the keys to a valet. "Look what happened the last time you parked it."

I strolled through the courtyard to a heavy oak door where an emperor penguin with a clipboard was checking the guest list. He studied my engraved invitation and scowled.

"Surely you are not Mrs. Emma Shaw of the *Providence Dispatch.*"

"What gave me away?"

"Do this job as long as I have," he said, "and you develop a sixth sense about this sort of thing." He looked me up and down. "I can see that your eyebrows haven't been plucked lately." He paused to rub his chin

17

with his big left wing. "And your perfume is a little off. The last dame to walk through here was wearing Shalimar. You smell like Eau d'Cigars."

"You don't know any women who smoke cigars?"

"Not the kind made out of tobacco," he said. From his snicker, I could tell he took special pride in that one. "I'm sorry, sir, but I can't admit you."

"Oh yeah? Well, this isn't the only mansion in town, buster." I turned away to retrieve Secretariat, my pet name for the Bronco.

I'd drawn the assignment to cover the annual Derby Ball after Emma, our society reporter, quit last week, taking a buyout that trimmed thirty more jobs from a newsroom already cut to the marrow by last year's layoffs. Ed Lomax, the city editor, had pretended he was doing me a favor.

"I can guarantee you the cover of the 'Living' section," he said.

"Let me get this straight," I said. "We can no longer afford to have our baseball writer travel with the Red Sox. We don't have a medical writer or a religion writer anymore. Our Washington bureau is down to one reporter. And *this* is a priority?"

"The ball is the final event of the week

long Newport Jumping Derby," he said. "It's one of the biggest hoity-toity events of the year."

"So they say, but who gives a shit?"

"Other than the horses?"

"I'm a little busy with *real* stories right now, boss. I'm trolling through the governor's campaign contribution list to figure out who's buying him off *this* year. I'm looking into the toxic waste dumping in Briggs Marsh. And I'm still trying to figure out how that little girl's arm ended up as pig food last week."

"Look, Mulligan. Sometimes you have to do things you don't want to do. It's part of being a professional."

"And I have to do this particular thing because . . . ?"

"Because the publisher's seventeen-year-old niece is one of the equestrians."

"Aw, crap."

But if I couldn't get in, I couldn't be blamed for not covering it. Lomax didn't need to hear how readily I took no for an answer. I'd almost made it out of the courtyard when I heard high heels clicking behind me and a woman's voice calling my name. I quickened my pace. I was asking a valet where I could find my car when the high heels clattered to a stop beside me and their owner, a tiny middle-aged woman who'd had one face-lift too many, took me by the arm.

"I am *so* sorry for the confusion, Mr. Mulligan. Your Mr. Lomax called to say you would be taking Mrs. Shaw's place, and I neglected to amend the guest list."

"And you are . . . ?"

"Hillary Proctor, but you can call me 'Hill.' I'm the publicity director for the Derby, and I am honored that you are joining us this evening. I do hope my lapse hasn't caused you any embarrassment."

Aw, crap.

"Look, Hill," I said as she escorted me past the shrugging penguin and into the mansion's antechamber, "I'm supposed to write about the important people who are here and describe what they are wearing, but I can't tell the difference between a Vanderbilt draped in a Paris original and a trailer park queen dressed by J. C. Penney."

"Of course you can't. You're the young man who writes about mobsters and crooked politicians. I *love* your work, darling."

"So you're the one," I said.

"Oh, I do love a man with a sense of humor. How would you like to be my escort for the evening? I'll whisper the names of

20

the worthies and what they are wearing in your ear, and the gossips will be all atwitter about the mysterious man on my arm."

"That's a very gracious offer, Hill, but I like to work alone. Do you think you could just jot everything down while I wander around and soak up a little color?"

"Certainly," she said, not looking the least bit disappointed.

I handed her my notebook, strolled across the antechamber, and stepped into a huge dining room with a mosaic pink marble floor and a wall of stained glass windows that bristled with Christian iconography. Men in tuxedos and women in ball gowns were loading china plates with shrimp, roast beef, and several dishes I couldn't identify, all of it tastefully displayed on a sixteen-foot-long walnut trestle table. The room was illuminated by nine crystal chandeliers. The grande dame who owned the house liked to boast that the largest of them had once graced the parlor of an eighteenth-century Russian count. The hunky plumber she had impetuously married and then divorced tattled that it had actually been scavenged from a dilapidated movie house in Worcester, Massachusetts. I made a mental note to include that tidbit of Newport lore in my story.

The *Dispatch*'s ethics policy prohibited reporters from accepting freebies, but the roast beef looked too good to pass up. I scarfed some down and then followed the sound of music up a winding oak staircase to the second floor. There, four chandeliers blazed from a vaulted cream-colored ceiling that arched thirty feet above a parquet ballroom floor. A fireplace, its limestone-and-marble chimneypiece carved to resemble a French château, commanded one end of the room. The hearth was big enough to roast a stegosaurus or cremate the New England Patriots' offensive line. At the other end of the room, a band I wasn't hip enough to recognize played hip-hop music I wasn't tone-deaf enough to like.

I snatched a flute of champagne from a circulating waiter and circumnavigated the dance floor, spotting the mayors of Newport, Providence, New Haven, and Boston; the governors of Rhode Island, Connecticut, Vermont, Kentucky, and New Jersey; one of Rhode Island's U.S. senators; both of its congressmen; three bank presidents; four Brown University deans; twelve captains of industry; two Kennedys; a Bush; and a herd of athletic-looking young women.

I found a spot against the wall between a couple of suits of armor and watched the mayor of Boston try to dance the Soulja Boy with a teenage girl whose last name might have been Du Pont or Firestone. When a waiter glided by, I nabbed another flute, but it just made me thirsty for a Killian's at the White Horse Tavern. After observing the festivities for a half hour, I figured I'd seen enough.

I was looking for Hill so I could retrieve my notebook when I spotted Salvatore Maniella. He was leaning against a corner of the huge chimneypiece, as out of place as Mel Gibson at a seder. What was a creep like him doing at a swanky event like this? I was still lurking a few minutes later when our governor strolled up and tapped him on the shoulder. They crossed the ballroom together and slipped into a room behind the bandstand. I gave them twenty seconds and then followed.

Through the half-open door I could make out red flocked wallpaper, a G clef design in gold leaf on the ceiling, and a grand piano — the mansion's music room, which the current owner had proudly restored to its original garishness. Maniella and the governor had the room to themselves, but they stood close, whispering conspiratorially in each other's ears. After a moment, they grinned and shook hands.

I slipped away as they turned toward the door.

3

In the morning, I ordered a large coffee and an Egg McMuffin at the McDonald's on West Main Road in Newport, took a seat by the window, and opened my laptop to check the headlines. I'd have preferred to hold a newspaper in my hands, but the *Dispatch,* in another cost-cutting move, had stopped delivering down here.

A federal judge had dismissed the labor racketeering indictment against our local Mob boss, Giuseppe Arena, because of prosecutorial misconduct. Someone had taken a potshot at the medical director of Rhode Island Planned Parenthood, the rifle slug crashing through her kitchen window and burying itself in her refrigerator. A pair of loan sharks, Jimmy Finazzo and his baby brother, Dominick, had been arrested for executing a deadbeat in their Cadillac Coupe de Ville while they were being tailed — and videotaped — by the state police.

The video was already on YouTube. And the coach of the Boston Celtics, who were training at Newport's Salve Regina University, announced he'd canceled a team tour of the Newport mansions after realizing most of his players owned bigger houses.

My story on the Derby Ball was on the paper's Web site, too. I'd pecked it out late last night at the White Horse, making liberal use of the names and gown descriptions Hill had jotted in my notebook. Sue Wong, Adrianna Papell, and Darius Cordell, I'd proclaimed, were the hot designers this season. I had no idea who they were, but I figured Hill could be trusted. Three Killian's later, I'd checked myself into a Motel 6, the cheapest bed to be found in Newport, and filed the story over the landline.

After breakfast with Ronald McDonald and the Hamburglar, I slid Buddy Guy's *Heavy Love* into the CD player and pointed the Bronco back toward Providence. I was halfway across the Jamestown Verrazzano Bridge, named for an Italian navigator who explored Narragansett Bay in 1524, when Don Henley interrupted some great blues with his thin tenor:

"I make my living off the evening news" — the ringtone that signaled a call from Lomax.

"Mulligan."

"On the way back?"

"Be there in less than an hour."

"Step on it. Obits are piling up, and I need you to cover a press conference at the health department at noon."

Aw, crap.

"Good job last night, by the way. I had no idea you knew so much about fashion."

"Yeah. I'm full of surprises."

I flipped the cell closed and let up on the gas. Knowing what was waiting for me, I was in no rush to get back to the newsroom. I set fire to a Partagás with my lighter, cruised north on Route 4, and let my mind wander back to last night.

Salvatore Maniella. He'd gotten his start in the sex business in the mid-1960s when he was an accounting student at Bryant College, talking coeds out of their clothes, snapping their pictures, and publishing them in his own amateur skin magazine. Today he was said to control 15 percent of the porn sites on the Internet, although no one could say for sure. According to some experts, Internet porn is a ninety-seven-billion-dollar-a-year business worldwide — bigger than Microsoft, Apple, Google, eBay, Yahoo!, Amazon, and Netflix combined. Chances were Sal didn't have to rent *his* tux by the day.

Sal had also broken into the brothel business in the 1990s after a clever lawyer actually read the state's antiprostitution law and discovered it defined the offense as streetwalking. That, the lawyer argued, meant sex for pay was legal in Rhode Island as long as the transaction occurred indoors. When the courts agreed, entrepreneurs leaped through the loophole, opening a string of gentlemen's clubs where strippers peddled blow jobs between pole dances. Maniella owned three of them, but the clubs were never more than a footnote to his pornography empire.

I was rolling slowly through North Kingstown and thinking about Sal when my police scanner started squawking. Both the Newport cops and the Rhode Island State Police were worked up about something. When I caught the gist, I turned around and floored it back to Newport.

In the harsh light of morning, Belcourt Castle wasn't as elegant as it had appeared the night before. The concrete cherubs and Grecian urns in the formal garden were crumbling from decades of acid rain and hard New England winters. Chocolate brown paint was peeling from window sashes. The side yard was a jumble of broken marble columns, refuse from restoration projects that had been started and then abandoned. Slate shingles that had tumbled from the roof littered the grass. I parked in the deserted drive and fetched my Nikon digital camera from the back. Don Henley started yowling again, but I let the call go to voice mail as I trotted through the mansion grounds toward the sea.

Newport's famous Cliff Walk is just what it sounds like. It skirts a rocky, guano-slick precipice that tumbles seventy feet to the mean high-tide line and another thirty feet or so to the shallow floor of the bay. From hoi polloi Easton's Beach in the north to exclusive Bailey's Beach in the south, the walk is a three-and-a-half-mile public right of way, much to the dismay of mansion owners who are compelled to share the spectacular ocean views with the rest of us. Occasionally, the patricians express their displeasure by trucking in boulders to block the path.

For much of its length, the walk is smoothly paved, and in places there is a guardrail; but those who press on past the Vanderbilt Tea House must negotiate crumbling paving stones, scramble between boulders, and maintain footing on slippery shelves of granite and schist. The late Claiborne Pell, a Newport aristocrat who represented the state in the U.S. Senate for thirty-six years, took a tumble here once while jogging and was fortunate he didn't go over the edge. The careless, the drunken, and the just plain unlucky fall with some regularity, and from time to time one of them gets killed. Judging by the chatter I'd overheard on the police radio, this was one of those times.

As I approached the Cliff Walk, the press was already swarming. Three bored Newport uniforms, arms folded across their chests, had the entrance blocked with yellow crime scene tape. Logan Bedford, a reporter for Channel 10 in Providence, was using them as a backdrop for one of his I'm-not-sure-what's-going-on-here-but-I-have-great-teeth stand-ups.

I swerved south, trespassed across forty yards of very private property, scaled a fence, fought through a tangle of dense brush, and emerged on a slab of rock overlooking the sea. Below, a dozen sailboats tacked in the light morning breeze. Above, a state police helicopter hovered. About thirty yards to the north, a uniformed Newport cop was waving his arms at a pair of tourists, ordering them to turn around and go back the way they had come.

Seagulls had strafed here, and the footing was treacherous. My cell played Lomax's ringtone again, but I ignored it. I crept as close to the edge as I dared, raised my Nikon, and studied the scene through the 135mm lens.

A body, its arms and legs splayed like a starfish, sprawled face up on a partially submerged, blood-spattered boulder. Three men in plain clothes — I figured them for two detectives and a medical examiner — were squatting beside it, one taking photographs and the others collecting bits of evidence and dropping them into clear plastic bags. The ropes they'd used to rappel down still dangled from the cliff. The tide was coming in, waves tossing foam on the investigators' trousers. In a few minutes, the scene would be underwater.

I snapped some photos, hoping for one or two usable shots. A real photographer would have done better, but as usual I didn't have one handy. Our photo department had been depleted by layoffs.

A couple of uniformed state troopers lowered a steel basket down the cliff face. As the detectives lifted the body and strapped it into the basket, I could see that the victim was dressed in a tuxedo. I took a few more pictures, but the Newport uniform who'd been shooing the tourists was heading my way now, his boots clicking on the stone path.

"Good morning, Officer Phelps."

He threw me a puzzled look, then nodded in recognition.

"Mulligan, right? From last night?"

"The same."

"You press?"

"Right again."

"Why didn't you tell me that when I pulled you over?"

"Would it have made a difference?"

"Ahhh . . . guess not."

We stood quietly for a moment, looking out over the sea. Phelps pulled a granola bar from his pocket, tore the shiny green wrapper, and took a small bite.

"Beautiful place to die," he said.

"That it is. Maybe that's why people come here to jump."

"This guy was no jumper."

"No?"

"Didn't fall, either," he said.

"And you know that because . . . ?"

"I could tell right off," he said, "just from the position of the body."

"Because he never tried to break his fall," I said.

"You noticed that, too, huh?"

"Yeah. It's a natural reaction. Even suicides usually do it. This guy just went over backwards and landed on his spine."

"There's some other stuff that seems suspicious, too," he said.

"Like?"

"Like the through-and-through bullet wound to his throat."

That explained the state police. They wouldn't have shown up for a jumper.

Phelps broke a crumb from his granola bar and tossed it into the air. A gull swooped in, snatched it, and dived toward the surf.

"I suppose that just encourages them," he said.

"Hey, everybody needs a little encouragement."

"Yeah? Well, the state cops said I should encourage *you* to stop taking pictures."

"That right?"

"Uh-huh. Also said to confiscate your camera."

"And?"

"And fuck them," he said. "They strut in here, bigfoot our case, treat us like errand boys. If they want your camera, they can come get it themselves. Far as I'm concerned, take all the pictures you want."

"Got an ID yet?"

"We're off the record, right?"

"Sure."

"The state cops ain't big on sharing, but from what I overheard, there was no identification on the body."

"Who found it?"

"Couple of early morning joggers spotted it and called 911."

"Anything else you can tell me?"

"Yeah, but it don't make no sense," he said. "The staties keep mumbling about salmonella. Seem pretty excited about it. What the hell does food poisoning have to do with anything? This dude got shot."

"Salmonella? You're sure that's what they said?"

"What it sounded like."

"Dirty Laundry" started playing again. I pulled the cell from my jacket pocket, told Phelps I had to take the call, and strolled out of earshot down the Cliff Walk.

"Mulligan."

"Been trying to reach you for an hour," Lomax said. "Why the hell aren't you answering the phone?"

"I've been a little busy."

"Listen, I need you to get your ass back to Newport. There's chatter on the state police radio, something about a body at the bottom of the Cliff Walk."

"Already on it," I said.

"And?"

"Guy in a tuxedo got shot and went over the edge."

"ID?"

"None on the body, but the state cops seem to think it's Sal Maniella."

"Holy shit!"

"Yeah."

"So Salmonella finally got what he deserved," Lomax said.

"Looks that way."

"ID good enough to go with?"

"Not even close. I got it secondhand from a Newport cop who eavesdropped on the staties and thought they were talking about food poisoning."

"Okay, but stay on it," Lomax said, "and for chrissake stay in touch."

4

Next morning I took the elevator to the *Dispatch*'s third-floor newsroom and tiptoed through a graveyard. By the windows that looked out on Fountain Street, a couple of technicians were dismantling Dell desktops. I could still picture Celeste Doaks, the bespectacled religion writer, hunched over one of those keyboards, cringing as Ted Anthony, the overweight medical writer, passed gas from his latest burrito. Malcolm Ritter, so damned good he had *me* understanding science, was always hidden behind a tower of books that couldn't muffle his asthmatic sniffs. Sometimes Mary Rajkumar, the travel babe, breezed in on her way to or from someplace exotic, reminding them that there was a life outside the newsroom. But none of them wanted to be anywhere else. Now two bored techs were pulling the plugs on their life's work.

I logged on to my computer and was skimming my messages when I sensed someone hovering. Whoever it was waited patiently, hesitant to intrude on my work. Someone genteel, then, and well mannered. Had to be the publisher's son. Anyone else would have had the sense to butt in. If I ignored him, maybe he would go away. I finished with my messages and reached for the phone.

"Excuse me, Mulligan. May I have a word?"

Aw, crap. "What is it now, Thanks-Dad?"

"I'd prefer that you stop calling me that. My name is Edward."

"So file a grievance."

"I just wanted to tell you that your Cliff Walk photographs were excellent."

"No, they weren't. Only good thing about them was that they were in focus."

"Well, *I* liked them."

"Maybe if your daddy hadn't laid off most of the photo staff, we could have had some professional pictures to go with the story."

He sighed. "It's not like he had a choice, you know."

Edward Anthony Mason IV was Rhode Island aristocracy, the scion of six inbred Yankee families that had owned the *Dispatch* since the Civil War. A year and a half ago, he'd been awarded a master's degree in journalism from Columbia, returned to Rhode Island, and moved back into the oceanfront Newport McMansion where he'd been raised. He'd been working as a reporter here ever since, learning the business that would soon be his by birthright. By the look of things, there wouldn't be much left of it by the time his daddy relinquished the corner office on the fourth floor. Given the size of Mason's trust fund, I wasn't about to start praying for him. In fact, I wanted to hate his privileged ass. But I didn't.

Mason had taken to hanging around me, eager to learn the things about street reporting that they didn't teach at Columbia — which was just about everything. Sometimes he got underfoot, but he *was* starting to pick up a few things.

"My father," Mason was saying, "deeply regrets the recent staff reductions, but they were necessary to preserve the financial health of our family newspaper."

"Yeah? Well, it's not working. The *Dispatch* is circling the drain."

"Perhaps, but it's hardly Father's fault. Every newspaper is having difficulties."

"Of course they are," I said, "and do you want to know why?"

"I'd welcome your opinion on the subject."

"Because they are run by idiots."

"A bit harsh, don't you think?"

"No, I don't."

"Newspapers have fallen victim to forces that are beyond their control," Mason said.

"Bullshit," I said. "When the Internet first got rolling, newspapers were *the* experts on reporting the news and selling classified advertising. They were ideally positioned to dominate the new medium. Instead, they sat around with their thumbs up their asses while upstarts like Google, the *Drudge Report,* the *Huffington Post,* and ESPN.com lured away their audience and newcomers like Craigslist, eBay, and AutoTrader.com stole their advertising business. By the time newspapers finally figured out what was happening and tried to make a go of it online, it was too late."

Mason stroked his chin, thinking it over.

"People like your daddy forgot what business they were in," I said. "They thought they were in the newspaper business, but they were really in the news and advertising business. It's a classic mistake — the same one the railroads made in the 1950s when the interstate highway system was being built. If Penn Central had understood it was in the freight business instead of the railroad business, it would be the biggest trucking company in the country today."

"A provocative analysis," Mason said. "Perhaps you might expand it into an op-ed piece."

"Already did. Your daddy declined to print it."

"Maybe if I had a word with him . . ."

"Don't bother," I said. "Writing about it isn't gonna change anything. What's done is done, and now thousands of journalists who devoted their lives to reporting the news are paying the price."

Mason fell silent for a moment, then said, "Did you know this is Mark Hanlon's last day?"

"Uh-huh."

"He doesn't want us to make a fuss."

"So he told me."

"Doesn't seem right."

"It's the way he wants it, Thanks-Dad."

"Lomax says he's the best feature writer the *Dispatch* ever had."

"Without a doubt."

Earlier this week, while perusing the obituary page, Hanlon noticed that the death of a seventy-seven-year-old Pawtucket woman had been given only three lines. It was the shortest obit he'd ever seen in the

Dispatch, and it offended him. So he talked to her only son, found the friends she worshipped with at St. Teresa's, tracked down people she once made G.I. Joes with on the assembly line at Hasbro, and wrote a story that celebrated her life. The lead was typical of his elegant, unadorned style: "This is Mary O'Keefe's second obituary." It was his final story for the *Dispatch.*

I stood and looked toward his cubicle near the city desk. He was still there, going through drawers and placing a few personal items in a shoebox. At fifty-four years old, he'd reluctantly accepted the paper's early retirement offer, knowing it was better than the alternative. I watched as he pushed back from the desk, rose on long, storklike legs, and shrugged on his denim jacket. Then he turned in a slow circle, looking the place over one last time.

Mason began to clap, the sound like gunshots in the cavernous space, and my opinion of him ticked up a notch. Lomax looked up from his computer screen, annoyed by the racket. Then he realized what was happening, pushed himself up from his fake leather throne, and joined in. One by one, throughout the football field–size newsroom, the survivors of the latest blood-letting got to their feet for a standing ovation. Marshall Pemberton, our fish-faced managing editor, rarely ventured from his glass-walled office that resembled an aquarium, but for this he made an exception. He waddled out of his door to join the tribute.

Hanlon lowered his head, tucked the cardboard box under his left arm, and trudged to the elevator. He stepped in, and the door slid shut behind him. He never once looked back.

Pemberton shook his head sadly, slipped back into the aquarium, and closed the door behind him. Once, he had managed the news department at one of the finest small-city newspapers in America. Now he was like a physician trying to keep his patient alive while the family debated whether to pull the plug.

5

Attila the Nun thunked her can of Bud on the cracked Formica tabletop, stuck a Marlboro in her mouth, sucked in a lungful, and said: "Fuck this shit."

"My sentiments exactly," I said.

"It's what, a week now? And the state police *still* can't ID the body? What is this, a *Naked Gun* sequel?" She paused to gulp more Bud. "Who's running this investigation, Frank Drebin?"

"Far as I know, it's still Captain Parisi," I said. "Think he might be stonewalling you?"

She hit me with a steely glare. "He wouldn't fucking dare."

Attila the Nun's real name was Fiona Mc-Nerney, but a *Dispatch* headline writer had bestowed the nickname on her, and it stuck. She was a member of the Little Sisters of the Poor religious order. She was also the Rhode Island attorney general. Both roles called for a more discreet vocabulary, but

43

she was always herself around me. We'd been friends since junior high. Over the years, the smiling kid with braces and a sprinkling of freckles across her nose had turned gruff and gray. Cigarettes and a holy determination that damned delicacy had graced her with a growl that rivaled John Lee Hooker's. Her red hair was chopped short like a boy's, and she never bothered with makeup. God wasn't the kind of husband who needed a trophy wife to boost his ego.

"So what's the holdup?" I said.

"Parisi says Salmonella's wife and daughter are both out of the country. He's not sure where and doesn't know when they're coming back."

"Makes sense," I said. "I've been checking their place in Greenville every few days. It's always dark and locked down tight. No one else can identify the body?"

"Apparently not. None of his dirt bag flunkies will even talk to a cop, let alone make an official ID."

"What about unofficially?"

"Unofficially, yeah, it's him — right down to the Navy SEALs tattoo on his right arm."

"Maniella was in the SEALs?"

"He was," she said. "He enlisted right after college. Ended up getting shipped to

South Vietnam, where the SEALs worked with the CIA in something called the Phoenix Program."

"What was that?"

"Code for hunting down Viet Cong sympathizers and slashing their throats."

I looked at my hands and thought about that for a moment. I hadn't realized Maniella had been such a tough guy — or that he'd served his country before stuffing his servers with smut.

"The ID sounds kinda tentative," I said.

"Best I can do, Mulligan. Maniella was so secretive about everything that our crack detective unit can't even find out who did his dental work. And he's never been arrested, so his prints aren't in the system."

"How about the navy?" I asked. "They should have his prints on file."

"So far, they aren't cooperating."

"Why the hell not?"

"No idea."

We both thought about that, but it didn't get us anywhere.

"What's happening with Scalici's pig?" I asked. "Frank Drebin and *Police Squad!* making any progress on that?"

"I think Lieutenant Jim Dangle and the misfits from *Reno 911!* are working that one," she said.

"Nothing, then?"

"The medical examiner found a couple of intact fingers in the pig's stomach. The crime lab pulled prints off them, but they don't match anything on file."

That figured. Groups like the Polly Klaas Foundation and Safety Kids had been urging parents to fingerprint their kids in case they ever went missing, but few people ever got around to it.

"If you use any of this, don't attribute it to me," Fiona said. "Just say it's from a source close to the investigation."

She took another pull from her beer. I sipped from my tumbler of club soda. I was jonesing for a Killian's, but my ulcer was grumbling.

Hopes hadn't changed much in the twenty-five years since Fiona and I started coming here with fake IDs to get blitzed on cheap draft beer. Same scarred mahogany bar. Same teetering chrome barstools and battered Formica-top tables. Same jukebox crammed with blind black men and fat black women singing the blues. The clientele consisted mostly of street hustlers, loan sharks, bookmakers, ambulance chasers, bail bondsmen, Providence cops, and firemen. *Dispatch* reporters and copy editors, too, although not nearly as many as there used to be. My favorite poet, a hot black babe who grew up on the West Side of Chicago, has a line about places like this:

When a woman rips a man open, this is where he comes to bleed.

Now that Fiona was the attorney general, she could afford better, but she still chose to drink here. Maybe it was the vow of poverty.

Sitting across the table from her, I felt good to be back on a real story again. Lately, I'd been getting stuck with a lot of routine assignments — duller-than-dirt stories that used to be handled by reporters who were now collecting unemployment checks. "Get used to it," Lomax kept telling me. "Unless we can figure out a way to blow up the Internet, it's only gonna get worse." The last week had been a nightmare of weather stories, obituaries, traffic accidents, and Providence planning commission meetings. Almost made me long for the Derby Ball.

"Salmonella's been grooming his daughter to take over the family business, so his murder won't change much," Fiona was saying. "The Maniellas have more money than God, and they know how to spread it around. The way I hear it, they own the governor, most of the superior court justices, and half the state legislature."

"Only half?"

"Half is all they need."

Fiona got elected last November after turning her campaign into a crusade to outlaw prostitution. Not everyone agreed with her. It was a close election. Since then, she'd made a lot of fiery speeches about the shame of Rhode Island — the only place in the country, outside of a few counties in Nevada, where sex for pay was legal. So far, she hadn't made any headway in persuading the state legislature to close the loophole. She figured the fix was in.

"I've been combing the campaign contribution lists for the governor and legislative committee chairmen," I said, "but I don't see any sign of it."

"And you won't," she said. "Salmonella conceals his campaign contributions by giving each of his porn actors five thousand dollars a year in cash and having them write personal checks to the politicians of his choice."

"How many actors are we talking about?"

"A hundred. Maybe more."

"And we don't know who they are," I said.

"No," she said. "Not unless their mothers

actually gave them names like Hugh Mungus and Lucy Bangs."

"How'd you hear about this?"

"Can't say, but my informant is reliable."

"Good enough to make a case?"

"No."

"With the millions Maniella makes selling virtual sex, why would he still care about a few Rhode Island brothels?"

"Maybe he's one of those guys who can never have enough money."

I wasn't much bothered by the Maniellas' prostitution business. The way I saw it, women could do whatever they wanted with their bodies, and men could do whatever they wanted with their money. But it bothered me a whole lot that the state government was for sale.

"I'll keep digging," I said. "If I can prove the Maniellas are doing what you say they are, it's a hell of a big corruption story."

"Good."

"But I gotta tell you, prostitution seems like a victimless crime to me," I said, and immediately regretted it.

"Tell that to the johns' wives when they come down with gonorrhea or HIV," Fiona said. "It's a filthy business. It exploits women, it enriches vile people like the Maniellas, and it's an ugly blot on the reputation of our state." Her tone did not invite further discussion.

She took a swig from her beer and added, "I just hope I can hang on to this job long enough to do something about it."

Back in 1980, when a fiery Jesuit priest named Robert Drinan was a Democratic congressman from Massachusetts, Pope John Paul II ordered priests and nuns to shun electoral politics. Now, thirty years later, it was still church policy. Fiona had chosen to ignore it.

"Better hurry," I said, "if you want to get the job done before the thunderbolt strikes from Rome."

"I'm hoping the Holy Father will understand that I'm doing the Lord's bidding."

"What's the bishop telling you?"

"That if I don't resign from public office, I could get excommunicated."

"Jesus, Fiona!"

"Don't take our Lord's name in vain in my presence, asshole."

She took another drag on her cigarette and brushed away the ash that fell on her jeans. Last year, the state legislature had finally gotten around to banning smoking in public accommodations. Nobody drinking in Hopes had the balls to mention it to her.

Attila the Nun excused herself and got up

to pee. I checked out her ass (some habits are hard to break) and noticed the brand name on the back of those jeans: True Religion.

6

I collapsed into my ergonomically correct office chair, booted my desktop, checked my messages, and found this from Lomax:

STILL NO ID ON THE BODY?

No, but thanks to Fiona I had enough for an update that might keep him off my back for a while. I opened a new file and banged out a lead:

Authorities believe the man who was shot to death and thrown from the Cliff Walk in Newport a week ago was Salvatore Maniella, the notorious and reclusive Rhode Island pornographer, but so far they have been unable to positively identify the body.

A few minutes later, I was putting the final touches on the story when Lomax plopped on a corner of my desk and read over my shoulder.

"Fiona your source for this?"

"One of 'em, yeah."

"Who else?"

"Captain Parisi."

"How'd you manage that? The tight-lipped SOB never tells us anything."

"I just got off the phone with him. When I asked him how the Maniella murder investigation was coming, he said he had no idea what I was talking about. But when I told him I got the ID from a 'source close to the investigation,' he let loose with a stream of curses about 'fucking leaks' and hung up."

"Good enough for me. Listen, you got plans for tonight?"

"I do." But I really didn't.

"Cancel them. Todd Lewan called in sick, so I need you to cover the city planning commission again."

Aw, crap. I checked my watch. Those meetings started at eight o'clock. If I hurried, there was still time to visit my bookie.

I shoved open the door to the little variety store on Hope Street and heard a familiar *ding*. Ever since I was a kid, that old brass bell had announced my visits to the storekeep, my old friend Dominic "Whoosh" Zerilli. For most of those years, it had dangled over a door on Doyle Avenue. The bell was one of the things Whoosh had salvaged after the arson there last year.

Teresa, who worked the register on week-nights, was hunched over the glass candy counter, studying the front page of the *National Enquirer*. Judging by her furrowed brow, it was hard going. I leaned down and plucked out her iPod earphones.

"And they say that young people don't read newspapers."

"Hi, Mulligan."

"How are you, Teresa?"

"I'm bored."

"Of course you are. It's the universal teen-age affliction."

"Finally ready to take me on that date?"

"Soon as you grow up."

"But I turned *eighteen* last week!"

I muffled a laugh. She pouted.

"So are you gonna buy something or what?"

"Just came by to see the old man."

She rolled her eyes. "He's in the back."

I strolled down a narrow grocery aisle. To my right, Ding Dongs, Twinkies, Fruit Pies, Honey Buns, and Devil Dogs. To my left, a rack of soft porn magazines with names like *Only 18, Black Booty,* and *Juggs.* Just ahead, coolers stocked with Yoohoo, Coca-Cola,

Mountain Dew, Red Bull, and twelve brands of cheap American beer. The illegal tax-stamp-free cigarettes were kept out of sight behind the counter.

At the end of the aisle, I climbed a short flight of wooden stairs and knocked on a reinforced steel door. When the dead bolt snicked open, I turned the knob, stepped into Zerilli's private sanctum, and was greeted with a low woof.

"He won't hurt you none," Zerilli said. "He's fuckin' harmless."

"Where'd you get him?"

"The pound."

"Got a name for him yet?"

"Calling him Shortstop."

"How come?"

" 'Cause Centerfielder's a stupid fuckin' name."

Shortstop got up from his spot in the corner and wandered over to lick my hand with a blue sandpaper tongue. He was a big dog, probably had a mastiff or two somewhere down the family tree.

"I turn him loose in the store at closing," Zerilli was saying. "Figured he'd discourage the neighborhood kids from breaking in again, but it ain't workin'. Useless fuckin' mutt loves everybody."

I almost asked if he was going to keep the

dog, but from the way his fingers were working behind its ears, I had my answer. The phone rang, and when Zerilli reached for it, I noticed a tremor in his right hand. That was new. He turned seventy-five last March and was finally starting to show his age.

"Eight points," he told the caller. "And the over-under is thirty-seven." He paused, then scratched some code on a scrap of flash paper with a yellow pencil stub. "Okay, you're in for a dime," he said, and hung up.

"Pats game?"

"Yeah. Want a piece?"

"Not this time, Whoosh."

"Don't blame you. Brady's third game back from knee surgery, it's hard to know whether he'll be throwing more touchdowns than interceptions."

He picked up the flash paper he'd recorded the bet on and dropped it into a metal washtub by his feet. If the cops ever raided the place, something that hadn't happened in years, he'd just drop a lighted cigarette in the tub and . . . *whoosh!* Which was how he got the nickname.

Zerilli fussed with his blue rep tie, loosening the Windsor knot. Then he drew a Colibri lighter from the inside pocket of his black Louis Boston suit jacket and set fire to the unfiltered Lucky that had been dangling from his lower lip. He took a drag, blew it out through his nose, and scratched his balls through his boxer shorts. As usual, he had removed his suit pants and hung them in the closet to preserve the crease.

I sat in the wooden Windsor visitor's chair, and Zerilli presented me with a box of illegal Cubans. I pried it open, took one out, and clipped the butt with my cigar cutter. Zerilli leaned over to give me a light.

"Swear on your mother you won't write about anything you see or hear in here," he said.

"I swear," I said, not mentioning that there was nothing to write because everybody already knew what went on in here. This was our ritual. The only thing that ever changed was the brand of Cubans. Sometimes Cohibas, this time Partagás.

"So," he said, "I'm guessing this ain't just a social call."

"Not entirely."

"You here to talk about Arena's labor racketeering case?"

"No."

" 'Cause I got nothin' to say about that."

"Of course you don't."

"Salmonella, then?"

"Right."

"The fuckin' prick dead or not?" he asked.

"Looks like, but I can't say for sure."

"Humph."

"What can you tell me about his operation?"

"The Internet porn, not a fuckin' thing."

"The clubs, then?"

"He don't bother with them no more," Zerilli said. "Turned them over to his daughter Vanessa a couple of years ago after she finally got her fuckin' business degree from URI. What I hear, she's a bigger cocksucker than him."

"She making a go of it?"

"Oh, yeah. Was her idea to put in private rooms so the strippers can screw the customers. 'Stead of just blowing them at the tables. Bitch calls 'em VIP rooms. Shitty little booths with cumstained vinyl couches. Jesus, what a joke."

"Any friction with the six clubs Arena and Grasso run?"

"Nah. The joints are all jumpin' on the weekend, pulling in customers from all over New England. Some of 'em come in on chartered buses from Boston and New Haven, for chrissake. Do a pretty good business most weekdays, too. There's enough fuckin' johns to go around, Mulligan."

"The Maniellas still aren't connected, right?"

"Business they're in, they gotta know some people. Back when porn was on videocassettes, before the Internet fucked up a good thing, crews outta New York, Miami, and Vegas handled the distribution — kept all the porn shop shelves stocked with filth. But the Maniellas ain't part of This Thing of Ours, if that's what you're gettin' at."

"So how much is Vanessa paying Arena and Grasso for the right to run her clubs on their turf?"

"Ah, shit." He stubbed out his cigarette, shook another from the pack, and lit it, the flame wobbling in his trembling right hand. "I don't wanna talk about that."

"No?"

"Fuck, no."

"Touchy subject?"

He looked away and started in on Shortstop's ears again. Drool dripped from the dog's maw and puddled on the linoleum. A minute passed before Whoosh turned his attention back to me.

"So," he said, "are you wasting my fuckin' time, or are you gonna lay down a bet?"

"Okay, Whoosh," I said. "What's the over-under on when the *Dispatch* goes belly-up?"

I expected a chuckle. Instead he dead-panned:

"Three years."

That stopped me.

"Seriously?"

"Three years from Columbus Day, to be exact."

"People are betting on that?"

"Come on, Mulligan. People bet on every fuckin' thing."

I let out a long sigh. "Give me fifty bucks on the under."

"Figures. All the guys from the paper are takin' the under." He picked up his pencil stub to record the bet.

I pulled out my wallet, paid him the twenty-five dollars I'd lost on Saturday's URI-UMass football game, and got up to go, still puzzling over why Vanessa's payoffs to Arena and Grasso were such a touchy subject. I had my hand on the doorknob when I tumbled to something.

"Wait a sec. They aren't paying *her,* are they?"

"What? Where the fuck did you get that idea?"

"Holy shit! They *are* paying her, aren't they?"

His eyes narrowed to slits. "No fuckin' way this came from me."

"Of course not, Whoosh."

"I better not see anything about this in the fuckin' *Dispatch.*"

"You won't."

"Swear on your mother."

"Already did."

"Do it again."

"Okay, okay. I swear."

He reached down to scratch his balls again, took another pull from his Lucky, and started talking.

"Ten years ago, when Maniella opened his fuckin' dives, couple of our boys paid them a visit. Said they'd be back every month to collect."

"How much?"

"Two grand per club."

"Sounds reasonable."

"We thought so."

"So what happened?"

"A couple weeks later, 'bout a half hour before the noon opening, a dozen guys with Navy SEALs tattoos come busting into Friction."

"Grasso's place," I said.

"Now, yeah, but it was Johnny Dio's before he got whacked."

"Uh-huh."

"The bouncer tried to stop them at the door, so they tossed him into the parking lot like he was fuckin' trash. Tore the place up pretty good. Smashed all the liquor bottles. Threw barstools through the fuckin' mirrors."

"No shit?"

"Yeah. You ain't heard about this? We tried to keep it quiet, but I figured you mighta heard about this."

"Anybody get hurt?"

"A few cuts and bruises. Nothin' worth cryin' over. Before the cocksuckers left, a couple of 'em climbed up on stage, un-zipped, and pissed on the stripper poles like they was fuckin' dogs."

"Marking their territory," I said.

"Dio figured right off Maniella must've sent 'em. Wanted to drive out to Greenville hisself and whack the sonuvabitch. After we got him calmed the fuck down, we asked Maniella for a sit-down."

"How'd that work out?"

"We invited the prick to a nice meal at Camille's so we could explain the situation. Arena did most of the talkin'. Said if Maniella's clubs were doing as well as ours, he was raking in the fuckin' dough. Said two grand a month per club was a fair price for the right to operate."

"Maniella didn't think so?"

"He said the money was fair and that his

boys would be by the first of every month to collect it."

"You're kidding me."

"Have I ever?"

"What did Arena say to that?"

"First he had to grab Dio by the legs to stop him from climbing over the table to get at the asshole. Then he said no fuckin' way."

"And Maniella said what?"

"At first he just smiled and looked at us over the rim of his fuckin' wineglass. Enjoying the moment."

"And then?"

"And then he rolled up his sleeve and showed us his Navy SEALs tattoo. Said he knew plenty of guys with the same ink. Said he figured a dozen was enough but that he had the scratch to bring in fifty of 'em if he had to."

"So Arena caved?"

"What the fuck could he do?"

"Arena and Grasso still paying?"

"To Vanessa now, yeah. Every fuckin' month. But we never talk about it." He took off his glasses and rubbed his eyes. "It's fuckin' humiliating."

"Not like the old days, huh?"

"Fuck, no," Zerilli said. "Back when Raymond L. S. Patriarca ran this town, no way anybody'd try somethin' like this. Bobo Marrapese, Pro Lerner, Frank Salemme, Dickie Callei, Red Kelly, Jackie Nazarian, Rudy Sciarra — just whisper the names of the guys in our crew and a dick like Maniella would have pissed his pants. But it ain't the 1970s no more."

"The ex-SEALs still around?"

"At least a couple are, yeah. Handling the collections."

I thanked him and got up to go.

"Hold on a sec," he said. "Could you use a GPS for the Bronco?"

"Don't really need one. I got a map of Rhode Island stored in my head."

"You go out of state sometimes, right?"

"I do."

He got up from his chair, unlocked the door to a little storeroom behind the office, and came back with a Garmin GPS in an unopened box.

"A thousand of 'em fell off a fuckin' truck in New Bedford last week," he said. "I bought 'em off the Arcaro brothers for ten cents on the dollar."

"What are you getting for them?"

"Forty bucks apiece, but yours is on the house."

If I turned it down, my friend would be insulted. "Thanks, Whoosh," I said. "And if you hear any chatter about the Maniella murder, give me a holler."

"Mulligan?"

"Um?"

"The gorillas who trashed Friction? We heard they signed on with Maniella after they got fired from Titan and Blackwater."

"No shit?"

"No shit."

"Know what for?"

"You won't fuckin' believe it."

"What?"

"Excessive force," he said. "Or as they call it at Blackwater, too much of a good thing."

By the time I got to city hall, the planning commission meeting was under way. I hadn't missed a thing. Wouldn't have missed much if I hadn't shown up at all. Two hours of wrangling about the future of a vacant lot off Elmwood Avenue was worth just three paragraphs on the bomber page — B-17.

It was raining when I stepped out of the *Dispatch*'s front door and dashed for Secretariat, and as I pointed him down Putnam Pike toward Greenville, it started coming down hard. The twenty-minute drive to the Maniellas' place on Waterman Lake took twice that. Should have used the GPS, because I was almost to Harmony before I realized I'd missed a turn in the dark.

I backtracked, found it this time, and rolled slowly down a country road, peering through sheets of rain for a glimpse of the white center-chimney colonial that had stood at the corner of Pine Ledge Road for two hundred years. When I saw it, I turned right onto an unpaved private track that the storm had churned into mud. It was narrow, barely wide enough for two cars to pass. A hundred yards in, it got narrower as it ran along the top of an earthen dike. The waters of Waterman Lake lurked on both sides, and I knew for a fact that Secretariat couldn't swim.

Rain caught the beams from my headlights and hurled them back at me, and halfway across, I lost sight of the road. I felt the Bronco dip as the right rear tire slid off the edge and grabbed air. I punched the gas, and the other three wheels slung mud as they fought to hold the road.

7

The Stillwater River, a tributary of the Woonas-quatucket, is just a creek, really, and in autumn it shrinks to a trickle. The earthen-and-masonry dam thrown across its course in 1838 is still there, holding back an amoeba-shaped lake of 270 acres. Water-man Lake is clean and the average depth is just nine feet, making it ideal for swimming and boating but unsuitable for disposing of a body.

The lake is privately owned, and so is the white-pine-and-maple-studded acreage that surrounds it. When I was a kid, most of the structures here were ramshackle summer cottages. In recent years, some of them had been ripped down and replaced by sprawling villas designed by architects who lifted their ideas from Philip Johnson and Frank Lloyd Wright. The biggest belonged to the Maniellas, or what was left of them.

Just past the dike, the dirt road curved to

the right. Drenched pine boughs swished against Secretariat's side, giving him an overdue scrubbing as we groped our way in the dark. Soon, the road split into five dirt trails that stretched toward the lakeshore like the fingers of an arthritic hand. The Maniellas' place was appropriately located at the tip of the middle finger, perched on a knoll overlooking the water.

When I pulled into the crushed-shell drive, the house looked dark and empty. I tugged the hood of my rain slicker over my head, sprinted through the storm, and climbed the stairs to the wide front porch. The doorbell chimed like Big Ben. No one answered. To be thorough, I sloshed around the house and peeked in the windows. Through a pane in the side door to the three-car garage, I could just make out the silhouettes of the year-old Maybach and the 2009 Hummer registered to Sal Maniella. Made me wonder how he'd gotten to Newport if he hadn't driven either of his cars. The stall reserved for Vanessa's Lexus was empty. Maybe he'd taken hers.

My jeans were soaked through with rain now, and the temperature was falling. I dashed for the Bronco, cranked the ignition, turned on the headlights and wipers, and could barely see the house through the windshield. Risking the dike again would be pushing my luck. I turned off the engine, opened my thermos, and sipped coffee for the warmth. It worked. It also triggered a gnawing pain just below my breastbone. I popped the glove box, cracked open a fresh bottle of Maalox, and took two big gulps. Then I let the seat down to catch a nap and wait for the rain to let up.

I'd just dozed off when Mick Jagger started growling the lyrics to "Bitch," a ringtone that alerted me to the frequent late-night calls from that special someone.

"Hello," I said, and received the usual salutation.

"You . . . fucking . . . bastard!"

"Good evening, Dorcas."

"Who are you out screwing tonight, you prick?"

"Five of the six Pussycat Dolls. Nicole Scherzinger couldn't make it."

"Always with the fucking jokes."

"Okay, you're on to me. Truth is, Melody Thornton couldn't make it, either."

"My lawyer call you today?"

"He did."

"And?"

"And I'm still not agreeing to lifetime alimony, Dorcas."

"You are *such* a prick."

"I did offer all the child support you could possibly want. He thought that was generous until he remembered we never had any kids."

"You think you're funny? Because you're not."

"I keep telling you, Dorcas, things are going downhill at the paper. Chances are I'm gonna get laid off. Even if I don't, the *Dispatch* is likely to close down in a few years, and I have no idea what I'll do then."

"Not my problem, asshole."

"Being a reporter is all I know, Dorcas. I've never been any good at anything else."

"You got that right."

"Do I need to point out again that you make twice as much money as I do?"

"Go to hell!"

"Sleep tight, Dorcas," I said, but she'd already hung up.

The rapping on the car window startled me. I opened my eyes to see Captain Parisi knocking on the glass with his knife-scarred knuckles. Across the lake, the sun had crept over the horizon and was peeking through the pines.

"Mulligan?" he said as I rolled down the window. "The hell you doing here?"

"Same thing you are."

I'd known Steve Parisi for years. Despite Fiona's grousing about the lack of results, he was a damned fine detective, although he did tend to be tight-lipped with the press. There was often a five-second delay before anything he said to me, as if he were afraid some juicy official secret would slip.

"House still empty?" he asked.

"It is."

"Doesn't explain why you're sleeping in a junk car in our favorite pornographer's driveway."

"I got caught in the storm last night and didn't dare risk the dike."

"Got an inspection sticker on this heap?" He checked and found it on the windshield. "How much of a bribe did you pay to get that?"

"The going rate is forty bucks."

Five seconds ticked off before he sighed and said, "Yeah, that's what I hear, too."

"If Rhode Islanders would stop killing each other for a week or two," I said, "maybe one of us could look into it."

That five-second delay again. Talking with Parisi was like conversing by radio signal with somebody on the moon.

"If I tell you not to come out here again," he said, "it won't do any good, will it?"

"It won't."

"How 'bout giving me a call if you find them before I do?"

"Sure," I said. "And if you find them first, you'll give me a heads-up, right?"

"I'll think about it. Watch yourself on the way out. The edge of the causeway broke away in a couple of spots last night, and from the skid marks in the mud, it looks like someone damn near went into the drink."

8

I was sitting at the bar nursing a six-dollar can of Bud when a bottle blonde sashayed up in a G-string and stiletto heels, thrust a pair of store-bought tits in my face, and said, "Want a blow job?" Well, sure, but not at these prices. I shook my head, and she stamped her heel in frustration. Then she spun away and scanned the room for another mark. I took a good look at her ass. Some habits are hard to break.

It was a slow Thursday night at the Tongue and Groove. There were no chartered buses in the parking lot, and the twenty hookers taking turns on the stripper poles outnumbered the paying customers. Most of the men looked as if they'd already had their fun. Now short on cash and stamina, they hunched over beers at the cocktail tables or slumped on stools by the stage to review the choreography. The girls gyrated in G-strings, but ten dollars would get you into the "all-nude room" upstairs. In the name of research, I pulled a Hamilton out of my pocket. As I handed it to the palooka watching the door, I wondered how I should phrase the entry on my expense account.

The room at the top of the stairs was dark except for the stage, where two naked women, one black and one white, were on their hands and knees, shaking their asses to the beat of a romantic mood setter by 50 Cent:

I'll take you to the candy shop,
I'll let you lick the lollipop . . .

Their genitals gyrated inches from the noses of two men sitting on barstools in a row of otherwise empty ones at the edge of the stage. One guy thrust a dollar in a garter and reached out to fondle the merchandise.

The Tongue and Groove was my last stop on a three-night tour of Vanessa Maniella's strip clubs. I'd been hoping to find out how they operated — and maybe pick up some gossip about the family's whereabouts. But the main thing I'd discovered was that Vanessa had learned a thing or two about merchandising at URI.

On Tuesday night, I'd hung out at Shakehouse. There, the cover was twenty dollars, which a large gentleman in a Joseph Abboud suit politely requested at the door. A poster-size photo of three naked stunners mugging with a linebacker from the New England Patriots was mounted just inside the entrance. Behind the gleaming granite bar, five mixologists in white shirts and black bow ties whipped up flavored martinis and drew mugs of premium draft beer.

The women, some fresh from appearances in Manhattan and Atlantic City, had spent a lot of time at the gym. They shimmied nude on three stages in a swirl of colored lights, moving as though Shakira had taught them to dance. The customers, most wearing business suits, lined up to tuck ten-dollar bills into garters strapped high on sweat-damp thighs. Now and then, one of the men would toss a fistful of bills in honor of a spirited performance. And I'd thought money showers went out when the recession came in.

After their turns in the spotlight, the women demurely donned lingerie before mingling with the customers. Buy one a twelve-dollar mixed drink and she'd sit with you and place your hand on her thigh. For fifty dollars, she'd lead you to a booth, remove her top, ask you to sit on your hands, and give you a lap dance that would last the length of a single song. Private rooms lined the back wall, and when I poked my head into an empty one, I found it was more enticing than the semen-stained sewer Whoosh had described.

"Your first time here?" one of the bartenders asked as I settled onto a stool to peruse the beer menu.

"It is."

"Like to know how it works?"

"I would."

"Two hundred gets you a half bottle of champagne and fifteen minutes in a private VIP room with one of the girls. For four hundred, you get a magnum and a half hour. The girls aren't allowed to hustle you. You have to approach them. Don't be offended if one of them turns you down. Not all of them are full-service girls. Some of them just dance for tips."

Last night I'd hit the second club, Rogue Island, and found the door blocked by six pickets from the Sword of God, a local group of right-wing religious zealots. They brandished hand-lettered picket signs proclaiming "Thou Shalt Not Commit Adultery," "Hades Is for Whoremongers," and "God Hates Fornicators." A pair of bouncers roughly shoved them aside and ushered me in. As the door banged closed behind me, I could hear them out there, howling about hellfire and immortal souls.

Inside, I paid the ten-dollar cover charge and took a stool at the bar. A few discreet inquiries determined that most of the girls were locals — single moms trying to make a living and college girls hustling for tuition. The bartenders served a good variety of decent bottled beer. The customers wore Dockers and button-down shirts, and it was apparent that some were regulars. The girls welcomed them by name, giving them the same greeting Norm used to get when he waddled through the door at Cheers.

The girls performed naked on a single stage, swinging from stripper poles and thrusting their hips in crude imitation of the sex act. The bills tucked into garters here were mostly fives. When their fifteen-minute sets ended, the girls pulled on G-strings and skimpy bras to mingle with the customers. Topless lap dances were thirty dollars, two for the price of one before five P.M. A Franklin bought a blow job in a dark booth, or for a hundred and fifty dollars you could take the girl of your choice to one of those private rooms Whoosh described and do whatever you wanted for fifteen minutes.

I was sitting alone at a cocktail table with

a good view of the stage when a slim brunette beauty approached and said, "Hi, Mulligan. Need another beer?"

"Marie? Don't tell me *you're* working here."

"Don't go all Oral Roberts on me. I just waitress."

"Nice outfit," I said. Her body stocking fit like a condom.

Marie used to wait tables at Hopes, and last year I took her to bed a couple of times, but it didn't lead anywhere. She was looking for a guy to raise a family. I told her to keep looking. "Tips good here?"

"Very."

"But not as good as if you were stripping."

"Of course not," she said, and sat down at my table.

"What kind of money do the strippers make?"

"The hookers, you mean?"

"Well, yeah."

"On a good night, the best girls take home a grand or so after expenses."

"Expenses?"

"Yeah."

"What expenses?"

"They have to pay a hundred fifty a night to dance here."

"The girls pay the club? The club doesn't

pay them?"

"Uh-huh. Candy, who used to strip at Shakehouse until she put on a few pounds, says it's three hundred a night there, but the hottest girls can make five or six grand on a big weekend."

"Any other expenses?"

"The girls pay the house twenty dollars every time they take a customer into a private room, and they're expected to tip the bouncers at the end of the night. Sometimes the bouncers take it out in trade, if you know what I mean."

"I do."

"On the plus side, the club buys condoms by the gross and provides them to the girls for free."

"Condoms?" I said. "The Maniellas are Catholic. They'll be saying Hail Marys till Easter if Pope Benedict finds out about this."

I had more questions, but the bartender bellowed from behind the bar, "Socialize on your own time, Marie. Orders are stacking up here."

"Gotta go," she said. "I'll bring you back a fresh beer on the house." A few minutes later, she did.

Tonight at the Tongue and Groove, admission was free. A lone bartender served two brands of beer, Bud and Bud Light. The customers wore jeans and T-shirts with Boston Bruins and New England Patriots logos on them. Most of the girls were fresh off the boat from Haiti, Russia, Brazil, and the Dominican Republic. They wore nothing but G-strings and smiles as they strolled among the cocktail tables to tempt the customers.

Garter tips were one-dollar bills here. Lap dances ran twenty bucks a pop, blow jobs were forty dollars, and for a hundred you could drag a girl into a private booth and make whoopie for twenty minutes. On a slow night like tonight, you could get two girls for the price of one.

Vanessa Maniella had built bordellos to suit every Rhode Island wallet. At each club, I asked for her and was politely informed that she was unavailable. When I asked if anyone had seen Sal lately, I drew icy stares.

I was standing now in the doorway of the Tongue and Groove's "all-nude room," waiting for my eyes to adjust to the dark. By the time 50 Cent stopped rapping, I could just make out the rows of cocktail tables, all of them empty. I chose one by the back wall and took a seat. It was shift-change time onstage. The girl who'd received the dollar tip slid down onto the lap of her benefactor and whispered in his ear. Then she dismounted, took him by the hand, and led him toward a row of private cubicles that lined the wall to my left.

The other girl pranced naked down the stage stairs and scanned the room for prey. I could barely see her when she moved out of the light, but I sensed she was heading my way. Two new girls strutted onto the stage on long legs made longer by fuck-me heels. You couldn't call them strippers because they didn't have anything to peel off.

"Bonsoir, beebe. Waz you name?"

"Mulligan. What's yours?"

"Destiny," she said, but it came out more like "DEZ-tin-ee."

"Sure it is," I said. "That's what all the Haitian mamas are naming their babies these days."

That made her giggle, and I noticed for the first time how young and pretty she was. She was still giggling when she wrapped her arms around my neck.

"Buy me a drink and mebbe I tell you my real name."

I pulled a twenty off the small roll of bills in my jeans, handed it to her, and asked her to bring me back a Bud. She snatched it and swung her hips as she walked to a little bar that I hadn't realized was there. When she returned with our drinks, she didn't give me change. I used my foot to push a chair away from the table for her, but she straddled my lap and pressed her small breasts against my neck.

"Marical," she said. "My name ees Marical."

"How old are you, Marical?"

"Ay-teen."

The same age as Teresa, the clerk at Zerilli's store, if she was telling the truth. I'd been trying to figure out what to do with my hands. I placed them now around her narrow waist.

"I show you a good time, beebe. Eef you get wit me, I make you world go round like craysee."

She moved her crotch in a circle against the front of my jeans, and I felt myself stiffen. Paul Simon's line from "The Boxer" popped into my head: "There were times when I was so lonesome I took some comfort there." But I'd never paid for something I could get for free, and I was too poor to start now.

"I got big love for you, beebe. I do you half price."

I shook my head no, and her shoulders slumped.

"Tonight I make no moany."

"Slow night."

"Slow, yes. The weekend be better, I hope so."

She twisted away from me, and I thought she was getting up to go. Instead, she reached behind her, plucked our drinks from the table, and handed me my bottle of Bud.

"How long have you been in Providence, Marical?"

"Tree muntz."

"Do you like it here?"

"Better than Haiti. I have no work dere."

"What do you have to pay to dance here?"

"I pay one hundred dollas a night. Tonight so far I loose moany."

Marical set her drink back on the table and ran her fingers through my hair, working on my sales resistance. She flicked open the buttons of my Dustin Pedroia Red Sox game jersey. Then she draped her arms around my neck, pressed her breasts against my bare chest, and humped the front of my jeans. That had to be worth something. I peeled off a five and slipped it in her garter. My hand had a mind of its own. It lingered on her inner thigh.

"I know you want me, beebe." And that was no lie.

She took my hands in hers, placed them on her ass, and humped some more.

That's when two guys shouldered through the door. I pegged them for college students — Providence College, maybe, or URI. They stood there until their eyes adjusted to the dark and then took seats at a table near the stage to study the action. Marical twisted around in my lap to look them over, then turned back to me.

"Love you, beebe, but I go to work now. Come see DEZ-tin-ee again when you have some moany, okay?"

She got up from my lap and walked toward the college boys, swinging her hips again as she went. She sat down at their table, and for a minute or two I listened to them laugh. Then I watched her bounce up, take them both by their hands, and lead them into one of the private rooms.

I wanted to kick the door in, pull her out of there, and take her away from all this. But I didn't.

Later I was sitting on a barstool downstairs, sipping another Bud and feeling vaguely guilty, when the bartender turned up the house lights and announced closing time with a twist on an old familiar refrain: "Time to go, dudes. You don't have to fuck at home, but you can't fuck here."

That's when I got a good look at one of the bouncers. His eyes were small and pale blue. His hair was the color of wet sand. At six feet three, he was my height but wider at his bulging shoulders, his torso tapering to a slightly pudgy waist. He looked familiar, but I couldn't come up with a name. He saw me, too, and headed my way as I drained my bottle and clunked it on the bar.

"Hey, Mulligan. Ain't seen you in a while."

The high, gravelly voice gave him away.

"Hi, Joseph." I hadn't seen Joseph De-Lucca since his house burned down during the arson spree in Mount Hope last year. "How'd you lose all the weight?"

"Cut my fuckin' drinkin' to two six-packs a week. Gave up doughnuts and pizza. Stopped chuggin' Coffee-mate from the bottle at breakfast."

"You drank Coffee-mate from the bottle?"

"It's fuckin' good, Mulligan. Oughta try it sometime."

"Looks like you've been working out, too."

"Most every day, yeah. Vinny Pazienza lets me use his private gym. Love pounding the heavy bag, man. Vinny says I got fuckin' talent. Started sooner and I mighta gone pro."

You lost, what, fifty, sixty pounds?"

"Closer to a hundred."

"Good for you, Joseph. So how long you been working here?"

"Since June. First time I had steady work in more'n three years."

The bartender wandered over and tapped Joseph's swollen, pasty forearm. "Friend of yours?" he asked.

"Yeah. Give us a couple of brews, Sonny."

"Sure thing," he said. He drew two Buds from the ice chest, popped the tops, and slid the bottles onto the bar. "Take your time. It'll take me a half hour to clean up."

I pulled a roll of Tums from my pocket, peeled off a couple, chewed them to calm my stomach, and chased them with beer.

"So whatcha doing here, Mulligan?" Joseph said. "Guy like you oughta be able to get his pussy for free. Never figured you for a john."

"I'm not. I'm workin.' "

"Saw you upstairs with Destiny on your lap. Nice work if you can get it."

"The *Dispatch* doesn't pay much," I said, "but the job does have fringe benefits."

"Mine, too. I watch out for the girls, make sure nobody gives 'em a hard time. And they take care of me."

"Complimentary blow jobs?"

"Complimentary means free?"

"It does."

"Then yeah, every fuckin' night."

"Do customers give the girls a hard time often?"

"Nah. Most of 'em know better. But every now and then, one of them South Providence pimps comes bopping in and tries to squeeze the girls for a cut. Miss Maniella don't allow that. Says the girls got a right to keep what they make."

"Good for her."

"Last month King Felix came in. Heard of him?"

"We've met." In fact, Felix and I went way back.

"Couple of the girls, Sacha and Karma, used to be in his stable. He seemed to think they still were."

"What'd you do?"

"Told him he was mistaken."

"How'd that work out?"

"Asshole went for a little silver pistol stuck in his waistband, so I took it away from him. Always heard he was a tough guy, but when I grabbed him by his fuckin' dreads and dragged him outside, he screamed like a little girl."

"Knock him around a little, did you?"

"Nothin' major. Smashed his nose. Cracked a few ribs. When I was done, I told him to go back out on the street and spread the word. Then I tossed the fucker in the Dumpster."

Joseph picked up his Bud and drained half the bottle in a swallow. The bartender wandered back our way and mopped a wet spot with his bar rag.

"You ain't told me what you're workin' on," Joseph said.

"I'm looking for Vanessa Maniella. Seen her around lately?"

He frowned, and his blue eyes turned to slits. "I don't want to read my name in your fuckin' paper."

"Okay."

" 'Cause if I do, I'll kick your ass."

"Understood."

The bartender was still mopping that same spot. Maybe he was eavesdropping. Maybe he was just being thorough.

"Ain't seen Miss Maniella in weeks," Joseph said. "She's got people what run the place for her. She don't come in much."

"How about her father?"

"Ain't never seen him in here."

"Think he's dead?"

"All I know about that is what you put in your fuckin' paper."

"No scuttlebutt about it around the club?"

"Scuttlebutt?"

"Gossip."

"Nah. Nobody here knows a fuckin' thing."

"That beating you gave King Felix. You said it was last month?"

"Yeah."

"Before or after the shooting on the Cliff Walk?"

He took a moment to think about it. " 'Bout a week before."

"Think he was mad enough about it to go gunning for Sal?"

"Wouldn't have been in any condition to go after anybody," Joseph said.

"He could have sent one of his peeps."

"King Felix is a fuckin' moron," Joseph said. "I doubt he even knows who Sal is. And the retards who work for him? They wouldn't be able to find Newport on a map. Besides, if they had the balls to come after somebody, it would have been me."

"They still might," I said, "so watch your back."

9

That night I logged on to iTunes and built a new thirty-song playlist: "Love for Sale" by Ella Fitzgerald, "Teen-Age Prostitute" by Frank Zappa, "Bad Girls" by Donna Summer, "Roxanne" by the Police, "Call Me" by Blondie, "What Do You Do for Money Honey" by AC/DC, "Lady Marma-lade" by Labelle, "The Fire Down Below" by Bob Seger, "Honky Tonk Women" by the Rolling Stones, "Christmas Card from a Hooker in Minneapolis" by Tom Waits, and a bunch more.

Musically, the sound track for my latest obsession was a mixed bag. My favorite was "867-5309/Jenny," by Tommy Tutone, who screeched about finding the number written on a wall — "for a good time, call." When the song hit the top of the charts back in 1982, pranksters all over the country called the number and asked for Jenny. I'd dialed it a few times myself, when my kid sister wasn't hogging the phone, and reached a humorless functionary at Brown University. Brown, like scores of other annoyed phone company customers, responded to the onslaught by changing phone numbers.

Next morning, I sat at the counter at my favorite Providence diner and skimmed the *Dispatch*'s sports section while sipping coffee from a chipped ceramic mug. Jerod Mayo, Matt Light, and Wes Welker were all doubtful for the Patriots' game on Sunday, making me regret the latest bet I'd phoned in to Zerilli.

Charlie, the short-order cook who also owned the place, bent over the grill and cracked eggs for my breakfast. Somebody's pancakes looked about ready. Beside them, strips of bacon popped and sizzled.

I flipped to the front page and saw that Fiona was back in the news, calling the governor a whoremaster because he wouldn't back her antiprostitution bill. Blackjack Baldelli and Knuckles Grieco, the two lunkheads who ran the Providence Highway Department, also made page one. A jury had convicted both of grand larceny, conspiracy, and income tax evasion for buying fifty thousand dollars' worth of manhole covers with city money, reselling them to a scrap dealer for fourteen thousand, and pocketing the cash. Two members of the Sword of God had been arrested for throwing rocks through the windows of the Planned Parenthood clinic on Point Street. And the Rhode Island unemployment rate had reached almost 12 percent, second highest in the nation after Michigan.

Charlie turned toward the counter to top off my coffee and noticed the headline on the unemployment story. "Damn," he said. "Why can't we ever be number one at anything?"

"We are," I said. "Rhode Island leads the nation in doughnut shops per capita."

"Really?"

"Yeah. We've got one for every forty-seven hundred people — nine times the national average."

"How do you know that?"

"Because I read the paper," I said. "You ought to try it sometime."

"No wonder Rhode Islanders are so fat."

"Your cuisine isn't helping any, Charlie."

He chuckled, turned back to the grill to flip my eggs, and tossed me a question over his shoulder.

"Anything new on Maniella?"

"There isn't."

"Think he's dead?"

"Looks like, but I can't swear to it."

He turned back to me and leaned his forearms on the counter. "Who would want to kill him?"

"Could be anybody," I said. "Business rivals. Born-again Christians. A porn actress's angry father." Or the Mob, I thought to myself. Grasso and Arena could hold a grudge for a long time. The pope might be miffed about those condoms, but since the Borgias passed into history, murder wasn't the Vatican's style . . . as far as I knew.

"Or maybe it was just a robbery gone bad," I said. "The cops didn't find a wallet on the body."

"In the old days, Sal used to come in here," Charlie said. "Back before he could afford champagne and caviar for breakfast. Seemed like a decent guy, but I guess he wasn't."

My eggs were ready now, so he turned back to scrape them onto a plate. Outside the diner's greasy windows, rays of morning sunshine broke through low, scattered clouds and turned the Beaux-Arts façade of city hall to gold. Seagulls had strafed the building again overnight, continuing their war of turds with the current administration. I shoveled Charlie's masterpiece into my mouth and tried to think things out.

Poking into the Maniellas' prostitution

business wasn't getting me any closer to proving they were paying off the governor. The mystery of Scalici's pig looked like a dead end, too.

Last night, I'd spent hours Googling investigative stories on Internet porn. The *Los Angeles Times* and *The Washington Post* had unearthed details about some of the big operators, but they'd run into a black hole when they looked at the Maniellas. They were too good at hiding their money and covering their tracks. The *Times* and *Post* had far more time and money to devote to the story than I did. If they couldn't find anything, there was no point in me trying.

Lomax could see I'd run dry and responded by jamming me up with a diet of obits, press conferences, and weather stories. I was starting to hate the job I'd always loved. I needed to find something big to work on to get Lomax to ease up, but I had no idea what that something might be. Cash for inspection stickers was a scandal, but it didn't qualify as news. Everybody already knew about it. Besides, for working people trying to keep clunkers on the road, it was a public service. A little graft was the only thing standing between Secretariat and the glue factory.

I opened the paper to the metro front and

read a police story under Mason's byline. Providence vice cops had kicked in the door to a second-floor apartment on Colfax Street last night and confiscated a computer containing hundreds of child porn videos. The occupants, who had rented the place under a phony name, were nowhere to be found.

I read the story carefully twice, but I couldn't see anything in it for me. The Maniellas had never stooped to child porn — as far as I knew. I doubted they had moral scruples about it, but with the millions they were making on adult porn, why would they get involved in something that would bring down so much heat?

Back at the office, I went over the computer printouts of the governor's campaign contributions again, looking for anything I might have missed the first five times. It was still just a blur of hundreds of names, addresses, and dollar figures. I learned nothing. I shoved it aside and started in on the stack of obits Lomax wanted by three o'clock.

"Hi, Mulligan."

"What's up, Thanks-Dad?"

"Need help with anything?"

"Want to try your hand with a few obits?"

"Not really, no."

Hadn't worked the last time I'd tried it, either. The publisher's son, surprise surprise, never got stuck with scut work.

"You know, there *is* something," I said, and handed him the computer printouts. "I could use a fresh pair of eyes on this."

"What am I looking for?"

"Any hint that the Maniellas have been funneling campaign contributions to the governor by using their porn actors as fronts. You might as well look at these, too," I said. I opened a file drawer and pulled out similar lists for the chairmen of the Rhode Island House and Senate judiciary committees.

He fanned the pages and whistled. "A lot to go through," he said.

"It is, but there's no hurry."

"Do we know the porn actors' names?"

"No, we don't."

He thought for a minute, then said, "Okay. Let me play around with this for a while and see what I can do."

Mason didn't know all the tricks of the trade, but he was damned smart. Maybe he *could* find something.

10

A half hour south of Providence, the little town of Warren clings like a barnacle to the eastern shore of Narragansett Bay. Here, the water is sometimes streaked with sewage, and quahogs angry with coliform bacteria pave the mucky bottom. Main Street, several hundred yards from and parallel to the shoreline, is a postcard from the Great Depression — old corner drugstore, red-brick town hall with Palladian windows, and ramshackle wood-frame storefronts with vacant office space on the second and third floors.

I parked Secretariat at a meter in front of a narrow storefront office two doors north of the police station. The office had housed a three-reporter news bureau until the *Dispatch* closed it down a couple of years ago to save money. Now, black lettering on the glass front door read "Bruce McCracken, Private Investigations." I entered and found him alone, sitting behind a computer at an oak desk that had seen better days. For the desk, like the town, those days were ninety years ago. A bank of dented metal file cabinets and an old black safe the size of a minifridge had been shoved against the back wall. The only decent pieces of furniture in the place were the black leather swivel chair he was sitting in and two client chairs lined up in front of his desk.

I'd known McCracken since our school days at Providence College. After graduation, he'd taken a job as an in-house investigator for a big fire insurance company and stayed for twenty years until he got laid off last spring. For the company, it was a brain-dead move. McCracken was good. Every year, his work had saved his employer hundreds of thousands, and sometimes millions, of dollars.

He held up his cell phone to show me he was occupied and pointed at one of the client chairs, inviting me to take a seat. Instead, I walked across the warped linoleum floor to the center of the room and scanned the framed autographed photos of Providence College basketball greats mounted on the cracked plaster walls: Jimmy Walker, Ray Flynn, Jim Thompson, Johnny Egan, Vinnie Ernst, Kevin Stacom,

Lenny Wilkins, Joey Hassett, Marvin Barnes, Billy Donovan, Ernie DiGregorio. I was still looking when McCracken finished his call, popped out of his chair, and walked over to grip my hand in his customary metacarpal-crushing handshake.

"When is my picture going up?" I asked.

"Soon as you get off the bench."

Fans of private eye novels have a warped idea of what real private detectives do. Most of their work is routine: delivering summonses in civil cases, locating child support delinquents, investigating pilfering from ware houses, spying on unfaithful spouses, checking the validity of insurance claims, and doing background checks on job applicants. From time to time, they might search for missing persons the police have given up on or help lawyers gather evidence in civil and criminal cases. Some P.I.s specialize, but McCracken, like most of them, did a little of this and a little of that. Unlike Raymond Chandler's Philip Marlowe and Robert B. Parker's Spenser, real private detectives rarely investigate murders. Most of them go their whole lives without beating somebody up or gunning somebody down.

"How's business?" I asked as I dropped into one of the visitor's chairs.

"Great!" he said.

"Really? Because this place is a dump."

"I'm trying to keep overhead down for now," he said, "but I'm getting so much work that I'm thinking about hiring a spunky secretary and moving into a two-room suite in the Turk's Head Building in the spring."

"Glad to hear it."

"Maybe I can get Effie Perine."

"She's spunky all right, but she's also loyal. You'll never lure her away from Sam Spade."

"Things keep going this good and I'll need a partner to help shoulder the load," he said. "You oughta give it some thought. From what I hear, the *Dispatch* is going down the tubes."

"Thanks. I will. That why you wanted to see me? To offer me a job?"

"One of the reasons."

"What else?"

"You looking into that Colfax Street child porn bust?"

"I'm not," I said.

"Maybe you should."

"And why would that be?"

"Day after the raid, this guy shows up in my office. Six two, blue eyes, gray hair, expensive razor cut. Wearing an Armani suit and a TAG Heuer watch. Maybe fifty or fifty-five. Wants to know do I have any Providence police contacts."

"Which you do."

"Of course."

"And?"

"He asks could I give him a heads-up if his name surfaces in the child porn investigation."

"What's this guy's name?"

"He says I don't need to know until I agree to take his case."

"What did you do?"

"I pulled out the top drawer of my desk, reached in, and told him I was going to shoot him if he didn't get the hell out of my office."

"Got a gun in the top drawer, do you?"

"I keep my Sturm, Ruger in the safe, but he didn't know that."

"Recognize him?"

"I didn't. But it was a busy morning. Hard to find a parking space on the street. I figured he must have left his car in the municipal lot behind the town hall. As soon as he went out the door, I slipped out the back, checked the lot, and watched him get behind the wheel of a black, year-old Jaguar XJ."

"Piece of shit," I said.

101

"Yeah. Shouldn't drive one of those unless you can afford to have a mechanic follow you around in a tow truck."

"Get the plate?"

"Of course."

"Run it?"

"Duh."

"So who is he?"

"Charles B. Wayne."

"*Doctor* Charles B. Wayne?"

"The same."

"No shit?"

"No shit."

I thanked him and got up to go.

"Mulligan?"

"Um?"

"If the good doctor is a chicken hawk, do me a favor?"

"What?"

"Bury the sonuvabitch."

11

The most interesting thing about Mary and Joseph Mendoza was that they had eight children and had named the three girls Mary and the five boys Joseph. I wondered how Joseph Sr. would manage now that his wife, just thirty-seven, had died from what the undertaker described as "a short illness."

I had two obits to go when Jimmy Cagney screamed, "You'll never take me alive, copper!" The line from his 1931 classic, *Public Enemy,* was my ringtone for incoming from law enforcement sources.

"Mulligan."

"Steve Parisi."

"Afternoon, Captain."

"Thought you'd like to know Vanessa Maniella and her mother came home Tuesday."

"Three days ago?"

"That's right."

"Guess you've been a little busy," I said.

"Be grateful I called at all, smart-ass."

"They ID the body?"

Five seconds ticked off. Maybe six. "No, they did not."

"It's not *him?*"

"We still don't know."

"*What?* Okay. Start from the beginning and tell me the whole story."

"You're joking, right?"

"Hey, you called *me,* remember? What can you tell me?"

Five seconds again. "Just that they're home. When I drove up to their place on the lake again Tuesday night, they were pulling a couple of big suitcases out of the Lexus."

"Where'd they been?"

"They declined to say."

"Did they say *anything?*"

"I asked when did they last speak to Sal."

"And?"

"Vanessa informed me that she and her mother had nothing to say to the police and referred me to her attorney."

"Why would she act like that?"

"Been asking myself the same question."

"Makes you wonder if maybe she had him killed, doesn't it?"

That five-second delay again. "The

thought crossed my mind."

"Got tired of waiting for the old man to turn the rest of the business over to her, did she?"

"I wouldn't want to speculate."

"Of course you wouldn't," I said. "So who's the lawyer?"

"Some broad named Yolanda Mosley-Jones."

"At McDougall, Young, and Limone," I said.

"You know her?"

"We've met."

"What's she like?"

"Girl of my dreams. Young, pretty, smart, honest, and legs that go all the way to the floor."

"If she's so honest," he said, "what's she doing representing the Maniellas?"

"Hey, porn's not illegal. And a girl's gotta make a living."

"Name like Yolanda, sounds like she might be black."

"That she is."

"Didn't know that was your type."

"The good-looking ones are all my type," I said. "So what did she have to say?"

"I left a message. She didn't return the call."

"Maybe she'll return mine," I said. I'd

been looking for an excuse to call her, and now I had one.

"And you'll let me know what you learn?"

"After three days or so, you mean?"

"Wiseass."

"Maybe I'll drop in on Vanessa, too. See if she likes reporters more than cops."

"I'm betting not," he said.

The Maniellas' front door had a mahogany frame, a round-top transom, four panels of stained glass, and a hand-wrought iron grill. This was the first time I'd seen it in daylight. I stood on the porch and admired it for a moment before I rang the fleur-de-lis-shaped doorbell. The door swung open to reveal a stout Hispanic woman in a demure black-and-white maid's uniform. Behind her, I caught a glimpse of a vast foyer with a sparkling white marble floor.

"Yes?" she said, although it came out sounding more like "Jes?"

"Is the lady of the house in?"

"Who may I say is calling?"

"Mr. Mulligan of the *Dispatch*."

"*Un momento, por favor,*" she said, and firmly shut the door.

I stood on the porch and looked out over the lake, its surface riffling in a stiff breeze. It was late in the season for water sports, but three teenagers in wet suits roared past on Jet Skis, throwing spray onto the Maniellas' floating wooden dock. It was a good five minutes before the maid swung the door open again and stood aside so Vanessa Maniella could block the entrance with her ample hips.

I knew her to be thirty-five, but she appeared younger in knee-high calf boots and the kind of short, clingy skirt favored by the Kardashian sisters. Bleached blond tresses tumbled to her shoulders in a style suitable for one of Sal's MILF videos. Vanessa looked me up and down and smirked.

"How was Rome?" I asked, trying an old reporting gambit. Pretend you know something you don't, and more often than not a source will either confirm it or correct you.

"Barcelona," she blurted out. "We were in Barcelona."

"Don't suppose your dad came along for the ride."

"I've got nothing to say about that."

"Do you know where he is?"

She was closing the door now.

"Is he in the morgue?"

I heard the dead bolt click.

"Why won't you ID the body?" I shouted. "Is the maid in the country legally? Are you paying her Social Security taxes?" Not that

I cared about that. It was just something to say.

I climbed into Secretariat, cranked the ignition, peeled out of the driveway, and tore down the narrow causeway at a reckless speed. After weeks of work on the Maniellas, I still had nothing worth printing. The frustration was getting to me. I felt like pounding on something.

12

It was nearly eight in the evening when I picked up a burger and fries to go at the lunch cart next to Providence City Hall and called Joseph DeLucca from the Bronco. He sounded groggy, as if my phone call had awakened him. Must have been his day off.

"Mulligan? Whassup?"

"I need a favor."

"Name it."

"I need to hit something."

"Sure. No prob. Vinny gave me a key to the gym. Meet you there in thirty minutes."

Vinny Pazienza's private gym was in an old brick fire house on Laurel Hill Avenue. Inside, the walls were hung with fight memorabilia: Everlast boxing gloves, framed sports pages, fight cards, and boxing posters from Foxwoods, Las Vegas, and Atlantic City.

Vinny was a local folk hero, partly because of his inspiring story and partly because he was small but tenacious — just like Rhode Island. He grew up as a skinny undersized kid who played a mean Little League short-stop, provoked on-field brawls, and kept the playground bullies at bay with his wild-eyed ferocity. When he was fourteen, he sat in the dark in the Park Cinema in his home-town of Cranston, watched Rocky Balboa and Apollo Creed beat each other half to death, and decided then and there that he wanted to become a boxer. He hit the weights, built himself a gladiator's body muscle by muscle, won a hundred out of a hundred twelve amateur bouts, turned pro in 1983, and defeated Greg Haugen for the IBF world lightweight championship in 1987.

In 1991, a few weeks after he pummeled Gilbert Dele to win the WBA world junior middleweight title, Vinny woke up in the hospital with a broken neck. A car crash had cracked his third and fourth vertebrae. Doctors told him he would never fight again. He was lucky he could even move his legs. Three months after the accident, he limped out of the hospital with a medieval-looking brace still screwed to his skull and went right into the gym. Just thirteen months later, he outpointed former WBC world super welterweight champion Luis

Santana in a tune-up fight and set his sights on bigger things.

Over his twenty-one-year ring career, Vinny took some beatings. Héctor "Macho" Camacho bloodied him. Roger Mayweather and the great Roy Jones Jr. knocked him around the ring. But along the way, he beat the legendary Roberto Duran twice, and by the time his final fight ended with a victory in 2004, he was a five-time world champion. His final pro record: ten losses and fifty wins, thirty of them by knockout.

When I walked into the gym Joseph was already at work, his fists thudding against one of the heavy bags hanging on a chain from the ceiling. Each time he slugged the bag, it swung away from him as if it feared for its life. He had to wait for it to swing back so he could punish it again.

"Hold this fuckin' thing still for me, will ya?" he said.

I stood behind the bag and steadied it while Joseph clubbed it with lefts and rights. He fired a ten-punch combination of hooks and uppercuts, backed off to catch his breath, and then went at it again. He completed his workout with a flurry of blows that traveled through the bag, up my arms, and down the length of my spine. Then he backed away, snorted like a bull, and said,

"Your turn."

Joseph showed me how to wrap my hands with strips of two-inch-wide cloth, weaving it between each finger, over each knuckle, and back around the wrist to protect the joints and tendons. When I was ready, I approached the bag and threw a couple of tentative left jabs. I tried a right cross, a left hook, a right uppercut, and found a rhythm. I liked the smacking sound my fists made when they met the bag. It felt good to be beating on something that didn't hit back.

Afterward, we reconvened over beers at Hopes.

"You beat the crap out of that bag," I said. "That how you hit King Felix when he pulled a gun on you?"

"Fuck, no. Asshole wouldn't still be walkin' around, I hit him like that."

He chugged his Bud and waved for another. "You know," he said, "you smacked the bag pretty good yourself. For a rookie. Got some pop in that skinny-ass frame."

"Maybe we can do it again sometime."

"Sure. Anytime you want."

When the waitress arrived with his beer, I ordered another for myself, but I was already two beers behind him.

"I need to ask you something," I said.

"If it's for the fuckin' paper, I ain't got

nothin' to say."

"Off the record," I said.

"That means you won't write what I tell you?"

"That's what it means."

"What, then?"

"Think the Maniellas could be making child porn?"

Joseph's face drained of color. "Do you?" he said.

"I don't know. That's why I'm asking."

"I ain't ever heard nothin' like that," he said. "If I thought they was . . ." He clenched his fist and shot a right jab past my ear.

"One more question."

"Still off the, uh . . ."

"Off the record. Right."

"What?"

"Ever heard the Maniellas or anybody who works for them mention a guy named Charles Wayne?"

"Who the fuck is that?"

13

The Brown University Medical School's official name is the Warren Alpert Medical School. Despite what it says on the stationery, nobody calls it that. Aside from getting sick and dying, Alpert didn't have anything to do with medicine. He was the founder of Xtra Mart, a convenience store chain that keeps America hooked on nicotine, caffeine, and high-fructose corn syrup. But he gave the medical school a hundred million dollars a couple of months before his death.

Dr. Charles B. Wayne, the school's dean of medicine and biological sciences, had an office on the third floor of the Metcalf Infant Research Laboratory just off Waterman Street. I had no reason to think he was connected to the Maniellas, but outing a Brown honcho as a pedophile would make a hell of a story.

I found a parking spot across from the

building and saw that the front door was blocked by a knot of people waving hand-lettered picket signs: "Brown Trains Abortionists." "Thank God for Abortion Clinic Bombers." "God Hates Brown." "God Hates Rhode Island." "God Hates America." And just so everything was covered: "God Hates the World."

As I started up the walk, a lean septuagenarian in a porkpie hat and a long black coat separated himself from the group, tottered up to me, and placed a skeletal hand on my shoulder. He reminded me of Reverend Kane, the creepy old man played by Julian Beck in *Poltergeist II*. For a moment, I was afraid he was going to deliver the scariest line in the movie: "Are you lost, sweetheart? Are you 'fraid, honey? Well then, why don't you come with me?"

What he did say wasn't much better: "Do not enter this house of evil, brother. Heed my words or you will be doomed to eternal hellfire."

"Thanks for the heads-up," I said, and brushed by him.

He yanked my shoulder with unexpected strength and spun me back to him. "Pray with me," he said, "and let us save your immortal soul."

"Don't go to any trouble on my account,"

I said. "It's too late for me anyway."

"It's never too late to turn your back on Satan and return to the righteous path, brother."

I extended my hand, and he shook it. "My name is Mulligan," I said, "and you must be Reverend Lucas Crenson of the Sword of God. I've seen your picture in the paper."

"At your service," he said, removing his hat to display a few wisps of white hair on a shiny bald pate. Then he honored me with a theatrical bow from the waist. Gee. I guess he'd seen the movie, too.

"Look, Reverend," I said, "I don't work in there. I'm a reporter for the *Dispatch*. I'm going inside to see if I can expose the evils that lurk within."

"Don't you lie to me, boy!"

"It's the truth. I swear."

"On your soul?"

"On my immortal soul," I said, although I wasn't sure I had one.

"Then you shall be allowed to pass."

"Thank you, Reverend," I said. "Say, do you think I could attend your service some Sunday? I'd like to hear you preach."

"Most certainly," he said. "Anyone seeking the path of righteousness is welcome in God's house."

He turned to his picketers, spread his

arms as if he were parting the waters, and smiled benignly as they opened a path for me. As I passed them, I counted five grown-ups, three kids who should have been in school, and two more who weren't old enough for it yet.

I took the elevator to the third floor, strolled down a corridor, peeked through the glass in the door to Dr. Wayne's outer office, and saw a blonde sitting behind a computer on an otherwise clean desk. The nameplate on it read "Peggi Simmons, Administrative Assistant." I made her as one of the seven types of blondes Raymond Chandler described in *The Long Goodbye:* the perky little doll who's everybody's pal and has learned enough martial arts to throw a truck driver over her shoulder.

At five in the afternoon, I was loitering on Waterman when she popped out of the building and elbowed her way through the picketers. They howled at her — something about a she-devil, but I didn't catch all of it. She ignored them, dashed across the street, and turned north on Thayer. Accosting her on the sidewalk didn't seem like the best idea, so I trailed behind her on the College Hill business strip as she strode past fast-food joints, copy centers, the Brown University Bookstore, and several bars. I was hoping she'd pop into one of the student watering holes so I could follow her in and strike up a conversation. Instead, she walked six blocks, turned left on Keene Street, and disappeared into a three-story Victorian that had been broken up into student apartments.

I was standing on the sidewalk, contemplating the wisdom of knocking on her door, when she popped back out with a Bernese mountain dog on a leash. He was just a pup, maybe nine months old, but he was already closing in on a hundred pounds. He took one look at me, broke into a doggie grin, and bounded straight for me. "Brady, no!" she shouted, but Brady wasn't listening. He kept coming, ears and big pink tongue flopping. She outweighed him, but not by much, and he was a lot stronger. He dragged her right to me. Good doggie. I squatted on my heels to meet him at his level. He draped his front paws over my shoulders and worked that tongue into my ear.

"Brady!" she said again, and tugged on the leash with no discernible effect.

"He can't help himself," I said. "Dogs and women love me."

I peeled Brady's paws from my shoulders and stood. He nuzzled my leg, so I reached down and rubbed him behind the ears.

"I'm so sorry," she said.

"No need to apologize. He's a magnificent dog."

"Thank you. I just wish he had better manners."

"He's about nine months old, right?"

"Nearly ten."

"How were your manners when you were ten months old?"

"I see what you mean," she said, and stuck out a hand for me to shake. "I'm Peggi Simmons. You've already met my Brady."

"Named after Tom Brady?"

"How'd ya guess?"

"Half the dogs in Rhode Island are named after Patriots, Red Sox, or Celtics players," I said. "A lot of the children, too. By the way, *my* name is Mulligan. I'm a reporter for the *Dispatch*. And you're Charles Wayne's secretary."

"How do you know *that?*"

"Because I'm a reporter for the *Dispatch*. We reporters know all kinds of stuff."

"Including how to get Brady to stop pulling me down the street on his walks?"

"Sure," I said. "Hand me the leash."

She did, and we strolled together on the sidewalk.

Brady walked nicely for ten yards or so. Then he spotted a kid on a bicycle and bolted, nearly jerking the leash from my grip. I pulled hard on it, freezing him in place. Brady tugged harder. When that didn't work, he reared on his hind legs like a spooked horse. I held on tight, cut in front of him, and pointed at my nose.

"Brady, look at me," I said. Brady looked. "Brady, sit." He sat. I held my hand, palm out, in front of his face and said, "Brady, stay." He stayed. I kept him sitting there for twenty seconds. Then I gave him a little more leash, said, "Okay," and started walking.

"Brady wants to be in motion," I said. "We have to teach him that walking is his reward for not pulling."

The dog trotted along by my side for a few yards. Then he spotted a woman pushing a baby carriage and bolted again. I reined him in and made him sit. After we repeated the routine a dozen times, Brady got the idea and stopped pulling.

"Smart dog," I said. "Now let's see how he does when you hold the leash."

Sensing his opportunity, Brady started pulling again. Each time he did, I grabbed the leash to stop him from dragging Peggi down the sidewalk, and she repeated the series of commands I'd shown her. Before long, Brady was walking nicely with her, too.

"How do you know so much about dogs?" she asked.

"I studied up a few years ago when my wife and I bought a Portuguese water dog pup that I named Rewrite," I said. "When we broke up, she didn't want him, and with my crazy hours I couldn't take care of him. Had to give him away. I really miss that crazy little guy."

Our walk had taken us back down Thayer Street. As we passed Andréas, I suggested we pop in for a drink.

"What about Brady?"

"We'll take him in with us."

"I don't think they allow animals."

"They make an exception for service dogs," I said.

I pulled sunglasses from my pocket, slid them on, gripped Brady's leash six inches from his collar, and groped toward the bar door. Inside, the maître d' took me by the elbow and led us to a booth. As we settled in, Brady scooted under the table, rolled over on his back, and started tugging on my shoestrings. When the waiter came, I gave him a Stevie Wonder head bob and remembered not to read the menu. We ordered, and within a few minutes he returned with a Samuel Adams for Peggi, a club soda for me, and a raw hamburger patty with water on the side for Brady.

"So," she said, "are you really this nice, or are you trying to pick me up?"

"Neither. The truth is, I'm working, Peggi. I need your help. I've got some questions about your boss."

"Oh."

"Yeah."

She stared at me for a moment before saying, "You really do like Brady, though, right?"

"Sure do. I like his owner, too."

"Why are you interested in my boss?"

"I think he might be involved in something bad, Peggi."

"How bad?"

"The kind of bad that rapists and murderers look down on."

"Oh, my God!"

"I could be wrong about this. All I've got so far are suspicions."

"And you want to know if I can confirm them?"

"Yeah."

"Well, I can't. I mean, I always thought he was a little creepy, but nothing like that."

"Do you have access to his computer?"

"His office desktop, sure."

"Does he have a laptop?"

"He does. He usually carries it around with him, but sometimes he forgets and leaves it in the office."

"Do you think you could look through his computer files without getting caught?"

She fell silent for a moment, thinking it over. "I guess I could," she said. "What would I be looking for?"

"Video."

"What kind of video?"

"You'll know when you see it."

Peggi checked her watch. "The office is empty now," she said. "We could go over there and take a look."

"I probably shouldn't go with you, Peggi. If someone walked in on us, you could say you were working late, but my presence would be hard to explain."

"Okay."

"Here's my card," I said. "Call me if you find something."

14

That evening, I stretched out on my Salvation Army mattress and cracked open the new Michael Connelly novel to see how Harry Bosch would solve his latest caper. Maybe I'd learn something I could use. Wouldn't be the first time.

My apartment was on the second floor of a crumbling three-story tenement house in the city's Italian section of Federal Hill. It wasn't much, but since my breakup with Dorcas, it was all I could afford. Besides, I felt at home in this working-class neighborhood of store clerks, hairdressers, and bus drivers raising big, close families. People here had a history of keeping their priorities straight. In 1933, Federal Hill voted to repeal Prohibition by a total of 2,005 to 3.

Angela Anselmo, the single mom who lived in the apartment across the hall, was cooking something spicy again tonight, the aroma seeping through the inch-wide crack at the bottom of my front door. My mouth watered. I switched off my iPod speakers so I could listen to Marta, Angela's ten-year-old daughter, practice the violin. She was getting really good.

She was in the middle of Hungarian Dance no. 5, for the fifth time, I think, when I heard someone trudging up the worn wooden stairs to the second-floor landing. Someone heavy, by the sound of it. Then a sharp rap on my door. I got up, walked into the kitchen, peered out the peephole, and got a good look at the center of a massive chest. Not a someone my door could keep out if he wanted to get in, so I unlocked it and turned the knob.

The someone turned out to be two someones. Both wore their hair military style. It was a chilly night, but they wore no jackets over their muscle shirts, one black and the other gray. I could see they were in shape, but there's a difference between iron-pumping shape and fighting shape. Then I spotted their matching tattoos — an eagle clutching an anchor and a Navy SEALs trident in its talons — and I knew these two were both.

They stepped inside, and Black Shirt gently closed the door.

"Mind if we sit?" he asked.

"Anywhere you'd like."

They looked around the kitchen and saw nothing but a greasy stove and a wheezing twenty-year-old Frigidaire.

"Sorry," I said. "The wife got all the furniture." I squatted on the floor, my back against the wall. They chose to remain standing.

"You dropped in on the Maniellas' place at the lake yesterday afternoon," Black Shirt said.

"Guilty," I said.

"Never a good idea to go there uninvited," he said.

"Thanks for letting me know."

"You've also been hanging around the clubs," Gray Shirt said.

"Didn't know I needed an invitation for that."

"You're welcome there anytime," he said. "But you were asking questions."

"Kinda goes with the job."

"Miss Maniella would like you to stop," Black Shirt said.

"Okay," I said.

"Cuz we might not be so polite if we have to come back," he said.

"And none of us want that," I said.

"We understand each other?" Gray Shirt said.

"We do."

That's when Black Shirt spotted my only piece of artwork suspended in a shadow box on the chipped plaster wall.

"What's with the forty-five auto?"

"My grandfather carried it when he was on the force," I said.

"Providence PD?"

"Yeah. I keep it there to remind me of him."

"Is it in working order?"

"I don't really know. I don't think so. It's pretty old."

"Good," Black Shirt said. "Listen, Miss Maniella said to give you this."

He reached into his hip pocket, pulled out a thin piece of plastic the size of a credit card, and handed it to me. On the front, a glossy picture of Marical in her birthday suit and the words "Compliments of Tongue and Groove."

"What's this?"

"Good for one trip around the world with the whore of your choice," Gray Shirt said. "Compliments of the house."

"Gee, thanks! And I thought you guys didn't like me."

"We don't," Black Shirt said.

"How about another one for Shake-house?"

"Don't think so," Gray Shirt said. "The girls there are out of your league."

"Hey," I said, "a boy can dream."

"Who's playing the violin?" Black Shirt asked.

"Neighbor's daughter," I said.

"She's good," he said. And with that, they took their leave.

When they were gone, I turned the dead bolt and took the shadow box down from the wall. I pried the pistol from the frame, fetched the gun oil and the cartridges from the cabinet over the refrigerator, and spread an oilcloth on my scuffed, fake-brick linoleum kitchen floor. I'd gotten a permit to carry last year, after the trouble in Mount Hope. I'd never made use of it, but if I broke my promise to Black Shirt and Gray Shirt, it might come in handy.

I sat on the floor, broke down the weapon, cleaned it, and reassembled it. Then I got up, assumed the combat shooter's stance I'd learned at the Providence Revolver Club — left leg forward, knees bent, both hands on the grip — and dry-fired at the refrigerator. It didn't fall down or shoot back. I sat back down on the floor and loaded the magazine with standard military-load cartridges.

15

Lomax stood over my desk, a printout of the obituary I'd just filed clutched in his hand. He smiled wanly and began to read aloud:

Margaret O'Hoolihan, 62, of 22 Hendrick Street, Providence, died yesterday at Rhode Island Hospital after a short illness. Her reputation as a whimsical flibbertigibbet was belied by her lifelong love of Proust.

"Precisely so," I said.
"Unusual lead for an obituary, though, don't you think?"
"I thought I'd try to liven things up."
"Maybe not the best approach for the obit page."
"I see your point."
"Flibbertigibbet?"
"It means flighty chatterbox."

"I know what it means, Mulligan."

"Of course you do."

"Because I looked it up."

"Okay."

"Tell me, Mulligan. How many of our subscribers do you suppose are in the habit of reading the paper with a *Webster's* in their laps?"

"I don't know," I said.

"I do."

"Enlighten me."

"None of them."

"Ah."

"Rewrite this piece of shit so I can put it in the paper."

"Right away, boss."

"Something else I need to ask you about," he said. He lowered his voice to a whisper. "Planning to gun somebody down today?"

"Not just now. Maybe later."

That morning, the big Colt dug into the small of my back as I smuggled it into the newsroom under my leather bomber jacket. At my desk, I slipped it out and locked it in my file drawer. I thought I was discreet about it, but Lomax must have caught a glimpse.

"Some reason you feel the need to be armed?"

"There is."

"Care to share?"

"Last night a couple of Schwarzeneggers who work for Vanessa Maniella paid me a visit."

"Oh, shit. You okay?"

"Fine and dandy."

"What did they want?"

"For me to mind my own business."

"But you're not going to, are you?"

"Of course not."

"Sounds like she has something to hide."

"It does."

"Any idea what?"

"Not a clue."

"Maybe we should call the police," he said.

"Won't do any good."

"I suppose not."

"So I figure on being ready when the Arnolds come back."

"Got a permit to carry?"

"I do."

"There's a rule against firearms in the newsroom, Mulligan."

"I suppose there would be."

"You're breaking it."

"I guess I am."

"People start bringing guns in here and this might as well be Dodge City."

"Only if we lay in a case of rotgut whiskey and hire some dance hall girls."

"You could get canned for this, Mulligan. The bean counters are itching to trim a few more bodies."

"Then maybe we could keep this between us."

"Just keep it locked up and out of sight, okay?"

"Sure."

"And don't shoot any copy editors no matter how much they deserve it."

16

Late that afternoon, I nursed a Killian's at Hopes and pondered my next move. Mason strolled into the place, claimed the stool next to mine, and slapped his Dunhill briefcase on the bar.

"Ready for another?"

"No thanks, Thanks-Dad. I was just heading out."

"Going home for the evening?"

"Not just yet. I thought I'd make a courtesy call on one of our local hooligans."

"Mind if I tag along?"

"You sure you want to? Where I'm going, you won't exactly blend in."

"That's okay," he said. "Just consider it part of my continuing education at the Mulligan School of Journalism."

"Fine," I said, "but when we find my guy, it would be best for all of us if you keep your mouth shut."

"I can do that."

"See that you do."

Fifteen minutes later, Secretariat cruised slowly down Broad Street past KFC, where fat mamas and their fat toddlers trudged ankle-deep through crushed fried chicken buckets and flattened paper cups. The roadway was rotten with commuters. Most of them were heading to their homes in the Elmwood section of Providence and the neighboring city of Cranston, but a few were hunting for the stroll that migrated up and down the main drag through South Providence. We crawled by Miss Fannie's Soul Food Kitchen, Jovan's Lounge, Empire Loan, the Bell Funeral Home, and the Rhode Island Free Clinic. Just past Calvary Baptist Church, at the corner of Broad Street and Potters Avenue, we found what we were looking for. I rolled through the intersection, pulled to the curb, and parked.

We were still sitting there five minutes later when two hookers, both shivering in halter tops and hot pants, separated from the pack, dashed across Potters, and startled Mason by rapping on his window. One of them was a tall, ample black woman pushing forty. The other was a short, skinny Asian who looked young enough to cartwheel for the Nathanael Greene Middle School cheerleaders. I powered down the window on Mason's side of the car.

"Ready for your booty call, baby?" the tall one asked. "Girlfriend and I are *bop!*"

Mason turned to me and said, "Bop?"

"They are proficient at oral sex," I said.

"You got *that* right," the short one said.

"I appreciate the offer, ladies, but no, thank you," Mason said.

"Come on, baby," the tall one said. "You got the green." She smacked herself on the ass and added, "You *know* you want to hit dat donk."

Mason looked at me and raised an eyebrow.

"Baby got back," I said.

"Huh?"

"Her ass."

With that, the hookers turned their backsides to us and dropped their drawers.

"I'm sorry," Mason said, "but we are not in the market for your services."

The short one stuck her head in the window, scowled, and looked at me.

"Yo' friend is buggin'," she said.

"Buggin'?" Mason said.

"Acting weird."

"Fo' shiggidy, my weeble," the tall one said.

Mason glanced at me again. "Sorry," I said. "No idea. I think she's just playing

135

with us now."

The hookers spun on their heels and trudged back across the street. I slid Mason's window up, started the engine, and cranked the heater.

"Getting anywhere with the campaign contribution lists?" I asked.

"I'm still working on it," Mason said.

"Want to tell me what you've got so far?"

"Not until I have something solid."

I took a Partagás from my shirt pocket, set fire to it, and cracked my window to let the fumes escape. On the corner behind us, commuters pulled their cars to the curb to check out the stroll. Now and then, one of them opened a car door so a girl could climb in. Others, displeased with the price or the merchandise, pulled out alone. A squad car crawled by, but the girls didn't scatter the way they did in the old days. Instead, they gave the cops a wave. Under Rhode Island's weird prostitution statute the stroll was against the law, but few cops paid it any mind. Why bust streetwalkers when indoor prostitution was legal? It wasn't worth the hassle of paperwork and court appearances.

"What are we waiting for?" Mason said.

"That," I said, pointing to a skinny black girl in a gold lamé mini skirt who was climbing out of a red Toyota pickup. "The guy we're after sets up every night at a different abandoned house. Best way to find him is to follow one of his girls when she comes back from a job with cash in her bra."

"I don't think she's wearing one," Mason said.

I reached across him, popped the glove compartment, took out the Colt, and stuck it into the hand pouch on the front of my New England Patriots sweatshirt. I expected Mason to ask why, but he didn't. Probably figured the neighborhood was answer enough. We got out of the car, crossed Broad Street, and followed the miniskirt east on Potters Avenue. She loped down the sidewalk, her high heels clacking on the cracked concrete. She passed several two-story houses with peeling paint and drooping shutters, turned left up a short macadam walk, and tromped up the splintered porch stairs of a fire-scarred house with plywood across the windows. We followed her up.

She heard us coming, spun, and whipped a straight razor out of her halter top. Mason let out a little shriek and backpedaled down the steps.

The porch was furnished with a single yellow-and-white lounge chair made of aluminum tubes and plastic webbing. Beside it was an open Igloo cooler containing a revolver and a dozen longnecks. In this weather, there was no need for ice. Next to the cooler stood a huge bottle of Vicodin that must have been stolen from a pharmacy. No doctor would prescribe that much. A tall black man was stretched out on the lounge. He was dressed in red Converse low-tops, a matching red fedora with a black feather in the band, and a full-length mink coat. He was smoking the biggest joint north of Jamaica.

"Why you trippin', bitch?" he said. "Be easy. Mulligan my man. We been down since we wuz shorties."

The hooker shrugged, flipped the razor shut, stuffed it back in her top, and came back out with a small roll of bills. King Felix smiled benignly and took it from her. He counted it out with his long slim fingers, peeled off two twenties, and handed them back to her. Then he slid his hand inside the mink, pulled out a small aluminum foil packet, and dropped it in her hand.

She turned to me then, placed her palm on my zipper, and said, "Jonesing fo' some dark meat tonight, white boy?"

"Mulligan don't want none a yo' crusty ass," Felix said. "Get yo' butt back out on the fuckin' street and bring back some mo' cheddar."

He watched her clomp down the stairs. Then he turned to me and said, "So how you been?"

"I'm fine. You?"

"Can't complain."

"No? Then why the Vicodin?"

"Ran into a little trouble a while back, and my ribs are still sore."

"A little trouble named Joseph DeLucca?"

"Who's he?"

"The bouncer you tangled with at the Tongue and Groove."

"Oh. You heard about that, huh?"

"I did."

"I wasn't looking for any trouble. Just wanted to talk to a couple of girls that used to work for me, see if I could talk them into coming back. The asshole blindsided me."

"I see."

"Don't tell anybody, okay? It'll damage my street cred."

"No worries."

Felix handed me the joint. I took a hit and then offered it to Mason, who was cautiously coming back up the stairs. He shook his head.

"When in Rome," I said, and offered it to him again. Again he shook his head, so I passed it back to Felix.

"Who's the newbie?" he said, and tipped his head toward Mason.

"Pay him no mind," I said. "I'm just showing him the ropes."

Felix pulled two longnecks from the cooler, popped the tops with a church key, and handed one to me and one to Mason. Then he opened one for himself and took a swallow.

"Careful," I said. "Vicodin, marijuana, and alcohol don't mix."

"So I've heard," he said. "But the combination works real good, and it hasn't killed me yet."

He passed the joint. I took another drag and handed it back to him.

"Still playing ball?" he asked.

"Not since you schooled me in that pickup game last September."

"Yeah. My wind isn't what it used to be, but I still got my jump shot."

Felix and I had been teammates at Hope High School back in the day. He was better than me, but he tanked his SATs; so I moved on to play at Providence College, and he moved on to this.

"That a gun in your sweatshirt?" he asked.

"It is."

"Not planning to shoot me, are you?"

Two skinny black teenagers unfolded

themselves from a dark corner of the porch and jerked little silver revolvers from their pants pockets. Until they moved, I hadn't noticed they were there. They looked to be about fifteen years old. The one on the left was nervous, his left eye twitching. The one on the right was as cool as a Texas executioner. He took a step and looked through me with flat, dead eyes.

"Chill," Felix said. They put their guns away, glided back to their dark corner, and flopped back down on the porch floor.

Beside me, Mason had been holding his breath. He blew it out now and took a step back, signaling he thought it was a good time to go.

"Sorry about that," Felix said. "Marcus and Jamal can be a tad overprotective."

"Hope you're not planning on sending them after DeLucca."

"Not unless word about the beating gets around," Felix said. "If it does, I might have to do something to restore my reputation."

"What about the family that owns the club?"

"What about them?"

"Not gunning for them, are you?"

"No way."

"Your baby hit squad been down to Newport lately?"

"You'd have to ask them."

"Should I?"

"I wouldn't recommend it."

I was about to ask another question, but a long-legged white hooker with a gash over her left eye and a red skirt that barely covered her privates was coming up the stairs now. My old teammate Felix evaporated and King Felix returned.

"Dog," he said. "I ain't seen you in a minute. Where the fuck you been at?"

"Makin' scrappy for my man," she said, and handed him some bills.

He counted them slowly. "Two fuckin' hours an' dat's all you brung me?"

She looked at her feet and didn't say anything. He handed her the joint. She plucked it from his fingers, took a hit, and held it. Then she blew it out through her nose and took another.

"Don't bogart dat shit, Sheila," he said. He grabbed it back, peeled off two twenties, tucked them into the valley between her breasts, and gave her a hard look. "Get yo' pale ass back out on the fuckin' street and bring back some serious green."

17

The Capital Grille is located in Providence's old Union Station, a lovingly restored, yellow-brick structure erected by the New Haven Railroad in 1898. It's a fashionable luncheon spot, but one that lacks my favorite diner's affordable prices and greasy charms.

In honor of the occasion, I'd shed my usual sweatshirt, jeans, and Reeboks in favor of Dockers, a white dress shirt, a Jerry Garcia tie, and buffed brogans. I'd topped off the ensemble with a double-breasted navy blue Sears blazer that went out of style when Roebuck was still around. It was the only suit jacket I owned since I left my new one behind on an Amtrak train last year. I hadn't worn the blazer in a long time, but it still fit, more or less. It wasn't loose enough to conceal a large handgun, however, so I'd reluctantly left the Colt locked in my file drawer.

Yolanda Mosley-Jones had declined to see me in her office, explaining that nosy reporters were banned from the firm's inner sanctum. After some whining on my part, she'd agreed to meet for lunch. When I slipped into the place, she was already there, sitting at the bar sipping a pale yellow something from a martini glass and fiddling with her BlackBerry. She didn't see me come in, so I stood there and watched her for a moment, admiring the legs she came in on.

Yolanda was more alluring fully clothed than the babes at Shakehouse were naked. I stood there a little longer, trying to come up with a good opening line, but the sight of her had me flustered. She spotted me in the mirror over the bar, tucked the Black-Berry into her purse, and spun toward me, giving me a better look at those perfect legs entwined around the luckiest barstool in town.

I never understood how some women can dress so simply yet ooze elegance. Yolanda was encased in a black silk suit that must have been made for her. Beneath the jacket, buttoned just low enough to jump-start my imagination, no blouse was evident. Instead, a cascade of thin gold chains sparked against skin so black it was nearly blue, and fell *there.*

"Sit," she said, patting the adjacent bar-stool. "Our table will be ready in a couple of minutes."

I sat and discovered my blazer didn't fit as well as I thought. The top button strained to hold the fabric across my belly.

"What are you drinking?" I asked.

"A wildberry apple vodka Hawaiian sher-bet."

Good God, I thought, but what I said was, "Ready for another?"

"Not quite yet." Her voice was so smoky I could smell it.

The bartender sidled over, and I asked for a Killian's. They didn't carry it, so I settled for a Samuel Adams.

"I hear they gave you Brady Coyle's old corner office," I said.

"Yes."

"And made you a partner."

"True."

"Things are working out for you, then."

"They are."

"No blowback from that favor you did for me last year?"

"I have no idea what you are talking about."

"No, of course not. It never happened. But if it *had* happened and you'd gotten

145

caught, which you didn't, you could have been fired. Even disbarred. I don't think I ever properly thanked you. That was a noble thing you never did."

She stared at me now as if she were being accosted by a lunatic. I was about to blabber something equally incoherent when the maître d' came to the rescue. He seated us at a cozy table for two, and romance was in the air. Or maybe it was just the smell of something spicy she'd dabbed on her skin.

Yolanda studied the menu while an elderly waiter too short to ride the Cyclone at Six Flags fetched fresh drinks and filled our water glasses. I scanned the prices. The *Dispatch*'s bean counters might have preferred paying for that blow job.

"Claus," she said without looking up, "I'll start with the pan-fried calamari and hot cherry peppers. And for my entrée, the sushi-grade sesame seared tuna with gingered rice."

"An excellent choice! And for the gentleman?"

"Ah . . . I'm gonna skip the appetizer and have the signature cheeseburger with fries."

Claus sniffed at me and went away.

"I've been reading about the layoffs at the *Dispatch*," Yolanda said. "I guess they must be clamping down on expense account lunches, too, huh?"

"That they are."

"Oh, Claus?" She waved the little waiter back. "Scratch the gentleman's order and bring him the smoked salmon appetizer and the sliced filet mignon with cipollini onions and wild mushrooms."

"Certainly, madam," he said. Then he smirked at me and turned away.

"Trying to get me fired?" I said.

"No worries. It's on the firm."

"I can't let you do that."

"Why not?"

"It's against *Dispatch* policy."

"And why would that be?"

"Afraid it might make me beholden, I guess." Her lips parted in a half smile, as if she knew what I wanted to be holdin'.

"So we won't tell them," she said.

"Ah," I said. "You lawyers know all the tricks."

"Besides," she said, "this way I can snatch a few morsels from your plate." And when Claus returned with the appetizers, she pinched a sliver of my salmon with her fingers and popped it into that mouth.

"So I understand you are representing Vanessa Maniella," I said.

"I'm not at liberty to confirm that."

"She gave your name to the state police,

147

Yolanda."

"I can't confirm that, either."

"Do you also represent her father?"

"Same answer."

"He *is* dead, right?"

"I couldn't say." She lifted another chunk of my smoked salmon and added, "I warned you I wasn't going to be much help."

"So far, you haven't been any."

"Told ya."

"Except, of course, for the inspiration I get from your presence."

"There is always that," she said. That half smile again.

"You know what puzzles me most?" I asked.

"Rap music? Black Republicans? How we lawyers can live with ourselves?"

"Well, yeah, but I was also wondering why Vanessa Maniella refuses to go to the morgue to ID the body."

"Maybe you should ask *her* about that."

"I would," I said, "but some very large men in her employ have advised against it."

"I see."

"I was going to tell them where to go," I said, "but I was afraid I might scare them to death."

Claus was back now, refilling water glasses and whisking our empty plates away to the

148

kitchen. Moments later he returned with the entrées, and we dug in.

"Mulligan?"

"Um?"

"Know what puzzles *me* most?"

"What would that be?"

"Why haven't you unbuttoned that blazer? It's obviously a bit tight on you, and I can tell you're uncomfortable."

"Not as uncomfortable as I'd be if I unbuttoned it."

"And why is that?"

"It's embarrassing."

"Tell me."

"Well, it's like this. There was an old coffee cup on my desk. I thought it was empty, but . . ."

She was chuckling now, and I hadn't even reached the good part.

"When I stood up to come here," I said, "I knocked it over and, uh . . . I didn't have time to go home to change."

"So you have a coffee stain on your nice white shirt."

"A little spot, yeah."

"Open up," she said, nodding toward the groaning button.

"What for?"

"Because it would amuse me."

"If that's what it takes," I said, and unbuttoned the jacket.

"Oh, snap!"

"Yeah."

"You sure it was just a cup? Looks like the whole damn pot."

She was laughing harder now, her head thrown back. It made her look even more beautiful.

That's when Claus reappeared and said, "Are we ready for dessert? Coffee, perhaps?" His timing was impeccable.

"No coffee for me," I said. "I already have some."

Yolanda put her elbows on the table, folded her hands, and rested her chin on them.

"You really are charming in a klutzy sort of way."

"Thanks. I think."

Claus spotted the stain and smirked at me again.

"Two Irish coffees," Yolanda told him, "and we'll share a slice of cheesecake with strawberries."

"Right away."

"And Claus?"

"Yes, madam."

"Stop throwin' shade at my friend if you expect the usual tip."

Claus skittered away. I'd never seen anyone skitter before, but I'm pretty sure that's what it was.

"You didn't have to defend me," I said after he'd gone. "I think I could have taken him."

She rested her chin on her hands again and gave me an appraising look. I tried my best to appear irresistible, no easy thing with my torso drenched in Folgers.

"Hey," I said, "do you like the blues?"

"I'm a Chicago girl, West Side. Damn right I like the blues. On the drive in from East Greenwich this morning, I jammed all the Littles on my iPod."

"The Littles?"

"You know. Little Milton, Little Walter, Little Buddy Doyle . . ."

"Cool."

"On the way home, I'm gonna switch to the Bigs. Big Bill Dolson, Big Pete Pearson, Big Time Sarah . . ."

"I never thought to sort them by weight class."

I opened my mouth to say something more, but Claus was back with the coffee and cheesecake, and I saw no need to make him a party to my imminent rejection. Yolanda scooped a bit of the cheesecake into her mouth, closed her eyes, and went, "Mmmm." I wanted to hear that sound again, but without cheesecake in the picture.

"So listen," I said when Claus was gone, "Buddy Guy's at the House of Blues in Boston a week from Saturday. Why don't we go?"

"Not happenin', Mulligan."

"You don't like Buddy Guy?"

"You just don't know. I *adore* Buddy Guy. It's you I've got a problem with."

"Problem?"

"I told you before, Mulligan. I'm not into white boys."

"It's been a long time since I was a boy."

"I'll give you that, but you can't outgrow being white."

"Didn't I tell you? I'm black Irish."

"Doesn't count," she said, but her eyes were dancing.

"I've got rhythm, too."

"Yeah, right," she said. "You're a regular James Brown."

"We have so much in common, Yolanda."

"This I've *got* to hear."

"There's the blues, for starters. We both dig Buddy Guy. And we're city kids, both of us raised in one of America's throbbing metropolises."

"I thought you grew up here."

"That I did."

"Providence throbs?"

"Daily."

"I haven't noticed any throbbing."

A thought popped into my head, but I suppressed it before it escaped. Instead, I said, "Buddy Guy's from Chicago, too."

"Actually, he was born in Louisiana."

"Well, yeah. But his club's in Chicago."

"Before I moved here," she said, "I used to hang out at his joint all the time. Don't hear music like that anywhere else. Sometimes Buddy even showed up to jam."

"You're talking about Legends," I said.

"Damn straight." She eyed the colossal coffee stain. "Maybe you're smarter than you look."

"I'd almost have to be."

She smiled at that, but part of her was still in Chicago. "The chitlins and cornbread at Legends were as good as my mama's."

I'd never met a chitlin, but it seemed unwise to bring that up. Instead, I played another card.

"My favorite poet's from Chicago. She's West Side, just like you."

"Gwendolyn Brooks?"

"Patricia Smith."

Yolanda looked skeptical, so I tossed out a few lines:

I always shudder when I pray,
so your name must be a prayer.
Saying your name colors my mouth,
frees loose this river, changes my skin,
turns my spine to string. I pray all the
    time now.
Amen.

"My, my," she said. "Aren't *you* full of
surprises. What next? Maybe warble a verse
or two of 'Lift Every Voice and Sing'?"

"I can if you want me to," I said, "but
Claus would ask us to leave."

"Better wait till we finish dessert."

"You know," I said, "Patricia reads in
Boston every now and then. Next time, we
should go see her."

"Got a thing for sistas from Chi-Town, do
you?"

"Just two of them."

"Maybe you should ask *her* out."

"She's married."

"So are you, last heard."

"Yeah, but mine's all over except for the
lawyering."

She thought about that for a moment
while I idly compared her with Dorcas and
almost laughed out loud.

"So Buddy Guy's in Boston next week,"
she said.

"Yes, he is."

"Buddy's no joke."

"And I have two tickets."

"Okay, let's do this."

"Great."

"But we're just going together. We're not *goin'* together."

"Of course not."

"So you better keep that mouth and those hands to yourself."

Not the final disposition of the case, I hoped. After a change of venue, perhaps she might entertain a plea bargain.

18

I was on my way back to the office when Peggi called.

"I didn't find anything weird on his desktop," she said.

"What about the laptop?"

"He left it behind when he headed out a few minutes ago for a meeting at the Rhode Island Hospital. I've got it open in front of me, but it's password protected."

"Try his birthday?"

"Yeah. Forward and backward. Also tried his wedding anniversary, his wife's name, his kids' names, his dog's name, and all their birthdays. Except for the dog's. I don't know that one."

"Well, it's not something random," I said. "He would have picked a name or number that means something him. Does he have a boat?"

"Yeah. The *Caped Crusader.* I tried it already."

"His wife's maiden name?"

"Tried it."

"Siblings?"

"Tried them, too."

"Parents' names?"

"Don't know what they were."

"What about his middle name?"

"It's Bruce. Already tried it."

"Charles *Bruce* Wayne?"

"Yeah."

"That explains the boat. Try 'Batman.' "

She chuckled and said, "Didn't think of that. . . . Nope. Doesn't work. . . . Hold on a sec." She put down the phone, and it was several minutes before she picked it up again. "I tried Robin, Batgirl, Joker, Penguin, Riddler, Catwoman, Poison Ivy, Two-Face, Commissioner Gordon, Gotham, and Batmobile. None of them worked."

"Try Alfred."

"Oh, right. The butler. . . . Nope."

"Dark Knight?"

"Bingo! I'll go through his files and call you back."

An hour later, she did.

"I didn't find any videos at all," she said. "He must keep them on a home computer, or maybe a portable hard drive."

"Or maybe I was mistaken, Peggi. Go

home, cuddle with Brady, and try to forget the whole thing."

19

A state police cruiser, its lights flashing, had the entrance to the driveway blocked, so I pulled off the country road and parked Secretariat in weeds beside a rusted barbed-wire fence. Gloria Costa and I had smelled pig excrement a half mile down the road, and as we got out of the car, it was all we could do not to retch.

"Scalici *lives* here?" Gloria asked.

"He does. With his wife and two young daughters."

"How do they stand it?"

"I don't know. Guess they've gotten used to it."

I fired up a cigar, and Gloria gave me a dirty look.

"That," she said, "isn't helping the situation any."

"Is for me," I said.

Gloria, one of the *Dispatch*'s few remaining photographers, had lost some weight during her comeback from a vicious assault last year. Her emotional recovery was still a work in progress, but physically she looked strong now, with curves reemerging in all the right places. Except for the black, pirate-style patch over her right eye, she resembled a young Sharon Stone.

"They gave me a glass eye, but I think it makes me look deranged," she'd told me. I told her the eye patch was hot. I would have been tempted if I didn't know Gloria had started seeing somebody — and if I weren't looking to lawyer up.

Gloria was the best one-eyed photographer I knew, better than most shooters with two. I opened the back of the Bronco, and she fetched her camera bag. Cops can be squeamish about citizens carrying concealed weapons, so I left the Colt locked in the glove box.

As we approached the driveway, a trooper rolled down the window of the cruiser, looked us up and down, and said, "The *Dispatch,* right?"

"Right."

"The captain figured you'd show. Said you should go up to the house and ring the bell."

Halfway up the long gravel driveway, we veered away from the house and slogged across a muddy field toward the hog pens.

There, three grim detectives wearing rubber boots and plastic gloves were pawing through an SUV-size mound of garbage. On the ground beside them, a sky-blue tarp had been spread on the ground. In the middle of the tarp, a small lump.

"Hey, Sully," I shouted over the grunts and squeals from nine hundred tons of breakfast meat on the hoof. "Hope that isn't what it looks like."

"Mulligan? You're not supposed to be here," he shouted back. "The captain said to send you up to the house."

"Okay."

"And tell your photographer to stop taking pictures."

Gloria dropped her camera, letting it dangle from its strap while I inquired about the well-being of Sergeant Sullivan's wife and kids. That gave her time to shoot from the hip, sneaking in a few more frames. When she nodded that she was ready, we turned and walked toward the white-shingled two-story house. A few curled brown leaves clung to the red oak that shaded Cosmo's porch in summer.

"*Your* photographer?" Gloria said. "I hate that. Just once, I'd like to hear you addressed as *my* reporter."

We stepped onto the wide farmer's porch

and wiped our muddy feet on the Three Little Pigs welcome mat. Gloria stretched out a finger to poke the bell.

"Hold on," I said.

"What?"

"Let's see if we can learn something first."

Captain Parisi's muffled voice leaked through the door, but I couldn't make out his words over the symphony of the swine. They butchered the vocals to Aerosmith's "Walk This Way" and segued into a raucous, off-key rendition of Led Zeppelin's "Whole Lotta Love." But whatever Parisi was saying pushed the pig farmer's buttons.

"It's Friday morning," Cosmo bellowed. "Where the fuck do you think they are?"

Parisi said something else I couldn't make out. Then Cosmo again:

"In *school,* asshole! They're in fuckin' school!"

I caught the sound of a woman's voice then, and whatever she said seemed to calm Cosmo down. After a few more unproductive minutes of ear strain, I rang the doorbell. A uniformed state trooper with bowling-ball shoulders opened the door, a buff broad-brimmed Stetson clutched in his left hand.

"Sir?" he said.

"This is Gloria Costa, a photographer

from the *Dispatch*," I said, "and I'm Mulligan, her reporter. Captain Parisi left word for us to come up to the house."

"Wait here," he said, and shut the door.

"Thank you," Gloria said.

"You're welcome."

We were still waiting there ten minutes later when a satellite truck from Providence's ABC affiliate raced down the road and screeched to a stop beside the cruiser blocking the drive.

"We've got company," Gloria said.

The driver got out to talk with the trooper, and after a minute or so the conversation grew heated. The hogs were covering a Michael Bolton power ballad now, their version an improvement over the original, but I could see that the TV guy was yelling and waving his arms in frustration. Finally he got back in the van, backed it up, and parked behind Secretariat. The crew climbed out, opened the back doors, pulled out camera equipment, and started setting up behind by the barbed-wire fence.

"Parisi must like you," Gloria said.

"I'm not sure he likes anybody."

"Then how come he let *us* up here and not them?"

"Because he knows we'll get the story right. No dressing it up with space aliens, conspiracy theories, and Angelina Jolie."

"More company," Gloria said. Satellite trucks from the NBC and CBS affiliates were coming down the road.

Somewhere nearby, two powerful engines growled to life, giving the hog chorus a bass line. A moment later, a matching pair of Peterbilt garbage trucks with "Scalici Recycling" in red letters on their cab doors lumbered into view from behind the farm house. I assumed they were hitting the road for more pig food. Instead, they took a sharp right through the muddy field and rolled to a stop in front of the crime scene, blocking the view of it from the road.

At the end of the driveway, the cruiser moved aside so the medical examiner's van could rumble through. It rocked its way up the gravel drive, pulled into the field, and stopped ten yards from the garbage pile where the state troopers were still sifting. The door swung open, and Anthony Tedesco, the state's tubby chief medical examiner, rolled out lugging a large, stainless-steel case. Normally, his assistants did the crime scene work. It took a big case for him to venture out from the sanctity of his morgue.

Gloria snapped a few pictures with her long lens as Tedesco waddled to the blue tarp and knelt beside it. When he peeled it back, she put down the camera, turned her head, and said, "Jesus!"

"Maybe you shouldn't be on this one, Gloria."

"And maybe you should shut up and let me do my job."

I was fishing for a suitable response when the farmhouse door swung open behind me.

"The captain says you can come in now."

The trooper held the door for us, and we walked through it, following the sound of voices down a short hallway floored with polished bamboo. On both sides, the walls were hung with formal studio photographs of the Scalicis' pork-fed daughters, Caprina and Fiora. We found Cosmo and Parisi in the kitchen, seated on opposite sides of a retro dinette table with chrome legs and a red cracked-ice Formica top. Both men had empty coffee mugs in front of them. Between them, a heaping platter of biscotti and cannoli.

Cosmo's wife Simona, slim at the waist and ample where it counted, stood at the granite countertop and measured grounds for a fresh pot. She threw us a look over her right shoulder.

"Make yourselves at home. The coffee will be ready in a few minutes."

As Gloria and I seated ourselves at the table, I spied six color snapshots on the sculpted steel door of the Sub-Zero refrigerator, all held in place by Miss Piggy refrigerator magnets. Cosmo saw where my eyes had gone.

"Her name was Gotti," he said. "First sow I ever owned." Across the room, Simona sniffed resentfully.

"What happened to her?"

"After her breeding days were over, we ate her."

"Any Gotti left to share with your guests?"

"It was twelve years ago."

"No leftover chitlins in the freezer, then?"

"We don't eat the viscera. We feed it to the pigs."

"Then I'll settle for this," I said. I snagged a cannoli from the stack and took a bite. "Fantastic. Did you make these, Mama Scalici?"

"Can't say I did. They're from DeFusco's Bakery in Johnston."

"Really?" Parisi said. "*That's* what you want to ask about?"

"Yeah," I said. "But I do have a couple of other questions."

"Shoot."

"Caprina and Fiora safe at school, are they?"

Cosmo slammed his fist on the table so hard, the pastry platter jumped. "You too, Mulligan?" he growled, his face a tomato. "I can't fuckin' believe it."

"Now, Cosmo," Simona said. "These gentlemen are just doing their jobs. And such language in my house!"

Cosmo was always quick to take offense at any insult, real or imagined. He'd spent his entire adult life trying to prove that pig farmers and garbagemen were as good as anybody else. But no matter how hard he tried or how much money he made, his kids got picked on at school, he and his wife never got invited to the right parties, and he kept getting blackballed at the Metacomet Country Club.

"The girls are fine," Parisi said. "We called their school to confirm. And young lady," he said, pointing a finger at Gloria, "put the camera away or we're done here."

"So who's under the blue tarp?" I asked.

"Don't know."

"A kid?"

A five-second delay, and then: "Pieces of one."

"Which pieces?"

"So far we've turned up a female torso and a couple of limbs. Tedesco will have to test the DNA to be sure they're from the same kid."

"How old?"

"You'll have to ask him that."

"He never talks to the press."

"Not my problem, Mulligan."

The coffee was ready now. Simona poured us each a fresh mug, took a seat at the table, picked up a string of rosary beads, and wrapped them around her wrists. To me, they looked like handcuffs.

"Who found the body parts?" I asked.

"Joe Fleck," Cosmo said.

"One of your workers?"

"Yeah. He upchucked his breakfast and then came running for me. I took a quick look and called the captain."

"Fleck just found the torso," Parisi said. "My men unearthed the rest in the same garbage heap."

"That garbage been here long?" I asked.

"Came in on a truck this morning," Cosmo said.

"Any idea where it was picked up?"

Cosmo started to answer, but Parisi cut him off. "That's still under investigation."

"What about the arm from last month? Could it be from the same kid?"

"I can't talk about that on the record, Mulligan."

"No?"

"Absolutely not."

"Why is that?"

Parisi glared at me.

"Okay, off, then."

"Definitely a different kid."

"You know that how?"

Five seconds of silence, and then: "The torso's just starting to decompose. And the two limbs we found today?"

"Yeah?"

"They're both arms."

I squeezed my eyes shut. For a moment, no one spoke.

"What the hell are we dealing with here, Captain?"

"Hard to say."

"A serial killer?"

"Don't jump the gun."

"What it looks like."

"I'm going to ask you not to write that, Mulligan. It would cause a panic. If I see the words *serial killer* in the paper tomorrow, you and I are done."

"Okay, I'll play along. But it's gonna get crazy once the Van Susteren wannabes at the end of the drive get wind of this."

"From what I've seen of their journalism skills," he said, "that could take a while."

As it happened, it took only three days.

20

By the time I got to Hopes, Attila the Nun had three dead soldiers on the table in front of her and a fourth in her sights.

"You're late," she said.

"Sorry, Fiona. The copydesk was short-handed, so I got drafted to edit state house copy and just finished up."

"What'll you have?" she asked, and waved for the waitress.

"Club soda."

"Ulcer acting up?"

"It is."

"Maybe you should give up the cigars."

"I don't eat them, Fiona."

"No, but I read somewhere that they're bad for what you've got."

"Most good things are."

"I didn't see you at the press conference," she said.

"Lomax had me cover it off the TV."

"The attorney general holds a press conference to announce that a serial killer is on the loose, and the *Dispatch* doesn't bother to show up?"

"Appalling isn't it? But it's the sort of thing that's bound to happen after three-quarters of our reporters are given walking papers."

"Hard to ask questions if you're not there, Mulligan."

"Even harder to get answers."

"Anything you want to ask now?"

"Yeah. Have you heard from Captain Parisi yet?"

"I have."

"And?"

"He's mad as hell. Says I've turned his case into a quote, fuckin' circus, unquote."

"And you said?"

"That parents have a right to know someone out there is butchering kids."

The operatic theme song for Channel 10 Action News, which seldom offered much of either, burst from the TV set over the bar. Fiona lit a cigarette, and we both turned to watch the teaser.

"Is a serial killer stalking Rhode Island's children, hacking them to pieces, and feeding them to pigs? We'll be back in a moment with our exclusive investigative report. You'll be shocked!"

The exclusive investigative report turned out to be neither exclusive nor investigative. It consisted of a sound bite from Fiona's press conference, an angry "No comment" from Parisi, wild speculation by on-air reporter Logan Bedford, and a reassurance from anchor-babe Amy Banderas that "the monster among us is a threat to every child in Rhode Island." Then she beamed at the camera and exclaimed, "Get ready for an unseasonably warm weekend! Next up, Storm Surge with the weather." Probably not the name his mama gave him.

This is what will pass for local news once the *Dispatch*'s death rattle falls silent. I looked at my friend and shook my head sadly.

"Fiona," I said, "look what you did."

"Think I was wrong?"

"I think you should have listened to Parisi."

"If what I did saves just one kid . . ."

"It won't," I said.

"It's going to make parents more watchful."

"Not all of them, Fiona. Some of them are stupid. Some are on drugs. Some just don't give a shit. Besides, not even the best parents can stand guard over their kids every minute of the day. If the killer wants another kid, he'll snatch another kid. It's as easy as picking up a quart of milk at 7-Eleven."

Fiona didn't have anything to say to that. Her vanquished Bud joined its fallen comrades, and she ordered another.

"Got the autopsy report yet?" I asked.

"It's not final. Tedesco's waiting on the DNA."

"What's he saying about cause of death?"

"That unless we turn up more body parts, we'll never know. Of course, he's pretty much ruled out natural causes."

"Anything else?" I asked.

"Off the record?"

"Okay."

"I'm afraid there is."

"What?"

She just stared at me and shook her head.

"Rape?"

"Yeah," she said. "Violently and repeatedly."

We sat quietly for a while, she guzzling her Bud, I sipping my club soda and pretending not to notice that Attila the Nun had begun to cry.

On the TV, the sports guy was showing NBA highlights. Fiona locked her eyes on the screen as Paul Pierce drained a last-second three-pointer to ice a game for the

Celtics. Then she clunked her Bud down on the tabletop, looked at me with wet eyes, and said:

"I wonder what he's doing with their heads."

21

In the days following Fiona's press conference, parents all over Rhode Island showed up late for work and skipped out early so they could ferry their children back and forth to school. Elementary and middle schools held assemblies so Officer Friendly could repeat the customary warning to avoid strangers. Grandstanding local officials pledged stepped-up police patrols of schoolyards and playgrounds. The cops complied, knowing full well that it wouldn't do any good. The killer would hunt where the police weren't.

Four days after Fiona's press conference, on a clear and cold Tuesday morning, Angela Anselmo rapped on my apartment door and asked if I could drop Marta off at school.

"I hate to bother you with this," she said, "but the nursing supervisor yelled at me for being late yesterday, and I'm too afraid to let Marta walk to school alone."

"It's no bother," I said. "I'm happy to do it."

"Thank you. I really appreciate this."

"Need me to pick her up in the afternoon?"

"No. I'll be off by then, so I can do it."

"What about tomorrow?"

"I'm setting up a car pool with some of the other mothers in the neighborhood, so we should be okay."

"Good. But if you run into a problem, you can count on me."

"Thanks *so* much," she said. Then she turned and dashed down the stairs.

Fifteen minutes later I collected Marta from her apartment, led her to the Bronco, and asked her to buckle her seat belt for the short drive to Feinstein Elementary School on Sackett Street.

"I've been listening to you practice every night, Marta," I said.

"I hope it isn't disturbing you, Mr. Mulligan."

"It's not. I'm enjoying it. You play beautifully."

"Old Man Pelligrini doesn't think so. He bangs on our ceiling every night. Yesterday, he came to our door and yelled at Mama. Said he was going to call the police if I didn't stop making those awful screeching noises."

"He's just a grumpy old man. Don't let him get to you."

I pulled up in front of the school, let Marta out, and watched her skip up the walk. I didn't pull away until the door swung shut behind her.

That afternoon, just fifteen miles east of Providence, 492 kids spilled out of the red-brick elementary school in the little town of Dighton, Massachusetts. Most of them scuttled onto waiting buses, but thirty-eight of them lived close enough to walk, Patrolman Robert Dutra told me later as we sat together in his squad car and sipped cups of takeout coffee. Parents wary of the alarming news from Rhode Island were waiting for most of the walkers, but sixteen of them, mostly third- and fourth-graders, were on their own.

Dutra watched six of the walkers cut across the school parking lot and turn left onto a sleepy country road. The other ten scampered down the long macadam driveway toward Somerset Avenue, the closest thing the little town had to a main road. The small-town cop had been on the job for a year — long enough to know what he should be doing but not long enough to be bored by his baby-sitting assignment.

"A crossing guard was on duty at the corner of Somerset and Center," he told me. "I knew I could count on her to look after the kids." So he pulled his cruiser out onto the country road to keep an eye on things there.

Peter Mello, a nine-year-old fourth-grader, walked north on Somerset Avenue with three of his friends. The crossing guard helped Peter's friends cross Center Street and watched them scoot north. Then she stopped the light traffic on Somerset so Peter could cross it and head east on Center Street.

The crossing guard's name was Shirley Amaral. She'd been doing this job for eight years, and she'd always taken her responsibilities seriously, but the news from nearby Rhode Island had made her extra-vigilant. Normally she would have headed home once the children passed her post. This time, she remained on the corner so she could keep an eye on both Peter and his friends as they walked toward their houses. None of the kids lived more than a half mile from school.

About a hundred yards from the corner, Center Street drops steeply, beginning its decent to the Taunton River about a quarter mile away. Amaral watched Peter drop out of sight down the slope and then turned her attention back to the boy's friends. When she lost sight of Peter, he was sixty yards from his front door. He never got there.

"Think this has something to do with the child murders in Rhode Island?" Dutra asked me.

"I don't know."

"If you didn't think so," he said, "you wouldn't be here."

22

The Red Sox traded Manny Ramirez away two seasons ago, but I wasn't going to be the one to break the news to my best friend. He was Rosie's favorite player, and the news would surely break her heart. I unfolded the autographed Sox jersey with Manny's number 24 on the back and draped it over the shoulders of her gravestone, just as I did every time I visited.

It was late in the year for the grass to be this green. I knelt in it and read the inscription on the headstone for what had to be the hundredth time: "Rosella Isabelle Morelli. First Woman Battalion Chief of the Providence Fire Department. Beloved Daughter. Faithful Friend. True Hero. February 12, 1968–August 27, 2008."

Rosie had been racing to a house fire on a foggy night when her car crashed and burned. The fire had been deliberately set. I'd feed the arsonist to Cosmo's pigs while he was still breathing, if only I knew who he was. Rosie and I had been best friends since we were six years old. Over the years, dozens of other friends had come and gone. Work had gone from bad to good to bad again. Lovers had consumed and then abandoned us. Through it all, Rosie and I told each other everything. Some habits are hard to break.

"I'm carrying a gun now, Rosie. Got it right here under this loose jacket. I'd take it out to show you, but I know you never liked guns. Some very big guys warned me to keep my nose out of something, and, well, you know how I am. I hope I don't have to shoot anybody, but I might if they come back."

H. P. Lovecraft, the master of classic horror fiction, was at rest nearby, hidden behind a thicket of azaleas. Not far off, Thomas Wilson Dorr was entombed, his failed rebellion no longer a threat to Rhode Island's ruling class. Ruggerio "the Blind Pig" Bruccola was just behind a row of rhododendrons, buried with the last few secrets he'd managed to keep from the feds. My best friend was never at a loss for stimulating company.

"I'm tired, Rosie. Tired of watching the newspaper business collapse. Tired of the

Maniellas and their dirty business. Tired of writing about dead and missing kids. Maybe I just need a little time off, but all I can manage right now is a night out. I've got tickets for Buddy Guy at the House of Blues in Boston tomorrow night. Same place we saw him jam three years ago. I'm taking this woman I know. You'd like her, Rosie. She's smart and funny and loves the blues. Drop-dead gorgeous, too. Only thing is, she doesn't seem to like me very much."

Off to the east, gulls swooped over the Seekonk River. Rosie and I sat silently for a while and listened to their rusty-hinge cries. This was Swan Point Cemetery, but I didn't see any swans. I wrapped my arms around the cold granite headstone and gave Rosie a hug. Then I stood, removed the jersey from her shoulders, folded it, and walked past a dozen graves to my car.

I turned the ignition, popped Buddy Guy into the CD player, and growled along with him:

You damn right, I've got the blues.

That evening, I flopped on my mattress with a book by a former *Tampa Tribune* reporter named Ace Atkins. Crime novels were his parachute out of the newspaper business. If only I had that kind of talent. Ace was one of my favorite writers, but I couldn't keep my mind from wandering. After reading the same paragraph four times, I gave it up, snatched the remote, and tried channel surfing. A *Law & Order* rerun, *Dog the Bounty Hunter,* Rachael Ray cooking something I wouldn't eat on a dare, *Keeping Up with the Kardashians,* Jim Cramer bellowing bad investment advice, a *NOVA* special on frogs, *The Golden Girls* (which seemed to be on twenty-four hours a day), a meaningless game between two bottom-dwelling NBA teams . . . Finally I landed on a Charlie Rose interview with some economist I'd never heard of. Rose was the television equivalent of a bottle of Ambien and a whiskey chaser, but I was so restless that not even *he* could put me to sleep.

I spent ten minutes looking for my cell phone, found it in the pocket of my bomber jacket, and called Joseph DeLucca. Twenty minutes later, I was smoking a cigar in the doorway of Pazienza's gym when Joseph rolled up in a decade-old Mustang that was even money to beat my Bronco to the glue factory.

I held the heavy bag for him again as he gave it a good working over. When he was done, he helped me wrap my hands. I began with a flurry of jabs and then turned my hips and put everything I had into a left hook. I backed off to catch my breath and then attacked the bag again, jabbing, hooking, and looping overhand rights. Sweat streamed into my eyes. I could barely see, but I kept throwing punches. I hated that bag. I willed it alive so I could beat it to death. I drew a breath and pounded it some more.

"Mulligan!"

I threw a right cross and a left hook.

"Mulligan!"

Another hook.

"Mulligan!?" Joseph said. He grabbed me by the waist and dragged me away from the bag.

"What?"

"Look at your fuckin' hands."

Blood was seeping through the wraps.

Thirty minutes later, both of us freshly showered, we knocked on the door at Hopes. It was after hours and the lights were turned down. Annie, the barmaid, unlocked the door, let us in, and locked it behind us. A half-dozen copy editors were playing low-stakes poker at a table in back. A couple of off-duty cops sat at the bar, drinking from tall glasses of Guinness. Joseph and I grabbed a couple of cans of Bud from the cooler, slapped our money on the bar, and took our pick of the empty tables.

I smelled like Dial. Joseph smelled as if he'd bathed in Axe. I hated Axe. I pulled out a cigar, clipped the end, set fire to it, and glared in turn at each customer in the place, daring someone to tell me to put it out.

Joseph gulped from his can of Bud, set it back on the table, and said, "What the fuck's wrong with you?"

When I got home, I was still jumpy. I lay in bed drinking Bushmills from a pint bottle, hoping it would calm me down. I used the remote to snap on the TV and channel surfed until I stumbled on a favorite movie, *The Assassination of Jesse James by the Coward Robert Ford.* As the whiskey kicked in, I fought to keep my eyes open, afraid of what my dreams might bring.

I knew I'd lost the fight when a bloody little girl walked into the room and asked me to help her find her arms.

23

According to my grandfather, America lost its tenuous hold on civilization in 1967; but, the Summer of Love's flower children, acid rock, and LSD proved to be a fleeting madness. When the collapse he feared finally did come, he wasn't alive to see it. It happened in 1998, the year Joseph R. Francis released his first *Girls Gone Wild* video. Since then it's been a downward spiral of celebrity boxing, Carrot Top, *Jackass,* Paris Hilton, Flavor Flav, *Norbit,* Lindsay Lohan, Glenn Beck, Starbucks Pumpkin Chai, Octomom, Bob Dylan's *Christmas in the Heart* CD, and Jimmy Dean's Chocolate Chip Pancakes & Sausage on a Stick.

The scene at the House of Blues completed the picture. The crowd consisted mainly of unruly college jocks and their half-naked dates, most of them shit-faced before they pushed through the door, bellied up to the bar, and clamored for beer.

Recorded music blared from speakers as we waited for Buddy Guy to take the stage. Elmore James. Muddy Waters. Koko Taylor. A rowdy bunch in Boston College Eagles sweatshirts howled along, getting the words all wrong. When an asshole in a UMass-Boston jersey and a double-barreled beer helmet staggered into Yolanda for the second time, his arm mashing her left breast, I figured it had to be on purpose. Maybe she had a point about white boys. This was beginning to look like a mistake.

Late that afternoon, I'd spent more than my customary three seconds looking in my mirror. Getting ready for a date usually required a few simple steps. Sniff the armpits, drag a wet brush through my hair, pluck a relatively fresh shirt from a pile of laundry, and make sure my shoes matched. This time I peered at myself, wondering what I had to offer a woman as . . . well, as *woman* as Yolanda. Nothing changed no matter how hard I looked. Maybe I could spill some coffee on my shirt again. She thought it was cute the first time.

On the way to pick her up, I stopped off at the mall downtown and blew a hundred bucks on a pair of loafers at Bostonian. The last time I'd treated myself to a new pair of kicks was when my marriage to Dorcas was ending. They were running shoes. I'd heard somewhere that shoes say a lot about a man. I hoped the loafers were smooth talkers.

It was a short drive to East Greenwich, an artsy little town on the western shore of Narragansett Bay. Time enough to play just six tunes from my prostitution playlist. Just off Division Street, I pulled up to a cluster of roomy condos, stared at the tangle of identical door fronts, and realized that I'd forgotten to write down Yolanda's unit number. Was it 52 or 53? Or maybe 54?

I was pulling out my cell to call her when I spotted a window with a decal of a dark, clenched fist in the bottom corner. Fierce yet discreet. Had to be her. I switched off the ignition, brushed cigar ash from my pants, bounded up the walk, and rang the bell to No. 54.

The door to No. 53 opened instead, and there was Yolanda, suppressing a smile that said she'd been watching me. Then the door to No. 54 eased open, and a squat gray panther, her hair a mass of blue curls, said, "May I help you?"

"He's mine," Yolanda said. "Sorry to bother you, Mrs. Steinberg."

Mrs. Steinberg looked me up and down and winked at Yolanda before closing her door.

"Fooled by the fist, were you?" Yolanda said. "Wait a sec while I grab my coat."

She left me alone in a room that was all mint green and air, with lots of framed pictures on the walls and tables. Some were of an older woman with a face like Yolanda's, others of a man handsome enough to worry me.

"That's my brother Mark," she said.

I turned and saw she'd pulled on a sleek leather jacket that went well with her faded jeans and red Tony Lamas. Her hair was pulled back, and she wore very little makeup, as if she knew she didn't need improving.

"He used to be a reporter, *L.A. Times,* but he could see there was no future in it. He's in law school now."

"Good he's got a plan."

"It is, but he's not thrilled about it. All he ever wanted to do was be a newspaperman. He really misses it. You guys should talk sometime."

"Oh? So he's okay with white guys?"

She laughed, the sound I'd been waiting for. "Like me, he considers them a necessary evil."

I fumbled for the keys to the Bronco as she locked her door. Then she turned to me and said, "Where's your car?"

189

"Right there," I said, pointing to Secretariat, still wheezing and ticking in his stall. "I cleaned off a spot for you on the front seat."

"Let's take mine," she said, and led me to a new burgundy Acura ZDX. Settling into the ivory leather passenger seat was like sinking into a tub of warm butter. Yolanda touched something on the dash, and the engine thrummed to life.

I wondered what we'd talk about on the traffic-choked, hour-long drive to Boston. The Maniellas were a conversation stopper. Dismembered children had dubious romantic appeal. And I sucked at small talk. What could I say to convince her that white guys could be A-OK? Maybe I could remember not to say things like A-OK.

Yolanda touched something else on the dash, and John Lee Hooker started grunting "Hittin' the Bottle Again." We fell into a comfortable silence, breaking it occasionally to touch on the weather, the car's handling, and the quality of the selections from the satellite radio blues channel. We were two people who didn't know each other well, trying not to talk about work. I leaned back and envisioned the two of us, bodies scrunched together in a jam-packed club, swaying to the rhythms of the best blues guitar player in the world. Maybe Buddy would get Yolanda's mojo working.

Ninety minutes later, when Beer Helmet stumbled into her for a third time, it didn't seem to be turning out the way I'd planned. I grabbed the asshole's wrist and swung him around to face me.

"Apologize," I said.

He didn't. Instead, he tossed her a dismissive "she's nobody anyway" look and started to turn away. I threw a left. Behind it was the power of my loathing for beer helmets, Carrot Top, *Jackass,* and all the rest of the jackasses. The punch caught nothing but air. Beer Helmet was already on the floor, clutching his balls and writhing in agony. The point of Yolanda's Tony Lamas had scored a direct hit.

Beer Helmet's buddies moved toward us but then backed off as two bouncers plowed through the crowd. They must have seen the whole thing because they didn't throw us out. Instead, they gave Yolanda a high five, yanked the jerk to his feet, and dragged him off.

"My hero," I said.

"Just a little somethin' you pick up," she said, "when you're raised on the West Side."

Beer Helmet's ejection seemed to sober the crowd, or at least settle it down. A few minutes later, Buddy and his band strutted out. I put my arms around Yolanda's waist, and she let me keep them there, leaning back against me as we swayed to the music. That drew hard stares from the jocks and their dates. Blues fans are mostly white these days, and Boston is far from a postracial town. Except for Buddy and the band, Yolanda was the only black person in the place.

Buddy played not one, not two, but three encores. By the time he was done with a ten-minute version of "Slippin' In," we'd shouted our throats raw, and Yolanda's body had been pressed against mine for more than an hour. Buddy wasn't coming back for a fourth time, so the bouncers cleared the room for the second show. As we strolled out arm in arm onto Lansdowne Street, both of us were hungry, although not necessarily for the same thing.

On the sidewalk, one of the bouncers tapped my shoulder. "Hey, pal," he said. "Your lady can work security here anytime."

Yolanda laughed out loud. I hoped it was working as a bouncer that struck her as funny, but it might have been the idea that she was my lady.

I was worried about where we'd be heading for grub. I didn't figure Yolanda for a chili dog/cheese fries kind of gal, and I was short after shelling out for the tickets. As Yolanda turned west, I tugged her arm.

"The parking lot's the other way."

"Yeah, but it smells better in this direction, and a sista needs to eat."

"This is Lansdowne Street, Yolanda. The main food groups here are beer, grease, and Tabasco."

"Yum," she said, and kept walking.

We strolled past Fenway Park, and at the corner of Brookline Street, she stopped in front of the Cask'n Flagon.

"Will this do?" she said. "I've been thinking about their cheese fries all day."

And I fell for her a little more.

"So the show was tight, huh?" she said as we settled into our seats under a black-and-white photograph of a young Ted Williams. "I coulda listened to that brutha play all night. And damn, he's still ripped. The way he moves, it's hard to believe he's seventy-four."

She pulled her nose out of the menu and locked eyes with me. "Thanks, Mulligan. I forget to do things like this until someone reminds me that there's a world outside the law office."

"I could remind you more often."

She didn't say anything to that. Suddenly,

her menu was more interesting.

"I would never have pictured you in a place like this, Yolanda, but you look right at home."

The waiter was a young black man with more muscles than he needed for the job. "Miss Mosley-Jones!" he said. "It's been a long time. Having the cheese fries and two sloppy burgers again?"

"Damn right," she said. "It's my day to be bad."

I certainly hoped so.

The waiter turned his eyes to me, and his wattage went down a notch.

"The same," I said. "And bring us a pitcher of Samuel Adams."

"I didn't realize you were a regular," I said after the waiter left.

"I've only been here once. Last summer I got to missing the Cubs, so I caught a Sox game at Fenway. It reminded me so much of Wrigley I got a little weepy. After nine innings, I'm always starving, so I followed the crowd here."

"You've been here once, and the waiter remembers your name?"

"You don't think I'm memorable?"

"I think you're unforgettable."

Just then, my cell vibrated. I slipped it out, checked the number, and put it back in my pants pocket.

"Nothing important?"

"Just a blast from the past."

"The almost-ex?"

"How'd you guess?"

"What's *she* like? What kind of woman ends up with you?"

The phone started vibrating again. I pulled it out, flipped it open, placed it in the middle of the table, and pressed speaker.

"Mulligan."

"You . . . fucking . . . bastard!"

"Good evening to you, too, Dorcas."

"Who are you out whoring with tonight, you sonuvabitch?"

"I'm having dinner with a friend right now, Dorcas. Sorry, but don't have time for one of our friendly chats."

"Don't you dare hang up on me, you goddamn —"

I flipped the phone shut and put it back in my pocket.

"Damn," Yolanda said. "What the hell did you do to her?"

"Married her. She's never forgiven me for it."

"Gotta be more to it than that."

"She's unstable, Yolanda. She needs help."

"So get her some."

"I've tried, but she refuses. She thinks the

rest of us are the crazy ones."

"Whoa."

"Yeah."

We fell into an uncomfortable silence. Maybe introducing the object of my affection to Dorcas wasn't the smoothest move. The silence lengthened while I tried to think of something that would drown out the sound of my almost-ex's screech.

"She can make me sound like a monster," I said. "I'm not. I'm just a regular guy who made a bad choice."

Yolanda smiled, and the mood lightened. "You're not a regular white guy, Mulligan."

"I'm not?"

"Uh-uh. Most of them try to impress me by quoting the 'I Have a Dream' speech, telling me how many black friends they have, and dropping the names of rappers, getting most of them wrong."

"Gee," I said. "And to think I was just about to tell you how much I dig Jay-Z Hammer."

She threw back her head and laughed. When the waiter finally showed up with our food, we spent the next half hour slurping, pulling fries from a gooey mountain of cheese, and licking our fingers. I loved watching her be so unlawyerlike.

Once we'd picked the cheese fries plate

clean and drained the last of the beer, she didn't look any thicker than when we came in. I wasn't sure I could get through the rest of the evening without unbuttoning my pants. And not in a good way.

On the drive home, we listened to more blues on the radio and talked about the show, the Cubs, and the Red Sox; but everything I said really meant "Please let me kiss you."

"Can't tell you how great this was, Mulligan," Yolanda said as she pulled the Acura into the space next to my Bronco. "I felt like a human being instead of a lawyer for a change."

"So where should we go next time?"

She turned off the ignition and turned toward me. "You gonna make me say it again?"

"You don't date white guys."

"You got it."

"No one would have to know. I promise not to go public."

"It's late," she said. "You should probably get going."

We got out of the car, and I walked her to the door. She unlocked it, and when she turned around to say good night, I was right there, my face close. She threw her arms around my neck and hugged me hard and quick. Then she pulled away, went through the door, and closed it. I'd been summarily dismissed.

As I drove up the interstate toward Providence, I held on to her smile, her laugh, her scent, those tight jeans and red Tony Lamas. Maybe all was not lost. When she'd pulled back from that hug, she'd tilted her head for a fraction of a second, the way a woman does when she wants to be kissed.

Or had I imagined it?

24

"Yes," I said, "I am a member of Joseph De-Lucca's immediate family."

"And exactly how are you related?"

"He's my brother."

"Why is it, then, that you have a different last name?"

"We're half-brothers."

"I'm skeptical," the hospital Nazi said.

"You are?"

"Yes."

"And why would that be?"

"Because I recognize you. You're that reporter from the *Dispatch*."

"Reporters can have brothers," I said.

"I imagine so," she said. "But this is the fifth time this year you have tried to get into a shooting victim's room by claiming to be a relative."

"The fifth that you know of," I said.

"You mean there were more?"

"Would you believe my family is having a

run of bad luck?"

"No."

"Give me a break," I said. "He's a friend, and I really need to talk to him."

"Get out of here before I call security."

"By security do you mean the geriatric rent-a-cop with a limp who waved to me in the lobby, or are you talking about the fat retired beat cop who's munching a cruller in the coffee shop?"

She reached for the phone. I shrugged and headed for the door.

It took a couple of hours, but I managed to piece together the story of what happened to Joseph by reading between the lines of the police report and chatting up three off-duty cops, two hookers, and a bartender. Of the sixty or so people who were in the Tongue and Groove when the shooting started, they were the only ones willing to talk to a reporter with a notepad. Logan Bedford, the asshole from Channel 10, had better luck. A few dozen witnesses had queued up for the opportunity to talk into his microphone. Anything to get on TV.

From what I gathered, it went down this way:

By the Budweiser clock on the wall, it was a little after nine P.M. when Jamal, King Felix's nervous triggerman, entered the club, pimp-walked up to the bar, and asked where he could find Joseph DeLucca. Jamal's full name, it turned out, was Jamal Jackson; and he was a little younger than I thought — just fourteen. The boy's father wasn't in the picture. His mother worked the day shift as an orderly at Rhode Island Hospital. Nights, she made beds at the Biltmore. No, she told police, she didn't know Jamal hadn't been to school all year.

Jamal made the bartender nervous. He didn't like the tic in the kid's left eye, and he especially didn't like the fact that he was a kid.

"Far as I know, there's no state law against a kid buying a blow job," the bartender told me later, "but he's not permitted to be in an establishment that serves alcohol. If Attila the Nun ever found out he was in here, the bitch would have another excuse to scream bloody murder." I didn't like his choice of words for my friend, but I needed to hear the rest of the story, so I didn't make an issue of it.

He told Jamal to get out, the bartender went on. His exact words, if he remembered them right, were "Get lost and come back when you're eighteen."

"Ain't leaving till I see DeLucca," Jamal

said, the twitch in his left eye growing more violent.

What the hell, the bartender figured. Joseph *was* the bouncer. He asked Chloe, the plump waitress with the green hair, to fetch Joseph from the all-nude room so he could throw the kid out.

Two minutes later, Joseph walked up to the bar and said, "Somebody lookin' for me?"

"You DeLucca?" Jamal asked.

"Yeah," Joseph said. "Who the fuck are you?"

Jamal didn't answer. He just reached into his waistband and pulled out his little silver pistol.

He had not picked the best evening for this.

There were twenty-two hookers and roughly forty customers in the club. Eighteen of the customers were there for Mike Scanlon's bachelor party. The festivities had just gotten under way, so the celebrants hadn't drunk themselves into a stupor yet. They'd had one beer apiece, and the first round of tequila shots had just arrived at their tables. Most of the guys had strippers on their laps. The girl who called herself Sacha, a couple of the celebrants told me later, was on her knees in front of the groom-to-be, her head bobbing up and down.

"Can you keep that part out of the paper?" Scanlon asked me. "My fiancée would fuckin' kill me."

"Sure thing," I said, "as long as you fill me in on what happened next."

When Sacha's work was done, Scanlon expelled a sigh of satisfaction, opened his eyes, and saw the glint of bar light on nickel as Jamal's pistol emerged from his waistband. Scanlon shoved the hooker aside and reached for the revolver in his ankle holster. His pals weren't sure what was happening at first, but instinctively they went for *their* guns, too.

Scanlon was a Providence cop. So were his buddies.

In the next fifteen seconds, approximately a hundred rounds were fired, according to the official police estimate. One slug grazed Joseph's thigh. Another ricocheted off a metal post and tore a ragged hole through the impressive rump of a stripper named Jezebelle. Dozens more slammed into the mahogany bar and the club's black-painted walls. And some hit what the room full of sharpshooters were aiming at. An assistant medical examiner was still counting the holes in Jamal's body. Every time he counted, he told me, he came up with a different number.

The cop who recovered Jamal's gun at the scene told me the kid never got off a shot.

25

Friday morning the executive editor, Marshall Pemberton, sent an all-hands e-mail directing the staff to assemble in the newsroom for a mandatory late afternoon meeting. I didn't figure he was about to announce that we'd won a Pulitzer, so it had to be more bad news. Maybe he was finally going to tell us the old girl was closing down for good.

Once, Smith Coronas clicked and clacked here on long banks of dented metal desks. Teletype machines chattered day and night, spewing AP copy onto long rolls of yellow paper. Copyboys sorted it by subject and hightailed across the ink-stained tile floor to hang it in streams from spikes by the business, sports, and national desks. Every time the door to the back shop swung open, the football field–sized newsroom rattled with the clanking from the linotype machines. That was all before my time, but I loved listening to the old-timers on the copydesk, the three that were left, reminisce about the old days.

When the paper's miserly owners finally got around to buying computers, the clicking and clacking ceased. Some of the old guys grumbled. Some had trouble adjusting. "Where do you put the paper in this damn thing?" Jim Clark had famously asked. But there was no arguing with progress.

Even after the typewriters and linotype machines were ancient history, the newsroom I loved was never quiet. Reporters relentlessly worked the phones. Assistant city editors scuttled from desk to desk, handing out assignments that were not always gratefully received. Photographers and photo editors huddled at the picture desk, arguing about what shots to use. Sports editors bellowed the latest scores. Copy editors cracked wise about bad leads. Some reporters needed earplugs to write their stories, but I liked the racket.

Six years ago the *Dispatch*'s owners, failing to recognize they were in a dying business, spent a million dollars to renovate the place. They laid a maroon carpet, installed recessed lighting, chopped the newsroom into cubicles, hauled in fake butcher-block desks, and plopped down potted plants. But the newsroom still thrummed with the thrill of putting out a daily newspaper. Evenings, when the first edition deadline passed and the giant Goss presses began to turn, I could feel the floor vibrate under my feet. Sometimes I'd trot down the back stairs and watch the rolls of newsprint race through those elegant machines. I loved their defiant roar.

Two decades ago, when the *Dispatch* hired me right out of Providence College to cover high school sports, those presses churned out a quarter of a million copies a day. Now they printed less than half that. The *Dispatch*'s news staff once numbered 340, but there were only 80 of us left — if you counted the 5 interns who worked for free.

At three P.M., Pemberton ventured out his glass-walled office in the middle of the newsroom and gathered what was left of the news staff around him. Lomax stood by Pemberton's side. They both looked grim.

"As you are all aware, the newspaper industry is experiencing difficult times," Pemberton began, and I felt the air go out of the room. "Over the course of the last two years, we have been forced to make significant cuts in the *Dispatch*'s news budget, including a number of regrettable staff reductions. This week, I was informed by the publisher that the cuts we have made to date have not been sufficient to restore the newspaper's financial stability. Therefore, we are taking the following steps:

"Effective a week from tomorrow, the *Dispatch* will cease publication on Saturdays. This measure will reduce our printing and delivery costs by fourteen percent. In addition —"

"Why Saturdays?" Gloria shouted.

Pemberton looked alarmed at the interruption, then said, "Because, Miss Costa, Saturday is the weakest advertising day of the week."

"But what if there's *news* on Friday?" Gloria said.

"There's always news on Friday," Carol Young, the sports editor, grumbled. "It's a big night for sports scores."

"And we'll report them in our online edition," Pemberton said. "Now if I may be allowed to continue?" He held up his right hand, asking for silence, and then pressed on.

"In addition," he said, "we are compelled to make further reductions in payroll."

The staffers present released a collective groan.

"We wish to accomplish this without additional layoffs," Pemberton said. "There-fore, we are reducing the work week of all news department employees, with a com-mensurate reduction in pay. Effective next Monday, each of you will be assigned to work four eight-hour days a week. Ed Lomax is revising the schedule for next week and will post it by five o'clock, so please check the bulletin boards before you leave for the day. That is all."

With that, he turned and slipped back into his office.

"Hold on," Lomax shouted as the group began to break up. "Mr. Pemberton forgot to mention one last thing. When the sup-plies on hand run out, you'll all have to buy your own pens and notepads."

That set off a stampede for the supply cabinets. I watched the mayhem for a mo-ment and then sidled up to Lomax as he headed back to the city desk.

"The copy editors might actually work four days a week," I said, "but most of the reporters care too much about their beats to do that. Hell, most of us have been work-ing six days a week for five days' pay as it is."

"I know that, Mulligan."

"Know what pisses me off most about this?"

"No, but I'm sure you're going to tell me."

"Waiting till three o'clock on a Friday afternoon to break bad news," I said. "It's one of those cheap tricks you can find in every management textbook. Pemberton figures that after we fume all weekend, the anger will die down by the time he comes back to work Monday morning."

"There's a hole in your theory," Lomax said.

"What?"

"Pemberton won't be coming back on Monday."

"Why is that?"

"His job has been eliminated."

"Oh."

"Yeah. Now I get to do my work *and* his."

26

Monday morning, the newsroom was as quiet and empty as Fenway Park in January. I'd just started working on the day's obits when Mason wandered in, dragged a chair into my cubicle, and dropped into it.

"I finally have something on that thing you asked me to look into," he said.

At first I drew a blank. I'd given him the campaign contribution lists weeks ago, and a lot had happened since then.

"I didn't know anything about the porn business," he said, "so I read everything I could find online. One of the things I learned is that most American-made porn is shot in the San Fernando Valley, but that some of it also comes out of Miami, Las Vegas, and Ypsilanti, Michigan."

"Ypsilanti? Really?"

"Yeah."

"Interesting," I said, "but how does any of this help us?"

"I figured there's a good chance Maniella has a studio in one of those places."

"But you looked and couldn't find it, right?"

"Not at first."

"Oh?"

"Most pornographers aren't as secretive as Sal Maniella. Wicked Pictures, Vivid Entertainment, Digital Playground, and a bunch of others with more, uh, more *colorful* names even have listed phone numbers. So I made a dozen blind calls and asked to speak to the owners. A couple of them hung up on me when I told them who I was, but most of them were eager to talk about Maniella."

"How come?"

"They don't like him. The guys I talked to — a couple of them were women, actually — said Maniella is notorious for stealing their best girls."

"I see."

"They also think he rats them out to the authorities."

"For what? It's a legal business."

"One guy said a couple of his actors — which is what he calls them — contracted HIV. He said he was dealing with it, but somebody reported him to the California State Health Department. Couple of others said someone called the cops on them for employing underage girls."

"Were they?"

"They said it wasn't their fault, that the girls had convincing fake IDs, but the studio heads — which is what they call themselves, like they're DreamWorks or something — are facing criminal charges."

"And they blame Maniella?"

"For some reason, they're sure it was him, yeah. Couple of them said they're glad he's dead. Saved them the trouble of shooting him themselves."

"So what did they tell you that's going to help us?"

"That the Maniellas have a studio in Van Nuys. Big brick ware house just off the San Diego Freeway with no sign on the building."

"That all you got?"

"There's more. Once I knew he was operating out of Van Nuys, I combed through the governor's campaign contribution list looking for people with addresses in or near there: Glendale, Burbank, Santa Clarita . . ."

"And?"

"And I found sixty-two."

"That's a lot of Southern California residents with an unnatural interest in getting the governor of Rhode Island re-elected," I said.

"That's what I thought."

"Any of them named Hugh Mungus or Lucy Bangs?"

"I don't think those are real names, Mulligan."

"Run the same check on the contribution lists for the legislative committee chairmen?"

"Not yet, but I will. I'm betting that will give us more names."

"That it?"

"Only twelve of the names I came up with have listed phone numbers," he said. "I called them, but they hung up on me."

"A lot of people just use unlisted cell phones these days."

"That's true. I guess one of us needs to fly to California and knock on doors."

"The paper will never spring for it," I said.

"Can this wait a couple of months?" he said. "I was thinking of taking some vacation time at the end of January."

"Knocking on doors isn't much of a vacation."

"I've got three weeks coming," he said. "I'll spend the first week on this and the rest lying in the sun in Malibu."

"Three weeks? Beginning reporters get

one. Must be nice to be the publisher's son."

"There are advantages."

"Well, you did some good work on this, Thanks-Dad. Maybe you can overcome your upbringing after all."

27

Thanksgiving sneaked up on me. It was Tuesday before I realized what week it was. By then my sister Meg, who lives in New Hampshire, had already flown out to spend the week with our brother in Los Angeles. Yolanda was on the way to Chicago to celebrate the holiday with her mom. And Rosie was still in her grave in Swan Point Cemetery. I didn't know what Dorcas was doing and didn't give a shit.

It was just as well. I wasn't in a festive mood. Last night, the little girl with no arms told me her name was Allison, that she loved the Celtics, and that she missed her mom. She'd become a regular nighttime visitor.

"I don't have any plans," I told Lomax. "Why don't I work the holiday so you can give somebody else the day off?"

"You sure?"

"I am. Otherwise I'll just be sitting alone at home, guzzling beer and watching football on TV."

"Okay," he said. "Come in at seven A.M. and you can play city editor. All you'll have to do is monitor the police radio, edit whatever breaking news the holiday skeleton crew scares up, and look over a couple of bullshit Thanksgiving Day features. Hardcastle will come in to relieve you at four."

"Give him the day off, too," I said. "I'll pull a double shift."

"You sure?"

"I am."

"No way I can pay you overtime."

"Didn't figure you could."

That evening I bumped into my neighbor Angela Anselmo in the hallway outside our apartment doors. She was on her way out, buttoning a cloth coat over a pale blue maternity dress. She looked to be about five months along now, but there didn't seem to be a man in the picture.

"Big plans for Thanksgiving?" she asked.

"No. It's just another workday for me."

"Oh. Well, the kids and I are having our turkey dinner around seven," she said. "Would you like to join us?"

"That's sweet of you, but I'm afraid I can't."

"You sure? I cook a mean turkey, and I could use a man to carve the bird and help

217

wash all the dishes."

"I'm working a double shift, Angela. I won't be home till eleven."

And so two days later I was sitting in Lomax's chair, editing a lame feature on cranberry bogs and watching the Cowboys bully the Raiders, when the desk phone rang.

"City desk, Mulligan."

"I've got an Angela Anselmo and her two kids down here," the guard in the lobby said. "They're asking can they come up."

"They look dangerous to you?" I asked.

"Not really."

"Then what are you waiting for?"

A minute later, Angela, Marta, and her fifteen-year-old brother, Nico, stepped off the elevator. Marta was carrying her violin case. Angela and Nico hefted plastic grocery bags.

"Happy Thanksgiving!" Angela and Marta cried in unison while Nico looked sullen and embarrassed to be in their company. Angela unpacked the bags, covering the city desk with Tupperware containers filled with what turned out to be roasted turkey, pomegranate-and-giblet gravy, sausage-and-mozzarella stuffing, sweet potatoes flavored with lime and ginger, and an assortment of Italian pastries. They'd also brought paper

218

plates, plastic utensils, and a ten-cup Dunkin' Donuts Box 'O Joe.

"You didn't need to do this," I said.

"We wanted to!" Marta said.

"It was Marta's idea," said her proud mama.

The little girl beamed, opened her violin case, tucked the instrument under her chin, and began to play "We Plow the Fields and Scatter." The holiday skeleton crew, a half-dozen reporters and copy editors, stopped tapping their keyboards to listen. When she was done, everyone in the room except Nico, who looked even more uncomfortable than before, applauded the performance.

"Enjoy your meal," Angela said as Marta packed up her violin. She and Marta both hugged me and then turned for the elevator, Nico slouching along behind them. I picked up a plastic fork and dug in. The food was as good as it looked, tasty but mild enough to soothe the gnawing pain in my stomach.

Late that night, I cracked open a fresh pint of Bushmills, collapsed on my mattress, and sipped from the bottle. The Irish whiskey did its job, keeping the little girl with no arms at bay. But in the morning, I woke up with a hot poker in my gut. I shuffled to the bathroom, felt the bile rise to my throat, and threw up in the sink. The vomit looked like bloody coffee grounds.

I drove myself to the hospital, where an emergency room doctor gave me a quick going-over and promptly admitted me. I spent the rest of the day getting studied, stabbed, and prodded.

Next morning, I awoke to find Brian Israel sitting by my hospital bed, a stethoscope draped over his Hugo Boss suit jacket so the hot young nurses would know he's a doctor.

"How long have you had pain in your abdomen?" he asked.

"Couple of years."

"And you didn't think it was worth seeing me about it?"

"I've been a little busy."

"So you've been self-medicating."

"I have."

"With what?"

"Rolaids and Maalox."

"And about a month ago that stopped working, right?"

"Pretty much."

"And still you didn't come see me?"

"I was going to, soon as I could make the time."

"When did your clothes stop fitting right?"

"How'd you know about that?"

"Just answer the question."

"Couple of weeks ago, I guess. Figured I'd just gained a little weight."

"More likely you were bloating."

"Because of what I've got?"

"Yeah."

"And what I've got is an ulcer," I said.

"Looked up your symptoms on WebMD, did you?"

"Matter of fact, I did."

"The EGD — the tube with the little camera on it that we stuck down your throat — told us you've got a one-centimeter gastric ulcer."

"How big is that in English?"

"About the size of a dime."

"Okay."

"Because you didn't get it treated, it perforated your stomach lining."

"That explains the bloody vomit?"

"Exactly. When we did the EGD, we cauterized the wound. We also biopsied your stomach lining and found *Helicobacter pylori.*"

"I'd *heard* he was missing."

The doc didn't crack a smile. "It's a bacteria," he said. "It's what caused your problem, but there were probably contributing factors."

"Such as?"

"Still smoking cigars?"

"One or two a day, yeah."

"Drink a lot of coffee?"

"Gallons."

"Skip meals? Eat at odd times?"

"Goes with the job."

"Well, there you go."

"So now what?"

He pulled some drug samples from the side pocket of his jacket and dropped them on the bedside table. "Amoxicillin to kill the bacteria and omeprazole to suppress stomach acid. I'll give you a prescription for the amoxicillin, which I want you to take twice a day for two weeks. You can buy omeprazole over the counter, and you'll be on that for life. Rolaids or Tums several times a day are a good idea, too. They protect the stomach lining."

"Anything else?"

"Yeah. Stop smoking, eat regular meals, and stick to a bland diet. No fried food, spices, cheese, caffeine, carbonated beverages, or alcohol."

"Aw, shit. You just described my entire diet," I said, and he chuckled like he thought I was kidding.

"Look, you need to take this seriously, Mulligan. If you don't, we might have to remove a piece of your stomach. Worst case, it could even be fatal."

"Okay, okay. So when do I get out of here?"

"Tomorrow morning," he said, so twenty-four hours later I walked out the door of Rhode Island Hospital, found Secretariat where I'd left him in the emergency room parking lot, took a Partagás from the glove box, and fired it up. I knew I'd have to cut back, but one or two a week probably wouldn't kill me.

28

It was getting dark when I swung the Bronco left onto Route 6, glanced in my side mirror, and saw a white Hummer lurch across two lines of traffic to make the same turn. It was three cars back when I turned north onto Route 295 and still behind me when I took the exit for Hartford Avenue in Johnston. I turned into a gas station, pulled up to the pumps, and watched the Hummer slowly roll by and keep on going. I couldn't see anything through its tinted windows.

Johnston Town Hall marked the halfway point between the *Dispatch* and state police headquarters in Scituate. When I turned into the parking lot, Parisi was already there. I nosed in beside his Crown Vic, and we both slid our windows down.

"Can't believe you're still driving that heap," he said.

"Shhh! You're going to hurt Secretariat's

feelings."

"You named your car?"

"I did, but don't let it fool you. He's slower than he looks."

"Doesn't seem possible," he said. "So tell me, did you ever talk to the Maniellas' lawyer?"

"I did."

"She tell you anything?"

"She told me she doesn't date white guys."

His eyes narrowed. "I don't give a shit about your love life, Mulligan. Did she tell you anything that would *interest* me?"

"That depends."

"On what?"

"On whether your interests include chitlins, the Chicago Cubs, and the blues."

"They don't."

"Well then, no."

He looked at me hard for a moment, then said, "We finally got a formal ID on Sal."

"How'd you manage that?" I asked, the question triggering Parisi's trademark five-second time delay.

"I did a little digging and found out the Maniellas illegally filled a thousand square yards of wetlands when they put their dock in last spring. If the state Environmental Protection Agency gets wind of it, they'll have to rip the whole thing out. I told

225

Vanessa it could be our little secret if she agreed to cooperate."

"So she made the ID?"

"At the morgue, she claimed she couldn't bear to look at the body, so she had her sixty-two-year-old mother do it."

"That's cold," I said.

"That's what I thought."

"Anything else on Sal?"

Five seconds of silence, and then: "Not that I can tell you."

"What about the body parts at the pig farm?"

"Still a dead end," he said. "Now your turn."

"I hear that a prominent citizen is worried his name might surface in the Providence PD's child porn case."

"Is that so?"

"Yeah."

"What's his name?"

"Right now it's just a rumor, so I'd rather not say."

"Are you suggesting a connection between that case and the Maniellas?" Parisi asked.

"Do you think there could be one?"

"As far as I know, Sal has never stooped to child porn, so I doubt it," he said, "but I'll keep an open mind. What else you got?"

"I dropped in on King Felix a few days

226

before the shooting at the Tongue and Groove."

"And?"

"He was still popping Vicodin from the beating DeLucca gave him."

"Meet his baby hit squad?"

"I did," I said. "Got to see Jamal before the Providence cops shot him full of holes."

"What about the other one?"

"Felix called him Marcus. A couple of inches taller and maybe a year or two older than Jamal."

"How'd he strike you?"

"Like a snake coiled to strike."

"His full name is Marcus Washington and he's sixteen," Parisi said. "We've got surveillance video of him shooting beer cans at twenty feet behind the Calvary Baptist Church."

"With a little nickel pistol?"

"Yeah."

"He hit any of them?"

"About a quarter of the time, yeah."

"That's pretty good shooting."

"It is," Parisi said. "If Felix sent *him* after DeLucca, things might have turned out different."

"Wonder why he didn't."

"Maybe he's saving him for something else."

"Think Felix had Sal whacked?" I asked.

Parisi took longer than usual to consider his answer. "I doubt it. His beef is with De-Lucca. The dumb shit probably doesn't even know who Sal is. So what else you got?"

"That's it."

"Then you got jack shit."

"No disrespect, Captain, but so do you."

"Unless I know more than I'm telling."

"You usually do," I said.

"You gonna stay on this?"

"Whenever I can break away from the routine crap."

"Let's compare notes again in a week or so," he said. "And get that muffler replaced, or next time I'm writing you up." With that, he cranked the engine of his Crown Vic and fishtailed out of the lot.

As I pulled onto Hartford Avenue, I didn't see the Hummer lurking. I drove less than a mile to the Subway on Atwood Avenue, ordered a veggie sandwich, and ate the vile thing standing up. Then I walked out of the place into a light rain and found the white monstrosity parked beside my Bronco. The Hummer's front doors swung open, and Black Shirt and Gray Shirt climbed out. This time, though, they wore matching XXXL Patriots jerseys. That made it hard to tell them apart. They leaned against the back of the Bronco and slowly shook their heads, letting me know I'd disappointed them.

"You and your pal Mason have been asking questions again," said the one on the left.

"Which we asked you nicely not to do," said the one on the right.

"So one of us is going to have to teach you a lesson," said the one on the left. He flexed and added, "You get to choose."

"What if I win?"

"If you pick *him*," said the one on the right, "you might have a one-in-a-thousand shot, but then you'll just have to fight me."

"Are you two carrying?" I asked, and they burst out laughing. The idea that they'd need a weapon to deal with me struck them as hilarious.

"Well, I am," I said, and I showed them the Colt. They didn't wet their pants, but they didn't come for me, either.

"You told us it wasn't in working condition," said the one on the right.

"I lied."

"Know how to use it?"

I thumbed the safety off and assumed a shooter's stance.

They shrugged, got back in the Hummer,

and drove away. I wondered if they were going home to fetch their guns.

29

Nighttime at Swan Point Cemetery was the perfect spot for a gunfight — plenty of cover and no one around to hear the shots — but I probably hadn't irritated Vanessa enough to provoke anything more than a savage beating. I had no trouble finding Rosie in the dark. I unfolded the Manny Ramirez jersey and draped it over her headstone.

"Rosie, I'm horny," I said. But she was in no position to help me with that.

"No, I'm still not getting any from that hot lawyer. She seems to be warming up to me, but not in that way. The good news is she hasn't said, 'Let's just be friends,' yet. Think I might still have a chance?"

I sat beside Rosie in the wet grass, and together we looked at the sky. A light rain was falling, so there were no stars to wish on.

"The little girl with no arms visits my dreams every night," I said. "Yes, it is hard on me. Probably hard on her, too."

With that, my imagination failed me. I could no longer hear Rosie's voice. I sat with her in the dark, my hand resting on the shoulder of her gravestone, until the rain turned to snow. By the time I got home, it was coming down hard.

30

Tuesday afternoon, I was dashing off a fender bender wrap-up for Lomax when "Confused" by a San Francisco punk band called the Nuns began playing in my pants pocket.

"Afternoon, Fiona."

"Let's talk."

"Hopes?"

"In ten minutes," she said, and hung up.

Except for a couple of alkies hunched over boilermakers at the bar, Hopes was nearly deserted, the snow keeping the regulars away. I asked the barkeep for a club soda. It probably wasn't the best thing for my ulcer, but I figured it was better than beer. I carried the drink to Fiona's table, draped my hooded army surplus parka over the back of a chair, and sat across from her. The gold wedding band God had given her gleamed on her ring finger.

"So what's up?" I asked.

"Frank Drebin and *Police Squad!* still aren't getting anywhere with the Maniella murder," she said.

"Same story with the body parts at Scalici's pig farm," I said.

"Problem with the body parts is we got no suspects," she said. "Problem with the Maniella murder is we got too many."

"Think Vanessa had Sal whacked so she could take over the family business?"

"No evidence to support it," Fiona said, "but she's got a hell of a motive."

"She's not the only one," I said, and told her about the rival porn producers boogying on Sal's grave.

"There's also the Mob," Fiona said. "Maybe Arena and Grasso whacked Sal to settle their old strip club beef."

"Could be," I said.

"What about your old pal King Felix? How does he fit into this?"

"I don't think he does," I said. "His beef is with DeLucca."

"Can't rule him out, though," she said. She took another swallow of Bud, picked her box of Marlboro 100's off the table, shook one out, and stuck it between her lips. I whipped out my lighter, and she leaned into the flame.

"Families of porn actresses?" I said.

"Parisi's working that angle. He's inter-
rogated a bunch of them who are angry
enough to have done it, but so far their
alibis are holding up."

"What about vigilantes?" I said.

"Like who?"

"A radical feminist group, maybe. Or
right-wing religious zealots like the Sword
of God. Did you know they've been picket-
ing the Maniellas' strip clubs?"

"So I've heard."

"I made Reverend Crenson's acquaintance
the other day," I said. "That's one scary
dude. Looks just like Reverend Kane in
Poltergeist II."

"Really? I think he looks more like Mr.
Burns from *The Simpsons*."

"Yeah, I can see that, too."

"We've had our eye on him since last
winter," she said, "when his parishioners
started sending hate mail to Sheldon White-
house and Patrick Kennedy."

"About what?"

"Their votes for Obama's 'death panels,'
their support for our 'coon' president's
'socialist agenda,' and their secret plan to
take everyone's guns away."

"The church has been around for what, a
couple of years?"

"More like ten, but they kept a low profile

235

until last year."

"Before he got canned," I said, "our religion writer told me the church took its name from a Roger Williams quote. I don't remember it word for word, but I don't think our gentle founder was advocating the use of firearms."

History preserved a lot of Williams's words, but no portrait — not even a description of him — has been handed down to us. The fourteen-foot-tall granite Roger Williams who stares down from Prospect Park, arms outstretched to bless the city he founded, is entirely made up. Leo Friedlander's statue has been up there since it was dedicated in 1939. Several years ago, vandals whacked the thumb and all five fingers from his right hand. I doubt they even knew who he was.

"Roger Williams was a pacifist," Fiona said. "The sword he wielded was the Word. The Sword of God seems to prefer bullets. I liked them for the shooting at the abortion doctor's house in Cranston last fall, but Parisi couldn't make a case."

We ordered another round, drank in silence, and pondered the possibilities.

"What we've got," I said, "is a lot of theories and nothing to back any of them up."

"The only thing we can be sure of," she said, "is that Sal Maniella is still dead."

31

The snow turned into a blizzard overnight. By first light, it was nearly two feet deep and still falling. Cars skidded into each other. Schools and businesses closed. Thirty thousand Narragansett Electric customers lost power. The mayor went on TV and urged everyone with a nonessential job to stay at home. Sugary flakes clung to tree branches, blanketed trash-strewn sidewalks, drifted across potholed streets, and transformed our hideous city hall into a fairy castle. I managed to write the weather story without using the phrase *winter wonderland.*

I'd just finished the piece when I heard "Who Are You?" by the Who, my ringtone for unrecognized numbers, playing in my pants pocket.

"Mulligan."

"It's Sal Maniella. I understand you've been looking for me."

■ ■ ■ ■

A stiff wind howled out of the northeast. Drifts formed, blew away, and re-formed across the streets. The plows couldn't keep up. Secretariat groped his way west at ten miles an hour on Route 44, struggling to hold the road. As we passed the deserted Apple Valley Mall, he skidded into a drift and stubbornly refused to budge. I fetched a collapsible shovel from the back, dug him out, threw rock salt under the wheels for traction, and pressed on. By the time I reached Greenville, I could barely see the road through the windshield. I switched on the GPS so I wouldn't miss the left turn onto West Greenville Road again, but the device couldn't locate a satellite through the thick cloud cover. I managed to find the turn anyway and crept along, searching for the big white colonial that marked the entrance to unpaved Pine Ledge Road.

I'd just spotted it when a figure in a navy-blue parka appeared out of the gloom and threw both hands in the air, directing me to stop. I pumped the brakes, and Secretariat skidded to a halt. I rolled down the window, and Black Shirt, or maybe it was Gray Shirt, filled it with his cinder-block head.

"I just plowed the access road," he said, "but it's still treacherous along the top of the dike. I damn near went into the drink. We're gonna leave the cars here and walk in."

I turned right onto Pine Ledge, nosed into a freshly cleared space at the side of the road, and parked beside a Jeep Wrangler with a plow mounted on the front. Next to it was another car that must have been there all day, or maybe even overnight. It was smothered with snow. As I walked behind it, I knocked enough off the back to identify it as a burgundy Acura ZDX.

Snow crunched under my Reeboks and the ex-SEAL's Timberland boots as we trudged west toward the dike, our hands buried in our jacket pockets. It was an eight-hundred-yard walk to the house, and my nose was already numb from the cold.

"Where's the forty-five at?" the ex-SEAL asked.

"Tucked inside my jacket."

"I won't undress you now, but when we get to the house I'll have to take it away from you."

"Still want to beat me up?"

"If I did, you'd already be turning the snow red."

We walked on in silence. New ice hugged

the edge of the lake. The tracks of a lone coyote danced across the snow cover.

Crack!

The big guy spun toward the sound, a Glock 17 suddenly in his right hand. Another crack, and then another as pine boughs snapped under their heavy burden of snow. The ex-SEAL smiled to himself and slipped the weapon back into his deep jacket pocket.

A drift blocked the Maniellas' wide front steps. We bypassed them, entered through the side door to the garage, and stomped the snow from our feet. I raised my arms without being asked, and the big guy unzipped my jacket, stuck his paw inside, and pulled out the Colt. We removed our jackets, shook the snow from them, and hung them on a row of brass pegs mounted on the garage wall. Then he led me inside and turned me over to the stout maid.

"Mr. Maniella say wait in library," she said, and led me across the marble floor of the foyer to a large room with a wood fire crackling in a fieldstone fireplace. I walked across a black-and-tan Persian carpet and knelt before the flames. When the feeling returned to my nose and feet, I stood and took a good look around. One wall was floor-to-ceiling windows with a panoramic view of the frozen lake. The other three walls were lined with built-in cherry bookcases that held the last thing I expected to find in a pornographer's house. Books. Many of them were bound in what appeared to be original eighteenth- and nineteenth-century calf and Moroccan leather. Titles stamped in gilt glittered on the spines. In a corner of the room, a spiral staircase led to a gallery, where more built-in bookshelves covered all four walls.

I turned to the nearest shelf and ran my finger along a row of books by Mark Twain: *Following the Equator, Adventures of Huckleberry Finn, The Innocents Abroad, Letters from the Earth,* and a dozen more. I slid *Life on the Mississippi* from the shelf, opened it to the title page, and found "S. L. Clemens" scrawled in brown ink. A signed first edition. I gingerly returned it to its place.

I strolled the room, stopped at a section filled with period books on the Civil War, and took the first volume of *Personal Memoirs of U. S. Grant* from a shelf. In the center of the room, two easy chairs and a sofa upholstered in matching chocolate calfskin surrounded a low marble-top table. The table had been set with a sterling coffee service and dainty blue-and-white cups and saucers. Beside them were two crystal decanters filled with amber liquid. I sat on the sofa and looked longingly at the decanters. Then I poured a cup of hot coffee, cut it with lots of cream, and downed it in a swallow. Beside the couch, a lamp with a stained glass shade rested on an antique cherry side table. I switched it on and nothing happened. The power was out. The day was fading now, the last gray light filtering through the wall of windows. I opened the book and could make out the words on the first page:

"Man proposes and God disposes." There are but few important events in the affairs of men brought about by their own choice. . . .

I was four pages into the first chapter when a deep voice rumbled: "I see you've made yourself at home."

I glanced up to see Salvatore Maniella, dressed in pressed jeans and a tan cardigan sweater, peering down at me with a kindly look on his face. I knew him to be sixty-five years old, but he looked younger thanks to good genes, clean living, or a skilled plastic surgeon. He sat beside me on the couch and stretched out his hand. I took it and didn't give it back.

"What are you doing?" he asked.

"Checking for a pulse."

The right corner of his mouth curled in a half smile. Then he took the book from my lap, checked the title, and handed it back to me.

"I always meant to read this," I said, "but I never got around to it."

"When we're finished here, why don't you take both volumes home with you," he said. "Just return them when you're done."

"I wouldn't dare," I said. "What if something happened to them?"

"Grant's memoir was the best selling book of the nineteenth century," he said. "It's not a rare book."

"But some of these are."

"Yes," he said.

"How long have you been collecting?"

"When I was a student at Bryant College, I picked up a Fitzgerald first edition for fifty cents at a library sale, and it got me hooked."

"I know what you mean," I said. "I found a stack of *Black Mask* and *Dime Detective* pulp magazines at a flea market when I was a teenager, and I've been looking for more ever since."

"You must have amassed quite a collection by now."

244

"Not really. A hundred, maybe, and a lot of them are chipped and torn."

"That the only thing you collect?"

I cast my eyes across the shelves and said, "Nothing that would interest you."

"Everything interests me."

I poured myself another cup of coffee. He poured himself a drink from one of the decanters and then looked at me expectantly.

"Over the years," I said, "I picked up about fifty old blues records from the 1940s and '50s. I also accumulated several hundred vintage paperback crime novels: Brett Halliday, Carter Brown, Richard S. Prather, Jim Thompson, John D. MacDonald. It's all gone now, though."

"Why is that?"

"The woman I've been trying to divorce for two years is keeping my stuff out of spite."

"That must upset you."

"Only when I think about it."

The maid waddled into the room carrying two silver candelabra. She placed them on the marble-top table, lit the candles, and exited without speaking. Then Vanessa Maniella entered, nodded to me, and sat facing us in one of the easy chairs.

"So, Sal," I said. "Where the hell have you been?"

32

Salvatore Maniella rose from the sofa, walked to the library door, opened it, and spoke to Black Shirt, or maybe Gray Shirt, who was standing watch in the hall. "Please ask our other guest to join us."

A minute later she strode into the room, sat in the other chair, and crossed those long, long legs.

"I understand no introductions are necessary," Sal said.

"Some reason you feel the need to have your lawyer present?" I asked.

"Just being careful."

"I'm gonna take a wild stab here and say the body in the morgue isn't you."

"No."

"So who is it?"

"His name was Dante Puglisi."

"Age?"

"Sixty-four."

"Address?"

"He lived here."

"A relative?"

"No. He was in my employ. Had been for a long time."

"How long?"

"Since we mustered out of the SEALs together."

"What did he do for you?"

"Little of this, little of that. Driver. Bodyguard. Workout partner. Sometimes he helped out around the place."

"Didn't his family wonder where he was the last three months?"

"His parents were killed in a car accident twenty years ago. We were the closest thing to family he had left."

"He looked a lot like you."

"He did."

"Similar features, same height and weight, same eye and hair color, same Van Damme arms and Schwarzenegger chest."

"That's correct."

"Was anything done to enhance this resemblance?"

"About ten years ago, he had a little work done, yes."

"Why?"

Sal glanced at Yolanda. She nodded, indicating it was okay to answer.

"Shortly after I opened our strip clubs, I

became involved in a dispute with some of our state's more unsavory characters."

"Carmine Grasso and Johnny Dio," I said.

"You know of this?"

"I do."

"Well, perhaps you can understand why it seemed advisable to employ a double."

"When the two of you were together, the Mob wouldn't know which one to shoot," I said.

"Quite right."

"And you could send him on errands posing as you."

"From time to time I did that, yes."

"Last September, he went to the Derby Ball in your place."

"He did."

"And it got him killed."

"Yes."

"What was he there for?"

"I'd prefer not to get into that."

"I was there, too," I said, "covering the event for the *Dispatch*."

"Were you now."

"I was. I saw him there, cozying up to the governor. Of course, I thought it was you. The governor probably thought so, too."

"Perhaps he did."

"Conducting some business for you with the governor, was he?"

"That's not a subject I am prepared to discuss."

"Does it bother you that you put a target on Dante Puglisi's back?"

"More than you know."

"Of course it bothers him," Vanessa broke in. "Dante wasn't just an employee. He was like family." She swiped at her eyes — maybe wiping away a tear, maybe just making a show of it.

"Yes, he was," Sal said. He reached for one of the decanters, poured three inches of whiskey into a tumbler, and drank it straight down. "Please help yourselves," he said. "The Scotch is Bowmore, a seventeen-year-old single-malt. The bourbon is sixteen-year-old A. H. Hirsch Reserve."

No one did. Sal poured himself another.

"Dante knew the risks," Sal said. "He volunteered for the job, and I paid him well for it, but that doesn't make us feel any better. I miss him every single day."

"The body looked enough like you to fool the state police," I said.

"Apparently so."

"So you decided to play dead."

"I did."

"Why?"

"Surely the reason is obvious."

"You didn't want the killers to know they

hit the wrong guy."

"Yes."

"Do you think the Mob was behind this?"

"I don't know. I haven't had any trouble with them in years."

"But they have long memories," I said.

"So I've been told."

"Anyone else who might want you dead?"

"I've made some enemies over the years."

"Families and boyfriends of porn actors?"

"A few of them, yes."

"Rivals in the porn business?"

"Perhaps."

"The Sword of God?"

"They're a dangerous bunch of lunatics, and they've made it clear that they disapprove of us," Sal said.

"The Sword of God hates everybody," Vanessa broke in. "Gays, Jews, blacks, liberals, moderates, feminists, abortion doctors, Obama, the media, the government. They scare the hell out of me."

"With so many enemies out there, why resurface now, Sal?"

"Something came up that required my attention."

"What would that be?"

"I'd rather not say."

"Can you tell me where you've been for the last three months?"

"Here and there," he said.

"That's a little vague."

"I prefer to keep it that way."

"Got a hideout you don't want anyone knowing about?"

"Something like that."

"The state police asked the navy for help in identifying the body and got stone-walled," I said. "You have something to do with that?"

Sal looked at Yolanda, and she shook her head.

"Still got some old pals working in the Pentagon, do you?"

Sal didn't answer.

"I assume your family knew you were alive," I said.

Sal glanced at Yolanda again. "We are not prepared to discuss that subject," she said.

I turned back to Sal. "Obviously your wife and daughter knew you had a double. You said he *lived* here."

"Yes," Sal said.

"Yet your wife positively identified his body as you," I said.

"Anita Maniella is an older woman," Yolanda said. "She was distraught and confused." I was surprised by how different she sounded. Her lawyer voice was nothing like her "I don't date white guys" voice. You might think she'd never met me before.

"Mrs. Maniella is only sixty-two," I said. "This is the story you're going to stick with?"

"That is our position, yes," Yolanda said.

"Oh, boy," I said. "Captain Parisi is gonna love this. Have you talked to him yet?"

"Not yet, no," Yolanda said.

"Figured you'd try the story out on me first?"

No reply.

"Well, if that was your plan," I said, "I can tell you right now there are a lot of holes in it."

33

Vanessa rose from her chair, walked to the hearth, and added a log to the fire. Then we all went to the wall of windows and looked out at the dark, still lake.

"The roads must be treacherous," Sal said. "You and Yolanda are welcome to dine with us and spend the night. We have plenty of room."

Being a pornographer's overnight guest wasn't on my bucket list, but it was better than the alternative.

We ate by candlelight, Sal's wife, Anita, joining us at a carved antique table that could have seated twice our number. Two uniformed servants piled slabs of roast beef, grilled vegetables, and mountains of mashed potatoes onto expensive-looking china plates. Classical music, something with a lot of strings, played softly from hidden speakers. Sal pulled the corks on three bottles of Pétrus, a pricey red wine whose virtues were wasted on me.

The conversation veered from the Patriots' playoff prospects, which we agreed were not good, to the Red Sox's signing of pitcher John Lackey, which we all deplored. I waited for Yolanda to soften up a little and throw in something about the Cubs or the Bears, but apparently she was still on the clock. After the servants cleared away our plates and returned with hot coffee and generous wedges of apple pie, Anita turned the conversation to President Obama's proposal to reform the banking industry.

"What he should do is restore the wall between investment banks and retail banks," she said. "Institutions that trade in derivatives, equity securities, fixed-income instruments, and foreign exchange should not be allowed to accept savings deposits."

I didn't understand much of that, but she didn't sound confused to me.

I stared at her, wondering how many plastic surgeons it took to keep a woman looking that good into her sixties. Then I stared some more, wondering what kind of a woman would marry a pornographer. She caught me looking and smiled.

"Go ahead and ask," she said. "I don't mind."

"Does it bother you?" I asked. "The way

your husband makes his money?"

"And my daughter, too," she said. "Don't forget Vanessa."

"Her too," I said.

She laced her fingers under her chin and studied me over the top of them. "You've never been a woman, have you, Mr. Mulligan?"

I thought it might be a trick question, so I went with a politician's answer: "Not that I can recall."

"Being a woman is all about choices. Long ago, I made the choice to support my husband's passion. Sal's passion is not pornography. It's not being surrounded by the naked women on his payroll. Sal's passion is making money and using it to buy his family nice things. I trust his path. And I like nice things, too."

"But —"

"Everyone involved in the business — the performers, the customers, even my daughter — is chasing something they've dreamed about. Most people just don't dream as big as Sal."

Sal chuckled at that. "Let me tell you what I'm dreaming about this week," he said, and steered the conversation to what I gathered was his favorite topic. Swann Galleries in Manhattan had scheduled a January auction of rare British mystery and spy novels, and he was pretty excited about it. I would have been, too, if the pre-auction estimates didn't make me choke.

After dinner, the Maniellas retired to their rooms. I went to the garage, found my parka still hanging on its peg, and pulled my antibiotics prescription and omeprazole tablets from an inside pocket. Then I reentered the house, passed Black Shirt and Gray Shirt standing watch in the foyer, and entered the library, where Yolanda was sitting on the couch.

"Not what you expected, are they," she said.

"No."

"You thought they'd be pigs."

"Maybe they are," I said. "All that dirty money can buy a lot of lipstick and deodorant."

"They're not," she said. "They're pretty nice when you get to know them."

"Nice for pornographers, you mean."

"I didn't realize you were such a *puritan,* Mulligan."

"Neither did I."

She gave me a searching look. "Pornography is legal," she said. "They're not doing anything wrong."

"A lawyer's answer."

"I *am* a lawyer. I leave the moralizing to the preachers."

"Perhaps I'd like them better," I said, "if they didn't keep sending their thugs after me."

"What do you mean?"

"The two ex-SEALs followed my car the other day and cornered me in a Subway parking lot."

"What did they want?"

"To beat me up."

"What happened? Are you okay?"

"I'm fine. I showed them my gun, and they went away."

"You carry a gun?"

"Only when I'm feeling threatened."

"Why were they after you?"

"Because I was asking questions about the Maniellas."

"They didn't seem to mind your questions today."

"They didn't answer the important ones."

The candles in the candelabra had burned to stubs, and one of them had gone out. I relit it with my lighter.

"When are you going to tell Captain Parisi that Sal is alive?" I asked.

"Tomorrow, if the roads are better," she said. "It's something I should do face-to-face."

"Taking Sal with you?"

"No."

"Parisi's going to want to question him."

"I'm not going to allow that," she said.

"Mind if I call the captain in the morning and give him the news myself?"

"Why would you want to do that?"

"Because it would amuse me."

"I'd rather you didn't, but I can't stop you." She paused and then added, "I guess it wouldn't do any harm."

I picked up the decanter of bourbon from the table and thought about how good it would feel on the way down. Then I thought about what would happen when it hit bottom and returned the container to the table.

"Patricia Smith is going to be at the Cantab in Cambridge the second week in January," I said.

"Is that so?"

"They say her readings are amazing. We should go."

"Maybe, but not together."

"Separate cars would waste gasoline," I said. "Don't you care about the environment?"

"Going together would just encourage you," she said.

Vanessa stepped into the library to announce that our beds would be ready shortly. Then she noticed the way I was looking at Yolanda and asked, "Will you be wanting one room or two?"

"One," I said.

"Two," Yolanda said.

Vanessa chuckled and slipped out of the room.

In the morning, Sal stood on the front porch with his wife and daughter and waved good-bye as Yolanda and I headed down the snow-covered dirt road to our cars. I helped her clear the snow from hers. Then I brushed off Secretariat. I locked my .45 in the glove box and placed a plastic bag holding Grant's two-volume memoir on the floor by the front passenger seat. I started the car, turned on the heater, and let the engine warm while I made the call to Parisi.

"Guess who I was just talking to," I said.

"I don't play guessing games, Mulligan."

"Sal Maniella."

That five-second pause, and then: "You talking to dead people now?"

"Sometimes I do," I said. "But he looked alive to me. He was walking and talking, and his breath turned white in the cold."

"Seriously?"

"Yeah."

"Because if this is your idea of a joke . . ."

"It's not."

"Then who the hell is in the morgue?"

"A retired Navy SEAL named Dante Puglisi. Sal had been using him as a double. They looked a lot alike, and Puglisi had some plastic surgery a few years back to perfect the illusion."

A five-second pause again. "Plastic surgery scars were noted in the autopsy report, but we chalked it up to vanity."

"I would have, too."

"Sal's been playing dead because somebody tried to kill him?"

"Yeah."

"His wife played along by falsely identifying the body?"

"Sal's lawyer claims she was distraught and confused."

"You met her?"

"I did."

"She seem confused to you?"

"No."

"Did Sal tell you who wants him dead?"

"He says he's got a lot of enemies."

"I'll bet. So where do I find him?"

"His lawyer," I said, "isn't going to let you talk to him."

Parisi fell silent for a moment. Then he said, "Swell."

34

"You sure you got it right this time?" Charlie said.

"I am."

" 'Cause you really fucked it up the first time around." He smirked as he cleared away what was left of my eggs and topped off my coffee.

I opened my mouth to argue but then thought better of it. I'd never flat-out reported that Maniella was dead. I'd just written that police *believed* he was. But I'd also believed it, and I'd made sure my readers did, too. The paper would not be running a correction, because by journalism standards my story had been *technically* accurate. But that didn't make it true.

Charlie was about to say something else when my cell phone interrupted with "Who Are You?"

"Mulligan."

"I'm only going to say this once," the

caller said, "so listen up." The voice was muffled — a man trying to disguise his voice. "Write down this address: 442 Pumgansett Street. Got that?"

"Got it. In the Chad Brown project, right?"

"Yeah."

"What's this about?"

"Big story for whoever gets there first. I suggest you haul ass."

"What kind of story?" I asked, but I was talking to a dead line.

The worst places always seem to be named after the best people. Any Franklin Delano Roosevelt High School, Martin Luther King Drive, or Dorothea Dix Hospital is likely to be a war zone. Chad Brown, Providence's oldest low-income public housing project, was named for one of the city's leading seventeenth-century citizens, a man Roger Williams once described as "a wise and godly soul." Its 198 cramped apartments were squeezed into twenty two-story red-brick row houses in the city's Wanskuck neighborhood three miles northwest of the statehouse.

When the project was completed in 1942, the apartments rented for as little as eleven dollars a month, with preference given to defense workers. By the 1970s, it had become Providence's most dangerous neighborhood, plagued by gangs, riddled with drugs, and terrorized by drive-by shootings. This year, the decent folks who lived there were working with the police, making another attempt to take back their neighborhood. Best of luck with that.

I parked Secretariat in the cracked macadam lot in front of 442 Pumgansett, got out of the car, and stepped in fresh dog shit. Folks who live on a battlefield don't bother with pooper-scoopers. I scraped my Reeboks on the curb and started up the concrete walk, my Nikon dangling from my left shoulder. My Boston Bruins sweatshirt hung low in front, weighted down by the .45 I'd shoved into the hand pouch. I didn't think I'd done anything to provoke the Maniellas and their goons again, but I had no idea what I was walking into.

" 'Scuse me, sir. *Scuuuuuse* me."

I turned and saw two scrawny teenagers sitting on the Bronco's hood. Gang tattoos on their necks identified them as members of the Goonies, the city's newest street gang. I wondered if they'd borrowed the name from the kid movie or if it was just a diminutive form of *goon*.

"Give us twenty bucks and we'll watch

the car for y'all, make sure nothin' happens to it."

I smiled and showed them my gun.

"The cracker got hisself a piece," the tall one said.

"Never seen one like dat," the short one said. "Looks fuckin' old."

"Prolly don't even shoot," the tall one said.

I pulled back the hammer. "Stick around," I said, "and maybe you'll find out."

They shrugged, slid off the hood, and pimp-walked down the street.

The guardrails flanking the row house's six concrete steps were loose and corroded. The shades on the apartment windows, two upstairs and one down, were drawn. The front door, dark green with two tiny broken windows, was open a crack. When I knocked no one answered, so I nudged it open with my shoulder, stepped inside, and elbowed it closed. I'd reported on enough crime scenes in the project to know the layout: an open living room–kitchen area on the first floor, two small bedrooms and a bathroom upstairs.

The living room held three fake-leather desk chairs, a daybed covered with a rumpled chenille bedspread, and two tipped-over aluminum worktables. Hundreds of DVDs in jewel cases were scattered

264

across the threadbare green carpet. Many of them were cracked, as if they'd been stomped on. On top of them were two open Apple laptops, their screens smashed.

"Hello. Is anyone here?"

When no one answered, I skirted the mess on the floor and checked out the kitchen. The rust-stained porcelain sink was piled high with food-encrusted dishes. A bottle of Early Times with two inches in the bottom stood on the yellow linoleum countertop next to a roll of paper towels. There was also a twelve-cup coffeemaker with a couple of refills left inside. I touched the pot with the back of my hand. It was warm.

A white Apple laptop, its power cord plugged into the wall, sat in the middle of a round, pressboard kitchen table. The screen was open but dark. On the keyboard, some-one had left a note, hand-printed in big block letters on a sheet of copy paper:

MULLIGAN!
PRESS PLAY.
WATCH TO END.
THEN CHECK UPSTAIRS.

Not sure what was going on here, I didn't want to risk leaving my prints, so I took a Bic pen out of my pocket and used it to nudge the note off the keyboard. Then I tapped the pen on the touch pad. The screen lit up, displaying a paused video. I dragged the pen across the touch pad, trying to move the cursor to the control panel, but it didn't work. I tore a paper towel off the roll on the counter, laid it on the touch pad, and slid my finger across it, moving the cursor to the play button. Then I reeled back.

A naked child was sprawled facedown across a queen-size bed. She was sobbing. A pale, skinny man climbed on top of her, and the child's mouth opened in a scream. Mercifully, the sound had been turned off. She couldn't have been more than seven or eight years old.

"WATCH TO END," the note said, but I couldn't take much of this. I hit the fast-forward button, slowing the video in time to watch the man complete his business, grab a fistful of brown curls, and pick up a buck knife. I averted my eyes too late to miss the big finish.

I don't know how long I stood there, immobilized by the shock of it. Maybe a few seconds. Maybe several minutes. Then I turned from the computer and threw up in the sink. When I finished heaving, I grabbed another paper towel, used it to turn on the cold water, and cupped some in my hands to wash the sour taste from my mouth. I hoped I wasn't washing any important trace evidence down the drain.

In twenty years as a journalist, I'd seen a lot of death: firemen burned to cinders in collapsed buildings, mobsters shotgunned against barroom walls, teenagers dismembered by fast-moving trains. But I'd never seen anything like this.

"THEN CHECK UPSTAIRS," the note said. I jerked the .45 out of my sweatshirt, craving an opportunity to use it.

The worn vinyl stair treads felt gritty under my Reeboks. As I nudged open the door to the first bedroom, the first thing that hit me was the odor. The room smelled as if an army had used it as a urinal.

Two men and a woman dressed in jeans and T-shirts were crumpled on a beige shag carpet beside an unmade queen-size bed. Beside them, several thousand dollars' worth of professional video equipment — two Sony video cameras, a couple of 5,500-watt Day-Flo lights, and a tripod — lay twisted and broken. The carpet, the bed, and the room's flowered wallpaper were splattered with blood and brain matter. It was the same wallpaper I'd seen in the video downstairs. The blood was still wet.

I stuck the Colt back in my sweatshirt, popped the lens cover off the Nikon, and snapped photos from as many angles as I could without stepping in blood. The paper would never print such horrific pictures, but my mind would try to block this out. I'd need photos to write an accurate story.

Careful not to touch anything, I backed into the hall. The bathroom was just ahead to my left, the door pulled closed. I shouldered it open. The room was empty.

I stepped back into the hall and saw that the door to the second bedroom was padlocked. I put my ear to it and thought I heard a whimper, but it was so faint that I couldn't be sure.

"Hello? Is anyone in there?"

No one answered. I put my ear to the door again. Another whimper.

My first instinct was to kick the door down, but I'd contaminated the crime scene too much already. Instead, I rushed down the stairs and fled the house. I had Captain Parisi on speed dial. He picked up on the second ring.

35

The day had turned bitterly cold. A stiff northwest wind blew McDonald's wrappers and old newspapers around the project parking lot. A half-dozen kids, one of them bouncing a basketball, strolled by. It was good to see children still pushing and pulling their own breath. I sucked in air to clear the stench of blood and urine from my nostrils. Then I unlocked the Bronco, slid in, and pulled a Partagás out of the glove box. As I lit it, my hands shook. I cracked the side window, smoked, and waited for Parisi to roll up.

After a few minutes, I started thinking more clearly. It wouldn't do to be carrying when the authorities arrived, so I tugged the Colt from my sweatshirt and locked it in the glove box. What else? Parisi might confiscate my camera. I ejected the memory card and concealed it between the passenger-seat cushions. Then I unzipped the pouch on the front of my camera bag, took out the spare card, and slipped it in the Nikon. I snapped a few shots of the front of the death house through the car window so there'd be something on the fresh card if anyone looked. Then I called Lomax, gave him the gist, and suggested he get a real photographer over here in time for the show.

Parisi must have made a courtesy call to the Providence PD, because they arrived first — two squad cars and an unmarked Crown Vic. The Vic's doors swung open, and out climbed the homicide twins: Jay Wargat, a big lug with a permanent five o'clock shadow and fists like hams, and Sandra Freitas, a bottle blonde with rumble hips and a predatory Cameron Diaz smile. I got out of the Bronco and met them on the sidewalk.

"Mulligan?" Freitas said. "You the one called this in?"

"I am."

"Been inside?"

"I have."

"And?"

"Two dead males and a dead female in one of the bedrooms upstairs. Looks like they were head-shot. And something worse in the kitchen."

"What would that be?"

"I don't want to talk about it. Go look for yourself."

"Touch anything?"

"Not so you'd notice. But I walked all the way through the place. Oh, and I threw up in the kitchen sink."

"You did, huh?" Wargat said, his face cracking into a grin.

"There's something else," I said. "The second bedroom is padlocked. I think someone might be locked inside, but I'm not sure."

"Stay here," Freitas said, "while we have a look."

I got back in the Bronco and watched the four uniforms mill around outside. Ten minutes later Wargat bolted out the apartment door, stumbled down the front steps, and gave the snuff film a thumbs-down review by emptying his stomach on the sidewalk. When he finished heaving, he walked over to the Crown Vic, opened the door, pulled out a Poland Spring bottle, and washed out his mouth. Then he shook himself like a dog, straightened his shoulders, and trudged back inside.

Another five minutes passed before Wargat and Freitas came back down the stairs, she holding the hands of two hollow-eyed

271

little boys and he with a little girl in his arms. The detectives loaded them into the back of an ambulance that had just rolled up. Freitas pulled a notebook out of her back pocket and climbed in with them.

Wargat watched the ambulance roll down Pumgansett Street toward Douglas Avenue. Then he turned and headed straight for me.

"Step out of the car, please."

So I did.

"Place your hands against the side of the car and spread your legs."

By noon, the lot in front of 442 Pumgansett was filling. Camera crews spilled out of three TV vans and set up on the sidewalk across the street. Gloria sat Buddha-style on top of her little blue Ford Focus and studied the scene through a long lens. Tedesco climbed out of his meat wagon and lugged his big steel case inside. Parisi and two of his detectives arrived in an unmarked car, spoke briefly with the uniformed Providence cops guarding the door, and then followed Tedesco in. From the back of a locked patrol car, I had a good seat for the show.

Twenty minutes later, Parisi and Wargat emerged together and headed my way. Parisi looked into the backseat of the patrol car and then turned back to Wargat.

"Why is Mulligan hooked up?"

"I don't want him going anywhere," Wargat said, "till we get this sorted out."

"Uncuff him."

"Sorry, Captain. He's in Providence police custody."

"He's in my custody now," Parisi said. "This is my crime scene and my investigation, Wargat. Get used to it."

The interrogation room at state police headquarters in Scituate smelled like fear, sweat, and nicotine. Parisi sat across from me at a heavy oak table scarred with cigarette burns and coffee cup rings. We were drinking coffee and going over my story for the third time.

"Could you recognize the tipster's voice if you heard it again?"

"I don't think so."

"Any idea why he called *you?*"

"The answer's still no."

"Think he's involved in this?"

"My gut says he is. A citizen would have called the police."

We reached for our paper coffee cups, then put them down when we found they were both empty. Parisi pulled my cell phone out of his shirt pocket, placed it on the table, and said, "Put it on speaker and try calling him."

The tipster's number was listed first under received calls. I hit send. After eight rings, a recorded voice: "I'm sorry, but the person you have called has a voice mail mailbox that has not been set up yet. Good-bye."

Parisi slammed his palm on the table. The empty coffee cups jumped. A zebra plant on the windowsill seemed to wither. I withered a little myself.

"If he was smart," I said, "he used an untraceable prepaid and then threw it in a Dumpster."

"Most criminals aren't smart."

"Some are."

"Yeah," he said. "They're the ones who keep me in business."

"So," I said, "are we done?"

"Not yet."

He took off his glasses, rubbed his eyes, and put them back on again.

"In fifteen years as a detective, I never had a homicide case with a pornographer as the intended victim. Now I've got two of them."

"Think this case and the hit on Maniella's double are related?" I asked.

"There's no evidence tying them together, but I don't believe in coincidences."

"Why do cops always say that? Co-incidences happen every day."

We sat quietly and thought about that for

a minute.

"So," I said, "are we done *now?*"

"Not just yet. Sit tight."

He snatched the phone from my hand to stop me from calling the *Dispatch* with what I knew, sprang to his feet, and went through the door.

Time crawled. My ulcer growled. Someone had left a newspaper on the floor. I picked it up, opened it to the sports section to pass the time, and found a feature on the Boston Bruins' new forward, a Slovak named Miro Satan. The third paragraph read:

Satan looks fit and is skating fluidly.

After today, I couldn't argue with that.

It was nearly an hour before Parisi returned and placed my phone, car keys, and camera on the table. He took the Nikon out of its case, switched it on, examined all the photos on the LED screen, said, "Humph," and put it back in the case.

"Mulligan," he said, "I'm going to ask you not to write about what you saw inside that apartment."

"But you know I have to."

He sighed. "Would it kill you to omit a few details — some things only the perps could know?"

"Perps? You think there was more than one?"

"Slip of the tongue," he said. "Don't read anything into it."

"Okay."

"So can you leave some things out for me?"

"Such as?"

"The snuff film."

"Sorry, but I have to mention that."

"Ah, shit. Well, how about this? Can you leave out the smashed laptops? And the note that was left for you? And the fact that there were no shell casings at the scene?"

"Meaning the killer used a revolver or picked up his brass," I said.

"Yeah."

I'd been too much in shock to notice that. "Sure," I said, "I can leave those things out."

"Screw me on this, and you and I are done."

"Understood," I said. "Can you release the names of the shooting victims?"

A five-second pause. "Local lowlifes. Can't release the names till we notify their lowlife next of kin. And no way we're gonna release the names of the kids we pulled out of there alive."

"We wouldn't print them if you did," I

said. "What about the little girl in the snuff film?"

"Not a clue."

"Think maybe she got fed to Scalici's pigs?"

"I won't speculate."

"So, can I go *now?*"

"Not yet. Wargat and Freitas want a crack at you. When they finish playing detective, I'll have a trooper drive you back to your car."

By the time I got back to the newsroom that evening, it was too late to update the sketchy murder story Mason had written for the next day's paper.

"The cops are keeping a lid on this one," Lomax said. "All they're saying is they've got three bodies, and foul play is suspected."

"I've got a few details I can add," I said.

"Give it to Mason so he can update our Web site."

"You don't want *me* to write it?"

"No way," Lomax said. "You found the bodies, so you're part of the story now. Mason's gonna interview you — treat you as a source."

"Okay," I said. "Soon as I get something in my stomach."

The something was Maalox chugged

straight from the bottle. Earlier, I'd retrieved my Nikon's memory card from its hiding place. Now I carried my laptop to a vacant office off the newsroom for privacy, slipped the card in a card reader, plugged it into the computer, and downloaded the photographs. I spent ten minutes studying them, jotting down a few notes for my chat with Mason. When I was done, I sprinted for the bathroom. The dry heaves reminded me I hadn't eaten since breakfast.

When I finally got home it was after ten. I picked up a Michael Connelly novel, hoping it would take my mind off the snuff film. It didn't work, but I kept reading anyway. Harry Bosch was about to lose his temper with his by-the-book boss when "Bitch" started playing on my cell phone. Not even Dorcas could make *this* day any worse, so I picked up the phone and said, "Hello."

"You sent them, didn't you, you sonuvabitch!"

"Sent who?"

"You know who!"

"I'm afraid I don't."

"I thought they were gonna *kill* me."

"What? Okay, why don't you calm down and tell me what happened?"

"Like you don't fuckin' know!"

278

"I really don't."

She drew a deep breath. "There were two of them," she said. "They knocked on the door, and when I opened it they pushed me aside and forced their way in."

"Are you hurt?"

"No, but I'm still shaking."

"What did they look like?"

"Big. Really, really big."

"John Goodman big or *WWF SmackDown!* big?"

"You trying to tell me you don't know anything about this?"

"Of course I don't."

"You're a fucking liar," she said. And then she hung up.

What the hell was that about?

I went to my bedroom window, opened it, sucked in a lungful of frigid air, and slowly let it out. I'm not sure how long I stood there before I heard a police siren cut the dark. It sounded close, but all I could see were the black windows of the tenement next door. I closed the window, flopped on my bed, and read for an hour. Then I put down the book and fiddled with the cell phone, trying to decide on a ringtone for Yolanda. I finally settled on a spare acoustic version of "Dance with Me" by Tuck & Patti. Of course, I had no reason to think

Yolanda would call.

First thing next morning, she did.

36

"Mulligan? Are you okay?"

"I'm fine, Yolanda."

"You don't sound fine. Where are you?"

I was slumped on a stool at my favorite diner, reading Mason's update about the murders on the paper's Web site and struggling to keep Charlie's scrambled eggs down.

"Sit tight," she said. "I'll be there in a few minutes."

I finished Mason's story and then checked the other headlines. The bishop was enraged at an enterprising young man who had leased an abandoned Fotomat drive-through across the street from St. Mark's in Cranston, laid in a new line of merchandise, and renamed it the Condom Shed. According to a survey of top fashion designers, cleavage was back in style again. And a national newsmagazine was reporting that New Jersey was the most corrupt state in the

Union but that Little Rhody led the nation in scandals per capita. Finally we were number one at something besides doughnut shops. I was checking the betting line for the Patriots-Panthers game when Yolanda strolled in on those long, long legs.

She was wearing a frown and a gray business suit with the top two buttons of her blouse undone. When she bent to kiss my cheek, Charlie sneaked a peek. She plopped her alligator tote on the counter, took the stool next to mine, and asked for black coffee.

"I read the story on the Web this morning," she said.

"The one about how cleavage is in this season?"

"Good news for the fry cook," she said, "but it's not the one I meant."

Mason had done a fine job with the murder update, laying out the facts and going easy on the gore. Still, it was grim reading.

"It must have been horrible for you," she said.

"A police reporter sees lots of blood, Yolanda. You get used to it."

"Bullshit. This wasn't a car crash or a Mob hit. A murdered child is *not* something you get used to. It's haunting you. I can hear it in your voice."

My phone was on the counter beside my cold, half-empty mug of coffee. It began to play "Dirty Laundry." I reached for it and grabbed a fistful of air.

"Mr. Mulligan's office," Yolanda said. "How may I be of assistance? . . . I'm a friend of his. . . . Yes, I'm with him now. . . . He *says* he's fine, but he's not. . . . Actually, I think a couple of days would be better. . . . Okay, I'll let him know," she said, and flipped the cell closed.

"What did Lomax want?" I asked.

"He said to take today off. I tried to get you a couple of days, but he insisted he can't spare you that long."

"Of course he can't. I'm indispensable."

"Is 'Dirty Laundry' your ringtone for everything, or just for your editor?"

"Just him."

"Perfect choice," she said. "Do you have a special one for me, too?"

"Maybe I do."

She dug her BlackBerry out of her purse and punched in my number.

"That sounds like 'Dance with Me' by Tuck and Patti," she said.

"It is."

"She's black and he's white," she said.

"Uh-huh."

"Aren't they married?"

"To one another, yeah."

She let out a long sigh. "I told you —"

"Yeah, yeah, you don't date white guys. But you *do* dance, don't you?"

She averted her eyes and sipped her joe.

Charlie turned from the grill, swept my cold coffee off the counter, dumped it, and gave me a refill. When I picked up the cup, my hand was shaking. As I raised the coffee to my lips, a few drops slopped over the rim and fell on the front of my Bruins sweatshirt.

"Still got that klutzy charm," I said.

I thought that would get a smile out of her, but it didn't. She plucked napkins from the dispenser and patted me dry. Then she called her office, told her secretary to cancel her afternoon appointments, and spun on her stool to face me.

"I've got a couple of things this morning that I can't get out of," she said, "but when I'm done, I'm buying you lunch."

Charlie watched me watch her as she exited the diner and strode down the sidewalk toward the Textron Tower, where she had an office on the fourteenth floor. I kept looking until she was out of sight.

"Classy dame," he said.

"I agree."

"And she's black."

"Very."

"The little doll you used to come in here with last year was Asian," he said.

"She was."

"Got something against white girls?"

"I like 'em all, Charlie. White, black, yellow, and brown are my favorite colors."

"I like 'em all, too," he said, "but you seem to have a taste for the exotic." He put his hands on the counter and leaned toward me, wanting a serious answer.

"It's not about skin color, Charlie. Most guys want a woman who votes like they do, cheers for the same team, likes the same kind of movies, drinks the same brand of beer. I prefer women who *aren't* like me. They're more interesting both in and out of bed."

Charlie furrowed his brow and thought it over. Then he nodded to show he understood and turned back to the grill.

I wandered over to the Biltmore, bought *The New York Times* and *Sports Illustrated* at the newsstand off the lobby, carried them back to the diner, and read them over cups of Charlie's decaf. I was admiring the magazine's photo spread on the ten greatest fights of all time when Yolanda called and said to meet her at the Capital Grille.

■ ■ ■ ■

The place was packed with bankers, lawyers, politicians, and ladies who lunch, so we had to wait at the bar for ten minutes before the maître d' showed us to a table. At first Yolanda stuck to small talk, chatting about music, movies, and the weather while wolfing down the cedar-planked salmon with fennel relish. I played along as I nursed a Coke and managed a few bites of the lobster-and-crab burger. After Claus, the pint-size waiter, smirked at my Bruins sweatshirt and served us Irish coffees, the conversation turned serious.

"Did you always want to be a reporter?"

"I always wanted to play for the Celtics. Journalism was my backup plan."

"Why that?"

"It's the only thing I'm any good at."

"Oh, come on! You're a smart guy. You could have done anything."

"Not true. I can't sing worth a damn, I suck at math, I have a short attention span, and I hate wearing a tie. My options were limited."

"It takes a lot of courage to do what you do."

"*Courage?* My friend Brad Clift has courage. He was water-boarded by the Sudanese for photographing the genocide in Darfur for the *Hartford Courant.* Daniel Pearl had courage. He investigated al-Qaeda for *The Wall Street Journal,* and terrorists in Afghanistan cut off his head. I've never dared to chase stories like that. I'm a coward, Yolanda. I stayed right here in Little Rhody, where the worst thing likely to happen to me is a paper cut."

Yolanda grabbed my hand and looked into my eyes.

"Baby," she said, "you don't have to travel to Darfur or Afghanistan to fight evil. There's plenty of it right here."

That was a thought worth pondering, but all I could focus on was that she'd called me "baby."

"Come on," she said. "Let's go for a walk."

She turned her jacket collar up against the chill and took my hand as we strolled along the river. For a while, we didn't speak. It was a comfortable silence. I stroked her palm with my thumb, craving the contact.

"I have to ask you something," I said.

"Okay."

"Do you think your clients are involved in this?"

"The murders?"

"Yeah."

287

"If I knew, I wouldn't be able to say."

"What about the snuff film?"

"If I thought they were capable of *that,* they wouldn't be my clients."

We walked on in silence. I tried to turn off the bloody slide show that was flashing through my brain. Overhead, a jetliner minutes from takeoff at T. F. Green Airport climbed through an impossibly blue sky. I wanted to toss the bloody images into its cargo hold and send them into the stratosphere. Sensing my agitation, Yolanda squeezed my hand tighter.

By a pedestrian bridge that arched over the river, she bought a hot pretzel from a street vendor, tore it into pieces, and tossed the scraps to a pair of mallards that had grown too fat on handouts to fly south for the winter.

"You look like you could use a drink," she said, so we rode the elevator to the top of the Renaissance Hotel and settled into a booth with a view of the statehouse dome. She ordered an apple martini. I ordered a Bushmills straight up. The first sip felt good on the way down and then tore into my stomach lining like a dagger.

"Hey, Mulligan?"

"Um?"

"Why don't you ever use your first name?"

"I was named after my maternal grand-father, Sergeant Liam Patrick O'Shaughnessy of the Providence PD. Thirty years ago, outside Bruccola's vending machine business on Atwells Avenue, somebody hit him in the head with a pipe, pulled his pistol from his holster, and shot him dead with it."

"Oh, Jesus! I'm so sorry."

"It's okay. It was a long time ago."

"It's not okay. If it were, you'd be able to use his name."

"Whenever I hear it," I said, "I picture the chalk outline of his body on a cracked sidewalk."

We sat in silence for a moment.

"Your byline is L. S. A. Mulligan, so you must have middle names you could go by."

"Seamus and Aloysius."

"Oh."

"Yeah. Mulligan suits me better."

"Isn't a mulligan a second chance?" she asked.

"A do-over, yeah. Lord knows I need as many of those as I can get."

"Okay, baby," she said. "Mulligan it is."

" 'Baby' also works for me."

"Don't take that wrong," she said. "I call the mailman 'baby,' too."

That was a conversation stopper, so we

sat quietly for a while and sipped our drinks.

"Mulligan?"

"Um?"

"Did they ever catch the guy?"

"No, they never did."

She picked up the bar tab, and we strolled the Riverwalk again as the golden globes lining the water snapped on. We stopped at a bench and sat together in the dusk. My grandfather's gun dug into the small of my back, making me wonder if I should buy something smaller. A beat cop stomped up and glared at us, figuring a black woman with her arm on a white guy's shoulder had to be up to no good. Then he noticed how well she was dressed and moved on. A minute later, a drug dealer shuffled up and offered us cocaine and marijuana. It was time to go.

"Thank you, Yolanda. It's been a lovely day."

"It's not over yet," she said.

We found our cars, and I followed Yolanda to her place, where she whipped up a tangy mix of chicken and vegetables. This time I managed to clean my plate. Later we sat together on her black leather sofa, and she opened a bottle of thirty-year-old single-malt Scotch. I was a Bushmills man, but I didn't let that or my doctor's advice stop me. To night I needed whiskey.

Yolanda placed her hand on my shoulder.

"How are you feeling?"

"Sitting here drinking with you? I'm great."

"You're not. You're so tense you're practically vibrating. You need to get your mind off what you saw yesterday."

"How do I do that?"

"By thinking good thoughts." She paused, then said, "Tell me what you're most proud of."

"Proud?"

"Uh-huh."

"Nothing leaps to mind."

"What about your Pulitzer? And the Polk Award you won?"

"How'd you know about that?"

"I Googled you."

"Awards are bullshit, Yolanda. You just stick them in a drawer and move on to the next story."

"There must be something," she said.

"That I'm proud of?"

"Yeah."

"Well . . . I guess I'm proud that I made the PC basketball team as a walk-on."

"That's a good one."

"I would have been prouder if I hadn't spent four years on the bench."

"What else?"

"That the classiest woman in New England wants to know what makes me proud."

I was exhausted and a little drunk. I must have nodded off because the next thing I knew, Yolanda was lifting my legs onto the couch. She untied my Reeboks, slid them off, and tucked a throw pillow under my head.

"Go back to sleep," she said.

In the morning, I awoke early. The condo was silent, so I pulled on my running shoes and let myself out, making sure the door locked behind me. I needed a shower and fresh clothes, so I drove to my apartment, parked illegally on the street, tromped up the stairs, and found eight cardboard boxes — each big enough to hold a child's head — stacked against my front door.

37

I unlocked the door and dragged the boxes inside. Then I rummaged in the kitchen drawer, pulled out a steak knife, knelt on the floor, and carefully slit open the first box. I reached in and pulled out the June 1935 issue of *Black Mask* — the one with a Raymond Chandler story, "Nevada Gas," listed on the front cover.

I unpacked the rest of my pulp magazine collection from the box, and as far as I could tell it was all there. I slit open the other boxes and found my turntable, my old blues records, and my hoard of paperback novels from the 1940s and 1950s.

I showered, pulled on fresh jeans, plucked a relatively odorless Tommy Castro Band T-shirt from the laundry basket, and headed to the diner for a breakfast of scrambled eggs and toast and a mug of Charlie's decaf. I took a sip, pulled my phone out of my jeans, and punched in a number.

"Sal Maniella."

"It's Mulligan."

"What can I do for you?"

"I found some boxes on my doorstep this morning."

"Is that so?"

"It is. Apparently a couple of big guys forced their way into my almost-ex's place and retrieved them for me. Scared the woman half to death."

"Must have been terrible for her."

"I don't suppose you know anything about this."

"Of course not."

"I didn't think so."

"The boxes. Was everything in them?"

"Yes."

"That's good," he said. "Be a shame if somebody had to go back and scare the poor woman all over again."

Maniella had done me a favor, and his banter showed that he wanted me to know it. I wondered why he'd thought it was worth his while. Call me a cynic, but I couldn't buy the possibility that he was just being nice.

"Hear about the murders at Chad Brown?" I asked.

"I did."

"Something you can shed light on?"

"All I know is what I read in your paper."

I signed off, finished my eggs, and walked to the *Dispatch.* The assistant business editor had called in sick, so I spent the morning and half the afternoon editing banking and technology stories I didn't understand. It was past two o'clock before I was able to break away to check in with my sources.

I tore open a bag of Beggin' Strips, pulled one out, and tossed it to Shortstop. He snatched it from the air, wolfed it down, and laid his head in my lap. I scratched him behind the ears. He rumbled contentedly and drooled on my jeans.

"Give me a dime on Miami to cover," I said. I hated betting against New England, but the Dolphins' wildcat offense usually gave the Patriots fits. Zerilli jotted my bet on a scrap of flash paper and tossed it into his washtub.

"Nice of you to bring something for the mutt," he said.

"No problem."

"He likes you."

"Good somebody does."

"Yeah," he said, drawing the word out. "Nothin' gets your head straight like spending time with a good dog."

I reached into the bag and gave the pooch

another treat. He swallowed it whole, tore the bag from my hand, retreated to a corner, and helped himself to the rest.

"So what are you hearing?" I asked.

"The Chad Brown murders?"

"Yeah."

"Not a fuckin' thing."

He opened his file drawer and presented me with a fresh box of Cohibas.

"Thanks, Whoosh," I said, and laid the box on the floor by my chair.

"Not lighting one up?"

"Not right now. My doc says I gotta cut down."

"That sucks."

"It does."

"Think the child porn racket was Maniella's?" he asked.

"I was gonna ask *you.*"

"No idea."

"Did Arena and Grasso try to have Sal whacked?" I asked.

"And risk a war with the ex-SEALs? No fuckin' way."

"If they did, would you tell me?"

"Ah . . . probably not."

"Okay, Whoosh," I said. "If you hear any chatter about the Chad Brown killings, give me a holler."

■ ■ ■ ■

Fifteen minutes later, I pulled my car into the lot at the Tongue and Groove just in time to watch Joseph DeLucca shove a half-dozen pickets from the Sword of God off the stairs into snow.

"Assholes have been hassling the customers all afternoon," he told me. "They keep hollering about how I'm goin' straight to hell. I told the fuckers I look forward to seeing 'em there."

We walked out of the light into the dark and took adjoining stools at the bar. Christmas was just two weeks off, and the place was festooned with pine boughs, tinsel, and twinkling colored lights. The bartender popped the tops on a couple of Buds, clunked them on the bar in front of us, and wandered off without asking for money.

"How's the leg?" I asked.

"It's healing up good."

"Glad to hear it," I said. "By the way, I want to thank you for that tip on the bodies at Chad Brown." It was a shot in the dark. When his small eyes flew open, I thought I might have scored a hit, but I couldn't be sure.

"No idea what you're talkin' about," he said.

I was about to press the point when a slim, small-breasted girl in high heels, a G-string, and a Santa hat bounced up and wrapped her arms around my neck.

"Alo, beebe. You come back to spen' some moany on DEZ-tin-ee?"

"Not today, Marical."

She stood on tiptoes, beamed at me, and brushed her brown nipples across my lips.

"Pleeze, beebe. I make you world go round like craysee."

The complimentary card for a trip around the world was in the wallet in my hip pocket. I swear I felt it vibrate.

"Sorry, darlin'," I said, and her face fell. She pouted, threw me a look that said her heart had just been shattered by the man of her dreams, and took her routine to a fatso in a plaid work shirt at the other end of the bar.

"My God, she's beautiful," I said.

"Yeah," Joseph said. "And she can suck a hard-boiled egg through a screen door."

"Know this from experience?"

"Oh, yeah."

I took a small sip of Bud and tried to block out the image.

"So, Joseph," I said, "do you think the

Maniellas have been making child porn videos?"

"How the fuck should I know?"

The bartender was lurking now, interested in our conversation, so we spun around on our stools to watch a lone dancer swinging from a stripper pole.

"Somethin' wrong with your beer?" Joseph said.

"My doctor says I've got to quit the booze," I said, and Joseph gasped as if he'd been told the worst news in the world.

Parisi's Crown Vic was already in the Johnston Town Hall parking lot when I pulled in beside it and rolled down my window.

"Somebody copied the address books and e-mails off the computers in the death house at Chad Brown," he said. "Loaded them onto some kind of portable hard drive. Was it you?"

"I'm a Luddite, Captain. I wouldn't have any idea how to do that."

"You better not be lying to me, wiseass."

"I wouldn't dare."

"Sure you would."

"Okay, I guess I would. But I'm not."

A five-second delay, and then: "If it wasn't you, it must have been the perps."

"Copied stuff from the smashed laptops, too?"

"Yeah."

"How can you tell?"

"*I* can't. The department computer nerd figured it out by fiddling with the hard drives."

"Fiddling?"

"Yeah."

"You sure know your techie lingo."

"Fuck you," he said, and shot me a look that could make Dirty Harry cry out for his mama. In all the years I'd known him, Parisi had always been as alert as an eagle and as well-groomed as a show dog. Today, his hair was tousled, he needed a shave, and the light had leaked out of his eyes. He looked as if he hadn't slept in days.

"What do you suppose they wanted the e-mails for?"

"Don't know."

"Did they wipe them off the hard drive after they copied them?"

"They did not."

"So what's in them?"

"Why should I tell you?"

"Because we're on the same side."

"Are we?"

"Neither of us is into snuff films, and I don't like child pornographers and assassins any more than you do. So yeah, this time we are."

He removed his glasses, rubbed his eyes, and softened his glare a little.

"Off the record?"

"Sure," I said, and then counted off five seconds.

"What we've got," he said, "are e-mails from twelve hundred and fifty-four perverts in the market for videos of adults raping children, five hundred and fourteen more who get hard watching kids diddle each other, and another seventy-six who asked specifically for videos of kids getting murdered after they've been violated."

"That's more than eighteen hundred people," I said.

"It is."

We looked at each other and shook our heads.

"Fuckin' case is giving me nightmares," he said.

"Tell me about it."

"If you ask me," he said, "the killers performed a public service."

"But you've still got to catch them."

"Yeah, but then what? Arrest them or give them medals?"

"Why not both?"

Parisi closed his eyes, nodded, and seemed

to doze off for a second.

"The e-mails," I said. "Are they traceable?"

"Mostly not. My tech guy says the senders used some kind of cloaking software to mask their IP addresses, whatever that means."

"*Mostly* not?"

"Six of 'em were careless. That means their Internet providers should be able to tell us who they are."

"They'll be willing to do that?"

"Once they're served with subpoenas, they will."

"Gonna share the names when you get them?"

"No."

"Got the ballistics report yet?" I asked, and counted off five seconds again.

"All three victims were shot once in the head with nine-millimeters," Parisi said. "Two of the slugs were too damaged to make a comparison, and the intact slug doesn't match anything on file. With no shell casings found at the scene, there's no way to tell if more than one gun was used."

"Maniella's double was shot with a twenty-five-caliber pistol," I said.

"That's right."

"Doesn't really tell us anything."

"It doesn't," he said. "Could be different shooters. Could be the same shooter with a different weapon."

"Can you release the names of the three dead lowlifes yet?" I asked.

"The Winkler brothers, Martin and Joseph, and their cousin Molly Fitzgerald."

"Part of the Winkler clan from Pawtucket?"

"Yeah. Both guys had records. Peeping and molestation as juvies. Larceny and narcotics distribution as adults. Molly didn't have a sheet."

"What else you got?" I asked, and then waited as he considered his reply.

"Neighbors said they saw five or six people coming and going from the apartment the last few weeks."

"So two or three snuff filmmakers are still on the loose?"

"Looks that way."

"Learn anything about the three kids found in the apartment?"

"Other than the fact that they'd been repeatedly raped?"

"Aw, fuck."

"The girl," Parisi said, "was a ten-year-old who ran away from home in Woonsocket last September. One of the boys was the nine-year-old who vanished on the way

303

home from school in Dighton a couple of weeks ago. The other boy is another story entirely."

"Oh?"

"The mother's a heroin addict. Claimed her eight-year-old son was kidnapped from their hovel in Central Falls last month, but she'd never reported him missing."

"Sounds fishy."

"Oh, yeah."

"What did she say when you grilled her?"

"Stuck to her story for a couple of hours before she copped to selling the kid for four dime bags and three hundred in cash."

"Jesus!"

"Yeah."

"She ID the buyer?"

"All we got is a generic description — white male, average height, brown hair, no distinguishing marks. Showed her photos of the Winklers, but she was too addled to make an ID."

"Did she know what the buyer wanted her kid for?"

"Says she didn't. I don't think she much cared."

"You charging her?"

"With everything we can think of. Attila wants to put the bitch *under* the jail."

"Give me a shovel," I said, "and I'll lend her a hand."

38

The Sword of God arrived in pickup trucks — Fords, Chevys, and a couple of Toyotas. Most of them were already there at nine A.M. when I pulled Secretariat into the gravel parking lot off Herring Pond Road just north of the little mill town of Harrisville. I parked beside a red Chevy Silverado with a bumper sticker that read: "Gun Control Means Using Both Hands."

It was a clear Sunday morning. The snow cover gathered light from the weak winter sun, magnified it, and hurled it back into the air. The effect was blinding. I plucked my sunglasses from the dash, put them on, and watched members of the congregation climb out of their cabs and greet one another with smiles, hugs, and handshakes.

The church was a converted Sinclair filling station, the two islands where the pumps had been now just parallel humps in the snow. The trademark green brontosaurus had been pulled down from the roof and left where it had fallen. In its place was a plain wooden cross. Out front, one of those portable signs with interchangeable letters sat in the bed of a rusted, 1960s-vintage Dodge flatbed that had probably been towed in. The sign read:

Sword of God Baptist Church
Today's Service:
The Blessing of the Guns

The men and teenage boys who crunched through the snow toward the church door cradled a variety of long guns. I spotted military assault rifles, deer rifles with scopes affixed, and a couple of shotguns. A few of the women toted rifles, too. Not to be left out, the children, some as young as five or six, lugged what appeared to be Daisy air rifles.

I took my Nikon out of its case, rolled down my window, and snapped a few shots — just in case I decided to write about this. Then I took my grandfather's gun out of the glove box, held it in my hands for a moment, and put it back. In the unlikely event of trouble, I'd be too outgunned for it to do me any good; and the .45 didn't need blessing. It had already been washed in my family's blood.

By the time I pushed through the door, most of the parishioners were already seated on folding metal chairs arranged in neat rows on an oil-stained concrete floor. I counted forty-two people in all. I knew one of them, a young guy who'd overdone it, strapping a bandolier across his chest in an attempt to blend in. I caught his eye, and he quickly turned away. I didn't see an organ or a choir.

I took a seat in back just as Reverend Crenson walked through the door of what had probably been the garage's office. He was dressed in black and carried what looked to be a Revolutionary War–vintage musket at port arms. He rested its rusted barrel against an oaken lectern that looked as though it had been scavenged from a school auditorium.

"Welcome, my brothers and sisters, to the house of God," he said, overenunciating so the word came out "*GOD*-duh." He held out his hands palms up, commanding the congregation to rise, and led them in a spirited off-key rendition of all five verses of "Onward, Christian Soldiers." Scalici's hogs could have sung it better, but they were into power ballads and 1970s arena rock. The folding chairs clattered as the members of the congregation returned to their seats.

The order of service was reminiscent of what you might see in any Baptist church: hymn, invocation, pastoral prayer, offering, doxology, hymn, scripture reading, hymn, sermon, benediction, closing hymn. But content was something else again.

"Brothers and sisters," Reverend Crenson began, "have you heard the troubling news? The loathsome pornographer still walks among us. The avenging angel sent by Almighty God destroyed one of this demon's disciples, but his work is not yet complete. Bow your heads and pray with me for the death of Salvatore Maniella."

He paused, surveyed his flock, rested his elbows on the lectern, and clasped his hands in prayer.

"Lord, if it be your will, choke the breath from this vile beast and condemn him to the fiery pit of hell. And while you're at it, Lord, if it's not too much trouble, please snuff out the life of our mongrel president, too. In Jesus' name we pray. Amen."

I'd read about right-wing preachers praying for the death of Barack Obama, but reading about it was one thing. Seeing it in person was quite another. My face was a mask, concealing revulsion.

Reverend Crenson opened his sermon

with a declaration that the United States Constitution had been divinely inspired — "as holy a document as any book of the *BY-a-bil.*" That got me wondering why a divinely inspired document had needed to be amended twenty-seven times, but the preacher soon set me straight. The amendments, too, were written "under the guiding hand of *GOD*-duh." That the Eighteenth Amendment, which established prohibition, and the Twenty-first, which repealed it, were both divinely inspired seemed unlikely to me, but this wasn't the time and place to make an issue out if it.

The rest of the sermon consisted of a warning that the Second Amendment, which seemed to be the reverend's favorite, was under attack by liberals, socialists, communists, homosexuals, and "a socialist president who seeks to take our guns away so that he can enslave us."

Then came the part that I'd come to hear:

"Dear Lord, we have faith that you did not place your children on this earth to be easy prey for the sons of Satan. We thank you for giving us the courage to defend ourselves and our families and to fight for what is right. Joyfully, we thank you for providing us with the tools to do so. Bless our guns, O Lord, and steady our hands so that our aim may be true. In Jesus' name, amen."

Afterward, the congregants arranged the chairs in a circle for an hour-long Bible study. Reverend Crenson surprised me with his tolerance for dissent on the topic of the day: whether Barack Obama was the Antichrist, as the preacher believed, or merely one of his minions.

As the members of the Sword of God gathered their guns and headed out, Reverend Crenson stood in the doorway and wrapped each of them in an embrace. When it was my turn, he grasped my right hand in both of his, curled his lips into a smile, thanked me for coming, and urged me to come again.

39

A couple of days later, Fiona joined me for breakfast at the diner.

"We got the names of the pedophiles from the Internet providers," she said, "and one of them fits the profile."

"The profile?"

"Yeah. He's a fucking priest."

"Oh boy."

"Father Rajane Valois of Fond du Lac, Wisconsin."

"Who are the others?" I pulled a notepad from my hip pocket and took notes as she rattled off the names, ages, and hometowns of five middle-aged men from Fort Worth, Texas; Naples, Florida; Cape Girardeau, Missouri; Andover, Massachusetts; and Edison, New Jersey.

"They in custody yet?"

"They're all out of state," she said, "so we have to turn this over to the FBI. Probably be a couple of weeks before they move on it."

"The names are off the record till they do?"

"Yeah. Don't want to tip the bastards off. After that, do me a favor and make them famous."

"I will," I said. "It's a big story. The AP will pick it up and move it on the national wire. The perverts will get to read about themselves on the front pages of their hometown newspapers."

"Good," she said.

"Think there's a connection between the Chad Brown murders and the Providence PD's child porn raid on Colfax Street a couple of months back?"

"There must be," she said. "I mean, what are the odds that there were two child porn factories in our little state? The way I figure it, the Winklers were running their operation out of Colfax Street, somehow got away when the bust went down, and moved their operation to Chad Brown."

"That's how I figure it, too."

"Of course, we don't know for sure," she said. "The Providence cops are pissed at the way Parisi's been bigfooting them, so they're stonewalling us."

"I don't suppose Dr. Charles Wayne's

name has come up in any of this."

That startled her. "Some reason it should?"

So I told her what I'd heard, leaving Mc-Cracken and Peggi out of it. "Be nice if we could get a look at his home computer," I said.

"It would, but we can't. There's no probable cause for a warrant."

We lapsed into silence as Charlie shuffled over to top off our coffees. The silence dragged when he moseyed back to the grill. We were probably both thinking the same thing: We didn't have a clue who was behind the Chad Brown murders. The body parts at the pig farm were still a dead end. And we had no idea why Sal's double had been whacked. We were just blundering around in the dark.

We broke the silence at the same time.

"Could it all be connected somehow?" I asked, just as Fiona said:

"What if it's all connected?"

"Parisi won't speculate," I said.

"But we will," she said.

So we started brainstorming, throwing out ideas that had been bouncing around in our skulls for weeks.

"A war between rival pornographers?" I suggested.

"Maybe. The Chad Brown creeps try to whack Sal so he whacks them."

"Of course, the creeps could have been working for Sal."

"In that case," Fiona said, "maybe Arena and Grasso whacked them all to settle their old strip club beef."

"Then again, what if this is all the handiwork of the Sword of God?" I said, and started to give her a rundown on Sunday's service.

"I heard all about that," she interrupted. "Parisi planted an undercover in the congregation to keep an eye on them."

"Jimmy Ludovich," I said.

"How'd you know that?"

"I saw him there Sunday."

I sipped coffee that was turning as cold as my investigation.

"Got anything solid yet on the Maniellas' illegal campaign contributions?" Fiona asked.

"Not yet."

"That's what you should be concentrating on. You're a reporter, not a cop. Murder investigations are way out of your league."

"You're probably right."

She picked up her cup of coffee, discovered it was cold, clunked it back on the table, and sighed.

"So we're still nowhere with all of this," she said.

"Only thing we can be pretty sure of," I said, "is that the body parts at Scalici's farm came from the Chad Brown snuff film factory."

"No, we can't," she said. "We can't be sure of anything."

40

Christmas Day I didn't have anything better to do, so I volunteered for a double shift on the city desk again. I edited the annual holiday traffic fatal — a family of five erased in a collision with a snowplow — and was scrolling the AP national wire when a story out of Fond du Lac, Wisconsin, caught my eye.

The parish priest at St. Agnes Roman Catholic Church had presided over midnight Mass on Christmas Eve, but he failed to show up for Mass on Christmas morning. Alarmed, the vicar went looking for him, found the back door of the rectory kicked in, and called the police. Two patrolmen arrived promptly and discovered that the place had been ransacked. They found the priest dead in his bed. Father Rajane Valois had been executed with a single gunshot to the back of his head.

I thought about calling Parisi to see if he'd

heard the news, but it *was* Christmas. I figured it could wait a day. Twenty minutes later, Jimmy Cagney's voice shrieked from my cell phone: "You'll never take me alive, copper!"

"Merry Christmas, Captain."

"Not so merry in Fond du Lac, Wisconsin."

"Is that so?"

"A parish priest was shot to death sometime early this morning."

"Father Rajane Valois," I said.

"You know about this?"

"I read about it on the AP wire."

A five-second delay, and then: "I just got off the phone with the chief of police in Fond du Lac. He says they found about a hundred child porn videos on the good father's personal computer."

"Doesn't surprise me," I said.

"Oh?"

"He was one of the names you got from the Internet providers," I said.

"How the hell do you know that?"

"A source."

"Jesus! This investigation leaks like the *Titanic.*"

"Now we know why the Chad Brown killers downloaded all those e-mails," I said.

"Looks like."

"How do you suppose they got the priest's name from the Internet provider?"

"Probably paid somebody off," Parisi said. "A bribe is as good as a subpoena."

"Better," I said. "You don't have to wait for it to be signed by a judge."

"They probably have the other five names, too," Parisi said.

"A hit list," I said.

"Be my guess. I called the FBI this morning, but nobody on duty today knows anything about our case. If the bureau doesn't move on this soon, we might end up with five more deserving corpses."

"Vigilantes," I said.

"Or Good Samaritans with guns."

After we signed off, I tried to remember what I knew about Fond du Lac. All I could come up with was that it was about the size of Providence and that Edward L. Doheny, an Irish American oil tycoon, was born there. Doheny was the inspiration for the fictional Daniel Plainview, the evil genius played by Daniel Day-Lewis in *There Will Be Blood*.

41

Three days later, the cops reporter called in sick, so I got stuck with writing the police briefs — a dozen short, pointless paragraphs about purse snatchings, break-ins, fender benders, and Peeping Toms. A few minutes after I turned it in, Lomax was standing over my desk with a computer printout in his hand. He gave me a dirty look and began to read out loud.

John Mura, 24, of 75 Chalkstone Avenue, was charged with burglary yesterday after four teenagers walking their Great Dane spotted him climbing through the window of an apartment at 21 Zone Street. Mura told police he would have gotten away with it if it weren't for those meddling kids and their dog.

"Exactly right," I said.

"I can't help but notice that you didn't quote Mura directly," Lomax said.

"I paraphrased."

"And why is that?"

"Because according to the Providence police, his exact words were 'those little cocksuckers and their fucking mutt.' "

"And do I detect, in your paraphrase, an allusion to *Scooby-Doo?*"

"I don't know," I said. "Do you?"

One corner of his mouth curled in a poor excuse for a smile. "I kinda like this one, so I'm gonna run with it," he said, "but I'm keeping my eye on you."

I was flipping through my notes on the Chad Brown murder, trying to see if I'd missed anything, when Johnny Rivers interrupted me with his rendition of "Secret Agent Man," my ringtone for McCracken.

"What's up?" I asked.

"Did you know Vanessa Maniella bought an old warehouse in West Warwick six weeks ago?" the private detective said.

"I didn't. Your source good on this?"

"A Realtor I know brokered the deal."

"Where is it exactly?"

"On Washington Street. Used to be a discount furniture warehouse. When that went belly-up, the Cunha brothers ran a flea market there for a while."

"What's she doing with it?"

"Don't know. Another strip club, maybe."

"Sounds like a lot of space for a strip club," I said. "Have you been out there?"

"No. Just thought there might be a story in it for you."

Late that afternoon, I drove out to West Warwick to check it out. The warehouse was a three-story red-brick structure sandwiched between a print shop and a pawnbroker. A "Half Price on Discount Furniture" sign, so faded that it was almost unreadable, stretched across the front of the building between the first- and second-floor windows. A "Cunha's Fabulus Flea Market" sign, misspelled and hand-painted on a barn door–size slab of plywood, was nailed across three of the second-floor windows. All of the windows were dark, but eight cars were parked head in against the front of the building. One of them was Sal Maniella's black Hummer. The others, low-end-model Fords and Toyotas, looked a few miles short of the junkyard.

I pulled in beside the Hummer, got out, and saw why the warehouse windows were dark. The glass had been painted black on the inside. I climbed the crumbling concrete steps to the front door and tried the latch. It was locked, and there was no bell. I pounded on the peeling green paint with my fist until I heard heavy footsteps. The door was shoved open by a big man wearing a leather shoulder holster over a green-and-white Celtics T-shirt with Kevin Garnett's number 5 on the front.

"Mulligan? The hell you doing here? This place is secret."

"Not anymore," I said.

"Mr. Maniella ain't gonna like this."

"He'll get over it," I said. "So what are *you* doing here, Joseph? Get tired of bouncing drunks at the Tongue and Groove?"

"I got promoted."

"To what?"

"Bodyguard."

"The two ex-SEALs aren't enough?"

"Them guys are fuckin' good, but they ain't always around."

"Out of town, are they?"

"Yeah. Took off a couple of days ago and won't be back till the end of the week."

"I'd like to have a word with Sal," I said.

"What makes you think he's here?"

"His car's right out front, Joseph."

"Oh, yeah. I told him he shoulda parked in back. Hang here and I'll see if he'll talk to you," he said, and slammed the door in my face.

I was watching an alarming number of

grackles gather on the telephone wires across the street when the opening guitar lick to "Bitch" started playing. I didn't see Keith Richards in the immediate vicinity so I pulled the phone out of my pocket and flipped it open.

"You . . . fucking . . . bastard!"

"And a good afternoon to you, too, Dorcas."

"Today is my birthday, asshole."

"Shall I break into song?"

"I'm still your wife, you know. You could have sent a fucking card."

"Have you checked your mail today?"

"What? No. Hold on a sec," she said, but Joseph was swinging the door open now.

"Happy birthday, Dorcas. Gotta go."

Joseph ushered me into a vestibule with peeling green walls and a splintered wood floor. A naked bulb burned in a fixture that dangled by its wires from the ceiling. In front of us was a new steel door with a keypad lock. Joseph punched in a sequence of five numbers. I managed to catch four of them. He turned the handle and led me inside.

There, a young woman in a forest-green business suit sat behind a kidney-shaped glass desk decorated with a framed family photo and a pink orchid in a ceramic pot.

Antique photographs of Rhode Island land-
marks, most of them long gone, hung in
bird's-eye maple frames on new drywall.
The off-white paint was so fresh that I could
smell it.

"Please take a seat," she said. "Mr.
Maniella will be with you shortly."

I dropped into a red leather couch —
probably better than anything that had been
in the place when it was a discount furniture
store — and Joseph sat beside me in a
matching easy chair.

"Where'd you get the gun?" I asked.

"Mr. Maniella give it to me."

"A Glock 17?"

"Just like his other bodyguards got."

"Seventeen-cartridge magazine, right?"

"Yeah. Lot more firepower than the Rem-
ington Arms piece of crap I got at home."

"Got a permit to carry?"

"It's pending."

The phone on the desk beeped. The
receptionist picked it up, listened for a moment, hung up, and said, "Mr. Maniella will
see you now." She touched something on
the desk, and the lock in a steel door to her
right clicked. Joseph and I got up and went
through it.

To our left, rusted fluorescent light fix-
tures, all of them dark, hung over a scarred

wood floor lined with rows of makeshift plywood display tables left over from the building's flea market days. To our right, two studio lights on tripods loomed over an unmade bed in a set built to look like a five-star hotel room. Joseph kept walking, so I followed him past another set, this one built to look like a room in a massage parlor. Over the massage table, bottles of oil glistened on a shelf that also held an impressive assortment of dildos.

The third and final set had pink walls hung with posters from the latest *Twilight* movie. A huge teddy bear sat at the foot of the bed. Piles of girl's underwear had been scattered on the floor. A teenager's room. A pretty young blonde who couldn't have weighed more than a hundred and ten pounds — maybe just a hundred without the implants — was on all fours on the bed's fresh pink sheet. She wore a Hope High School cheerleader's uniform, the top yanked up to expose her nipples and the skirt flipped to expose her ass. An older guy with a handheld camera moved in close to catch the spittle dripping from her lips as she sucked a grinning twentysomething's large black penis. A young guy with another handheld trained it on an enormous white phallus as its owner doused it with lubricant and then wedged it, with some difficulty, into the girl's rectum. Her eyes got wide, and she went, "Mmmm," pretending to enjoy it. White phallus saw me watching and winked. I gave him a wave. Dwayne Carter, a lanky murmuring dude who ran the Shell station on Broadway in Providence, had been helping me keep Secretariat on the road for years.

We tiptoed past the set and walked on until we arrived at an oak door in a new off-white wall. Joseph rapped softly, and a deep voice rumbled, "Come on in." Joseph opened the door, stepped aside, waved me in, and closed it softly behind me. Inside, the walls were decorated with movie posters from the 1970s, when feature-length porn played in theaters all over the country: *Debbie Does Dallas, Flesh Gordon, Deep Throat, The Opening of Misty Beethoven, Babylon Pink, The Devil in Miss Jones.* Maniella was seated behind an enormous cherrywood desk. He could have parked his Hummer on it and had enough room left over for a sorority house lesbian orgy. He rose and strolled across a newly laid rust carpet to greet me, taking my hand in both of his.

"Mulligan," he said. "It's good to see you. Please sit down and make yourself comfortable."

I dropped into a black leather couch, the back of my head inches from the blond tresses of Marilyn Chambers, the all-American girl star of the Mitchell Brothers' 1972 gang-rape fantasy, *Behind the Green Door.* In front of the couch, five AVN awards, the Oscars of porn, stood on a spotless glass coffee table.

"Can I get you anything?" Maniella asked as he opened a small refrigerator and rummaged inside.

"Whatever you're having."

He took out a bottle of Evian, poured the contents into two crystal glasses, handed me one, and sat down beside me.

"Are you enjoying the Grant memoir?" he asked.

"I'm nearly done with the first volume," I said, "and it really surprised me."

"How so?"

"I had no idea that he wrote so well."

"Yes, the prose is quite remarkable. He was a great general, too. It's a shame he wasn't a better president."

"So," I said as I cast my eyes about the room, "I like what you've done with the place."

"It's a work in progress."

"Moving your whole operation here, are you?"

"Just part of it. Can you tell me how you found us?"

"It's a small state, Sal. Hard to keep something like this a secret."

"True, but perhaps we could keep it between us for now."

"I don't know," I said. "The opening of a movie studio *is* a story for the business pages."

"I see."

"Then again, I don't write for the business pages."

Sal smiled and was about to say something else when the door flew open and a black woman with a narrow waist and enormous breasts burst in. The older man I'd seen holding a camera on the movie set stepped in behind her.

"I *told* this muthafucka I do *not* do anal," the woman screeched. Except for red high heels, she was stark naked.

"Then maybe you shouldn't have agreed to shoot a scene titled *Anal Action*," the older guy shouted.

"Okay, everybody calm down," Sal said. "Obviously, there's been a misunderstanding. Doreen, no one is going to make you do something you are uncomfortable with."

"That's for *damn* sure," she said.

"Would you be willing to do the scene if

we paid you an additional five hundred dollars?" he asked.

"No fuckin' way, Sal."

"All right, then." Sal rubbed his chin and thought for a moment. "Chet, why don't we just change the title to reflect Doreen's most appealing feature? Maybe we could call it *Black Boobs* or something. Doreen, would you be okay with Dwayne ejaculating on your nipples?"

"I can do that," she said.

"Great. Back to work, now. And Chet, please close the door on your way out."

"Actors," I said as the door clicked shut. "Always complaining about the size of the dressing room, the brand of sparkling water, or somebody trying to shove something up their ass."

"Story of my life," Sal said.

"So tell me," I said. "How's business?"

"Lousy."

"Really? I thought porn was recession-proof."

"It is," he said. "That's not the problem."

"What, then?"

"You really want to know about this?"

"I do."

"Off the record?"

"Sure."

"Then let me give you a little background."

"Okay."

"I saw you looking at my vintage posters."

"Hard to miss them."

"They're from the 1970s, when Cecil Howard, the Mitchell Brothers, Howard Ziehm, and Gerard Damiano were making feature-length hard-core films. People went to the theater to watch them. They attracted the raincoat crowd, of course, but some guys went with dates."

"So I've heard," I said. "I was in diapers then."

"The VCR changed all that," Sal said. "Once people could rent or buy videocassettes, they preferred to watch pornography at home. But the industry still made feature-length films. We employed scriptwriters. Our movies had plots. Then porn went online, and things changed again."

"How so?"

"Attention spans got shorter. Nobody cared about plots anymore. Ninety-minute feature films mostly disappeared. We still shoot a couple a year, but they don't make any money. We just make them to maintain our self-respect."

A half-dozen smart remarks ran through my mind, but I decided to keep them to myself.

"The thirty- and sixty-minute DVDs that replaced them were just compilations of ten-minute sex scenes that could be chopped and posted separately on Internet pay sites," Sal said. "Turned out even they were too long. Guys just watched the first penetration, fast-forwarded to the money shot, and jumped to the next video."

"But it was profitable," I said.

"Very."

"So what went wrong?"

"The market got flooded. Cheap hand-held video cameras made it easy for any fool to shoot a porno. The number of online pay sites exploded. A price war broke out. We used to charge forty-five dollars a month for a subscription to one of our sites. Now we're asking nineteen ninety-five, and it's hard to get people to pay even that."

"Because?"

"Because our videos are being pirated. People download them and then post them by the hundreds on porn-sharing sites where anyone can watch them for free."

"Like what happened with music," I said.

"Exactly. Then it got worse. Now guys are shooting videos of themselves having sex with their fat wives and skanky girlfriends and posting them online." Sal looked at me and shook his head. "I never dreamed people would be giving this stuff away."

"Sounds like you're in a dying business," I said.

"I don't think so. There are still people out there who want to see beautiful women having sex, and who want their videos to be in focus and well lighted. There's still a market for our product, but the margins are smaller now, so we have to keep our costs down."

"Which is why you opened the studio here," I said.

"That's right. The rent is lower, and the actors we've recruited locally work cheaper. In Southern California, we competed with Vivid, Digital Playground, and a dozen other studios for the best talent, so we had to pay the girls three to five thousand for each sex scene. Here, they take a grand and are grateful to get it."

"What about the men?"

"In the Valley, they get five to eight hundred per scene," he said. "Here we're paying them two hundred, and they're so glad for the chance to fuck girls like Doreen that they'd probably work for free."

"Know what all this reminds me of?" I asked.

"The newspaper business?"

"Yeah. Aggregators pirate our news, readers don't want to pay for something they can get for free, and we keep cutting costs to keep our heads above water."

"One big difference, though," he said.

"What's that?"

"The pornography business will survive." Sal rubbed his face and looked at me for a moment. "How much longer do you think the *Dispatch* will hold on?"

"I don't know. Two or three years, maybe."

"What will you do then?"

"No idea."

"Would you consider coming to work for me?"

"Doing what?"

"You are an expert at digging up hard-to-get information," Sal said.

"So I've been told."

"I could use somebody like you."

"What kind of information are you after?"

"That is something to be discussed after you take the job."

I considered asking Sal about the Chad Brown murders again but then thought better of it. He'd already told me the only thing he knew was what he'd read in the paper. If he wasn't involved, that was probably the truth. If he *was* involved, he wasn't going to tell me.

I told Sal I'd think about his offer. I shook

his hand, and I was on my way out when I ran into Vanessa in the hall.

"Did Dad offer you that job?" she asked.

"He did."

"Going to take it?"

"I don't know."

"You should. You'd look good in front of a camera."

"Oh God, no!"

She threw back her head and laughed. "Just kidding," she said, and walked on by. I turned and watched her step into her father's office.

I continued down the hall, pushed through the door to the outer office, and found it empty. The receptionist had left for the day, or maybe she'd stepped out for a smoke. I walked across the beige carpet and went through the steel door to the peeling green vestibule. Then I stopped, thought for a second, and decided to employ one of those investigative reporting techniques they don't teach at Columbia. I turned back just as the lock in the steel door clicked shut. I punched the first four numbers into the electronic keypad, guessed at the fifth, and hit it on the fourth try. At the receptionist's desk, I found the button that unlocked the inner door, slipped inside, and crept back to Sal's office. Standing outside the door, I could just make out the voices.

"When did this happen?" Sal said.

"A couple of hours ago," Vanessa said.

"Where?"

"Pawtucket."

"Sonuvabitch," Sal said. "It's not over."

Then the phone rang. Sal took the call and started arguing with someone about the price of a new video camera. I tiptoed down the hall, went back out the door, and headed for the *Dispatch.*

I'd just stepped into the newsroom when Lomax grabbed me by the arm and handed me a printout of a story under Mason's byline:

Nine-year-old Julia Arruda of 22 Maynard St., Pawtucket, was abducted at 3:15 p.m. today and remains missing.

Pawtucket police said the child had been playing with friends outside the Potter Burns Elementary School, which she attends, when she was struck in the face with a snowball and decided to go home. She had just stepped onto the sidewalk when a van pulled up and the back door flew open. A man wearing a black ski mask jumped out, grabbed her, and dragged her inside. Julia's best friend, Karen Rose, also 9, ran after the van, caught the license plate, and wrote it down in the snow, police said.

Twenty minutes later, police found the van abandoned on a side street a half-mile away. It had been reported stolen yesterday from a U-Haul lot on Harris Street in nearby South Attleboro.

42

Tuesday at dawn, FBI agents raided houses in Fort Worth, Texas; Naples, Florida; Cape Girardeau, Missouri; Andover, Massachusetts; and Edison, New Jersey. They arrested five middle-aged men and seized their computers. By Thursday, all five had been formally charged with possession of child pornography, released on bail pending trial, and fired from their jobs. According to Parisi, all five were warned that the charges might be the least of their problems — that someone out there might be gunning for them.

Shortly before noon on Friday, Charles H. Gleason of 43 Carmello Drive in Edison was waiting at a red light at the corner of Lincoln Highway and Plainfield Avenue when somebody driving a stolen Buick Regal pulled up next to him, rolled down the passenger-side window, and fired three shots from a nine-millimeter Springfield

XdM. According to the Associated Press account, cops found the Buick abandoned a few miles away on the Rutgers University campus. The handgun, reported stolen from a gun shop in Providence a month earlier, was under the driver's seat. Gleason's wife, referring to her late husband as "the pathetic little pervert," told the AP he'd been on his way to the state unemployment office to apply for benefits.

I didn't care. I had a date.

43

I liked to go into Boston for the games. Secretariat had memorized the directions to Fenway Park and the Garden and knew to drop me off at a couple of watering holes along the route. The bars on Yawkey Way always served up just what I needed — cheese fries, entertaining loudmouths, and the occasional Yankees or Knicks fan who wandered into the wrong place. I didn't often bother with the rest of the city. Providence had all the problems I could handle, and it was small enough to fit in my pocket.

Cambridge, just north of Boston, was a schizophrenic little place: halfway houses and mom-and-pop grocers interspersed with pretentious eateries and ivory towers that hummed with possibility. The center of the town was gritty enough to remind me of home.

As Yolanda and I headed to Central

Square for Patricia Smith's poetry reading, I pointed out everything I didn't like. "Another Starbucks," I said for the fourth time. "Another grill with an 'e' on the end. And there's another shop with an extra 'pe' on the end. Either folks around here can't spell, or we've wandered into an alternate universe."

Behind the wheel of her Acura, Yolanda shook her head and laughed, and I felt my breath catch on something.

"MIT and Harvard spell money," she said. "What did you expect?"

The Cantab Lounge was in the middle of a block that lifted my spirits a little. Although it held one of those ghastly fern-filled restaurants, there was also a pizza joint that sold sloppy slices and a 7-Eleven with ancient hot dogs spinning on hot rollers — cuisine for the tipsy, late-night connoisseur.

We grabbed a parking spot behind the bar, and I walked behind my date, getting a load of the scenery. Yolanda had tucked a man's blue oxford shirt into faded jeans that looked poured on. On the back right pocket was a familiar logo — True Religion. I don't consider myself a prayin' man, but . . .

"Mulligan, c'mon, the show's starting soon. What are you doing back there?" I looked up to see Yolanda smirking at me from beneath the brim of a Chicago Cubs hat. She looked so gorgeous that I'd already decided to forgive her for the ball cap.

She'd finally agreed to go with me because she really wanted to hear Patricia read, didn't want to go alone, and couldn't find anyone else who gave a shit about poetry. Her usual ground rule applied: We were just going together, not *goin'* together.

We opened the door to the Cantab and were greeted by the smell of cheap whiskey and old fried food, the sound of heartbreak on the jukebox, and dark the way drunks like it. Before my eyes adjusted, I could barely make out the forms of guys who'd probably been glued to their stools since breakfast.

We followed a stream of people down a narrow staircase to the basement, where the poetry reading was set to start in fifteen minutes. The buzz there hinted at an optimism sorely lacking on the first floor. The room was strung with colored lights. The stage was just a small area cleared at the front of the room. A DJ was playing songs that sounded like drums mumbling.

We found stools at the bar, the last seats left. Yolanda requested white wine. The barkeep, a gravelly-voiced gal named Judy, unscrewed the cap on a green bottle and poured liberally into a plastic cup. I wanted beer, but I asked for a club soda.

"I know why this place is called the Cantab," I said.

"Why?" Yolanda said.

"In England, a resident of Cambridge was called a Cantabrigian. So were students at the University of Cambridge. And here we are in Cambridge, Massachusetts."

"And just how did you know that?"

"I Googled it this morning while I was looking up ways to impress you."

The room had grown so crowded that folks were sitting on the floor beside the stage and on the stairs leading to the restrooms. We were approaching fire hazard, and Yolanda already had me a little sweaty. I could feel her thigh against mine.

"So where's my favorite poet?" I shouted. It was tough to hear.

"How many poets have you actually read?"

"That depends."

"On what?"

"On whether Dr. Seuss counts."

Yolanda laughed again, and my thigh quivered a little. "That's Patricia over there," she said.

I followed her eyes to a corner near the front of the room where a Hershey-colored woman was signing a slim volume of poetry.

I recognized her smile from the back of her books, but I was unprepared for the rest of her, looking good in black slacks and a blue silk blouse with an African print. She looked up just in time to see me staring, came straight for us, and gave Yolanda a hard hug. Seeing the two of them tangled that way sent my mind into all sorts of kinky places.

"I didn't know you two knew each other," I said. "I assumed Yolanda only knew you from your work, and she let me think it."

Patricia looked at me curiously.

"My name is Mulligan. I'm Ms. Mosley-Jones's boy toy."

Patricia looked at Yolanda. Then back at me. Then at Yolanda again.

"In his dreams," Yolanda said, and they both laughed.

Nobody told me that we'd have to suffer through something called an "open mic," which consisted of folks reading poems about their cats, poems about their orgasms, poems about their cats' orgasms, and poems that said over and over that the poet was angry, or in love, or horny, or all three. Then it was time for the main event.

Hearing Patricia was more mesmerizing than reading her. The poems, jazzy and full of language play, gave my emotions a workout. I hadn't been that close to tears since

I'd been forced to give away my dog. The dog wasn't too thrilled about it, either.

When the reading was over, I just wanted to go someplace with Yolanda and talk about what we'd heard. Preferably her place. Preferably in a horizontal position. But first it was burgers at the fern place. I suffered through a waitress named Ariel, shoestring fries, and parsley on the plate. Yolanda and I talked about Patricia's poetry, and she suggested names of other poets I might like. I promptly forgot them all.

The drive back to Rhode Island took too long, yet not as long as I wanted it to. We listened to Buddy Guy and John Lee Hooker and Koko Taylor and Tommy Castro. We didn't talk much, but it was a comfortable silence. At least her half of it. I felt sweat trickle under my shirt.

Finally we reached Yolanda's place, where Secretariat waited like a sentry at the curb across the street. I hoped he'd be waiting there for a while. Maybe until morning.

I walked her to her door. She held my hand part of the way, then broke the connection.

"That was great, Mulligan. I had a good time," she said. "You wear culture pretty well." She pulled her keys from her bag and unlocked her front door.

"Yolanda?"

She turned and locked eyes with me.

"I want to kiss you."

"I know."

She looked at me as if I were a puppy she had decided not to adopt. Then she stepped inside and closed her door so softly that I didn't hear the latch click into place.

44

Next morning I woke up thinking about Yolanda. I needed to stop obsessing about her and get my head back into the job. The cops were nowhere and so was I. Clearly we were missing something, but I had no idea what it was or where to find it.

Not knowing what else to do, I decided to take another look at Sal Maniella. He'd come out of hiding because, as he put it, "something needed my attention." He'd offered me a job because, according to him, I was "an expert at digging up hard-to-get information." And what was it I'd overheard him say on the afternoon of the Pawtucket kidnapping? Oh yeah. He'd said: "Sonuvabitch. It's not over."

Sal knew more than he was telling, and I had the feeling he was up to something more than making dirty movies.

I ran the possibilities over in my mind while I unloaded my grandfather's gun. I doubted Sal was involved in the child porn business, but it sounded like he was keeping tabs on it. If his interest wasn't business, maybe it was personal. I put the gun back in the shadow box and returned it to its place of honor on my wall. Whatever Sal was up to, there was no reason to think it would involve sending Black Shirt and Gray Shirt after me again.

In the newsroom, I spent the morning using every search engine I knew of to research him again online. I didn't find much, and I learned nothing new. After lunch at the diner, I walked across the Providence River to the red-brick courthouse and looked him up in the card catalog that lists the docket numbers of every criminal case filed in the state in the last fifty years. Nothing. Then I checked the card catalog for civil cases and learned he'd been sued a few times (payroll disputes with three of his employees, an alienation of affections suit, and a slip-and-fall on his front steps) and that he'd sued a few people himself (a manufacturer in a dispute over some faulty video equipment, a contractor who did a shoddy job roofing his house, and a neighbor he accused of poisoning his dog). No help there. To be thorough, I ran the same check on Vanessa and came up empty.

What next? I decided to try another long shot.

Police and social service records involving children are supposed to be confidential, but nothing really is if you know the right people. In a state you can throw a shot put across, a good reporter knows almost everybody. I rang up Dave Reid, a former *Dispatch* assistant city editor. He'd fled the crumbling business six years ago to join the police department in the little town of Smithfield, which includes the village of Greenville, where the Maniellas had lived for years.

"Seven tomorrow morning work for you?" he asked.

"Sure," I said, although it was awfully goddamned early. So at seven o'clock sharp, I stepped into the deputy chief's office and plunked a copy of the *Dispatch,* two large coffees, and a box holding a Dunkin' Donuts assortment on his supernaturally clean desk.

"Doughnuts? Really?" he said. "I thought you hated clichés."

"If you don't eat them, I will," I said, so he pried open the box and plucked the leaking jelly doughnut I'd had my heart set on.

"You sure Vanessa Maniella spent her entire childhood in Smithfield?" he asked.

"Yeah. The family owned a house near the Stillwater Reservoir before they built their Versailles on Waterman Lake."

"You understand I can't tell you anything officially," he said.

"Of course you can't."

"So we never had this conversation, right?"

"What conversation?"

"Our computerized records don't go that far back," he said. "I'll have to hit the file cabinets, and I can tell you right now they're a mess — a lot of stuff missing or misfiled."

"Whatever you can do," I said.

He got up, grabbed his cup of coffee from the desk, snatched another doughnut from the box, and said, "Wait here."

I sipped my vile, milk-diluted decaf, sank my teeth into a lemon doughnut, and settled down with the paper. The Pawtucket PD was begging the public to come forward with leads on the missing girl, a sure giveaway that they had nothing to go on. Three men in ski masks had invaded the statehouse, fired warning bursts with their Heckler & Koch 5.56mm machine guns, smashed the glass case outside the governor's office, stuffed the contents into canvas laundry bags, and made off with the antique Gorham sterling silver tea service that once

350

graced the captain's table of the battleship USS *Rhode Island*. And the Celtics, with Garnett still hobbling on a surgically repaired knee, were getting wiped out on their West Coast road trip. By the time Reid stepped back in, I'd been reduced to reading the obituaries, some of which I'd written. He looked at me and shook his head.

"Aw, crap."

"Sorry," he said. "Doesn't mean she was never molested. The file might be missing. Or maybe it was never reported."

"Could be," I said. "Maniella's the kind of guy who'd be inclined to handle something like that himself."

"Tell you what," Reid said. "Why don't you talk to my older sister, Meg. She's been the nurse at the middle school for thirty-five years; and don't tell her I said this, but she's quite the busybody. I'll call and let her know you're on the way."

A half hour later, Meg ushered me into her closet-size office, directed me to an uncomfortable metal folding chair, and made me wait for twenty minutes while she attended to a couple of gum-chewing malingerers whining about tummy aches. When she was done, she sat behind her little metal desk and clasped her hands together on the plain paper desk pad.

"If anything like that happened, I never heard tell of it," she said. "Before you got here, I called my friends Mary and Sylvia. They worked in the system forever. Mary was a nurse at the elementary school and Sylvia was a counselor at the high school before they both retired last year. Neither of them ever heard so much as a whisper."

"I see."

"Are you sure it's true?" she said, sounding a little breathless.

"If I were, I wouldn't be asking you about it," I said. "I'm just fishing."

"Fishing?"

"Yeah. It's what I do. I poke into things, ask a lot of questions, and once in a while I learn something."

"But you wouldn't be asking about this if you weren't pretty sure there was something to it, right?"

"Wrong."

"I see," she said. Rather coldly, I thought. "Well, I'm sorry I couldn't help you."

I thanked her and left.

It had been almost a week since I'd had a good cigar — or a bad one, for that matter. So I popped Memphis Slim into the Bronco's CD player and fired up a Cohiba. As I drove back to the *Dispatch,* I pictured Meg sitting at her desk, balancing her professional ethics against the merriment of spreading a malicious rumor all over town.

Allegra Morelli was nothing like her older sister. Rosie had been six feet five; Allegra was five feet one. Rosie had been outgoing; Allegra was withdrawn. Rosie had been drop-dead gorgeous; Allegra was as plain as a grocery bag. Rosie had been ambitious; Allegra settled for juggling a caseload of sorrow at the state Child Protective Services Unit. And the biggest difference: Allegra was alive; Rosie was dead.

"Give me an hour to check the files, and I'll call you back," Allegra said.

"I got a better idea," I said. "Why don't you meet me at the diner in Kennedy Plaza so I can buy you lunch?"

A couple of hours later, I walked into the place and found her sitting alone in a booth, perched like a nervous little bird on the edge of the red vinyl seat. Her black handbag was on the table in front of her, and she clutched it with both hands as if she were afraid somebody might try to take it away from her.

Allegra and I had fallen into the habit of talking on the phone every few weeks to reminisce about Rosie, but I hadn't seen her since the funeral and felt bad about that.

I sat down across from her and said, "It's good to see you. Thanks so much for coming."

"I probably shouldn't have," she said. "Being seen with a reporter could get me in trouble."

"I know."

"But Rosie would have wanted me to."

"God, I miss her," I said.

"Me too."

"Did you order yet?"

"No. I was waiting for you," she said, so I gave Charlie a wave, and he came right over.

"What can I get you, miss?"

"A small garden salad, please, with Italian dressing on the side."

"Anything to drink?"

"A glass of water."

"A burger and a cup of decaf for me, Charlie," I said. He nodded and went away.

"So, Allegra," I said, "what did you find out about the Maniellas?"

"Nothing," she said. "If either of them was ever molested as a child, there's no record of it."

"Oh. Well, thanks for checking."

"Sure."

"What about the three kids who were rescued from the Chad Brown child porn factory?"

"I can't talk about that if you're going to put something in the paper."

"I won't. I was just wondering how they're doing."

"Two of them are back with their parents. I assume they're getting psychiatric care, but they aren't in the system so we don't have files on them."

"What about the eight-year-old boy who was sold by his drug addict mother?"

"He's on my girlfriend Tracy's caseload," Allegra said, "so I got the whole story. The child's name is Phillip. Phillip Bowen. He was placed in a foster home in North Kingstown and will stay in foster care until his mother gets out of jail, which won't happen anytime soon, from what I hear."

"By the time that bitch sees sunshine again," I said, "Phillip will be all grown up."

Charlie dropped our orders in front of us with a clatter of plates and tableware. Allegra picked at her salad. I inhaled the burger.

"Tracy says Phillip's physical injuries are healing," Allegra said, "but his emotional health is another story. He goes to counseling once a week, but it's going to take a long time."

"I imagine so."

"Mulligan?"

"Um?"

"Do this job as long as Tracy and I have and you kinda get hardened to things, you know?"

"I do."

"And Tracy's always been a tough customer. But she couldn't even talk about Phillip without tearing up."

I didn't have a response to that, so I finished my coffee and reached for the check.

"Can you stay a little longer?" Allegra said. "I thought maybe we could sit for a while and talk about Rosie."

45

Mason, looking relaxed and deeply tanned, popped into my cubicle Tuesday morning and dropped a shopping bag on the desk.

"A present," he said.

I reached in and pulled out a black T-shirt. It had a blue surfboard on the front and the words "Surfin' Malibu U.S.A." on the back.

"Why, thank you, Thanks-Dad," I said. This would come in handy if I ever decided to wash the Bronco. "So how'd it go?"

"Great," he said. "I rented a town house right on the beach. Met a couple of fun-loving girls. And I took surfing lessons from a former ASP World Tour champion who called me 'dude.' "

"What else?"

"Don't tell anybody," he said, "but I got a tattoo." He took off his suit jacket, draped it over the cubicle divider, rolled up his left sleeve, and displayed a small blue tattoo of a sailboat on an angry red patch of forearm.

"I've got to hide it from Dad," he said. "He'll hate it."

"Judging from the grin on your face," I said, "I don't think you've told me the best part yet."

"Quite right."

"So?"

"I'll tell you over dinner. I made reservations at Camille's for eight this evening. We'll celebrate."

Camille's was the finest Italian restaurant on Federal Hill and had been for almost a hundred years. It was also the place where Vinnie Giordanno fell face-first into his plate of vongole alla Giovanni last year after two gunmen put one bullet each in his head.

"Don't worry, it's on me," Mason said. "And just a suggestion: You might want to skip lunch."

"I will."

"Oh, and don't forget to wear a jacket."

Mason had arranged a small private dining room for the occasion. After we perused the menu and placed our orders, he selected a hundred-dollar bottle of wine for each of us: something called Antinori, Cervaro della Sala, Chardonnay, Umbria, for me; Poliziano, Asinone, Vino Nobile di Montepulciano, for him. I'm no wine drinker, so I figured this was a good time to follow my doctor's orders. I told the waiter to hold the wine and bring me a bottle of San Pellegrino.

And then the food kept coming and coming and coming.

Appetizers: portobello strudel and shrimp Santiago. Soups: pasta e fagioli and escarole with bean and Speck ham. Salads: scungilli and cold antipasto platter. Pasta: linguine carbonara and rigatoni con formaggio affumicato. And finally the entrées: veal steak Giovanni for him and swordfish al cartoccio for me.

After they were served, Chef John Granata popped in to shake our hands and ask if everything was satisfactory. We assured him it was. My ulcer wasn't so sure. I popped a couple of omeprazole tablets and washed them down with San Pellegrino.

I kept trying to steer the conversation to Mason's big news, but he was having none of it. "After we dine," he said, and filled the space between us with small talk about surfing, Malibu, and the sorry state of the newspaper business.

I managed to eat about half of what was put in front of me. Mason, who was built like a Popsicle stick, cleaned his plate. If he weren't so well-bred, I think he would have licked it. We skipped dessert and went straight for the after-dinner drinks, cognac for him and decaf for me. After they were delivered, Mason clinked his glass against my cup and sipped.

"So, Thanks-Dad," I said, "don't you think it's time you told me what we're celebrating?"

Mason laced his fingers behind his head, leaned back in his chair, and said: "Nailed it."

"Could you be more specific?"

"I got seventeen porn stars on the record."

"Great."

"I knew you'd be pleased."

"I'd be more pleased if you told me what they went on the record *about.*"

"Let me tell it from the beginning," he said.

"Sure."

"At first I didn't think this was going to work out. The first six porn actors I located declined to talk to me, and most of them were quite rude about it. One even took a poke at me."

"That how you got the split lip?"

"No. I ducked and he missed." Mason laid a finger against the half-moon-shaped scab. "I got this when a whitecap flipped me and I got clipped by the board."

"So what happened next?"

"On my second day in the Valley, I knocked on the door of a little pink bungalow in Santa Clarita, and a very pretty blonde in shorts and a halter top greeted me with a smile. When I told her what I wanted, she didn't slam the door like the others. She invited me in and offered me iced tea."

"What's her name?"

"Her real name is Frieda Gottschalk, but she started calling herself Shania Bauer six years ago when she moved to Hollywood from Duluth to try to make it in the movie business."

"How'd that work out?"

"Not well. After a couple of years, she gave it up and started doing porn under the names Peachy Butt and Sugar Sweet."

"Does she have a peachy butt?"

"If that means what I think it does, I'd have to say yes."

"Is she sugar sweet?"

"I resisted the urge to taste."

"So what did she tell you?"

"First I showed Frieda the records indicating she had contributed five thousand dollars to the governor's reelection campaign three years in a row."

"I'd prefer that you refer to her as Peachy Butt."

"Why?"

"Isn't it obvious?"

"Okay. Peachy Butt confirmed that the records were accurate. She also acknowledged contributing two thousand dollars each to our house and senate judiciary committee chairmen. When I asked her why she made the contributions, she said Sal Maniella told her to."

"Did she tell you where she got the money?"

"She said Sal gave it to her."

"Did she know this was illegal?"

"She didn't say. I forgot to ask her that."

"Why do you suppose she told you all this?"

"She said Maniella trimmed his roster of actors a few months ago when he opened a new studio in Rhode Island. She's one of the ones who got dumped, and she's not pleased about it."

"Did she lead you to some of the others?"

"To five of them, yes. She even called them and said they should talk to me. Those five led me to still more, and by the end of the week I had seventeen on-the-record interviews. I could have gotten more, but I figured that was enough."

"They all told the same story?"

"Pretty much, yes."

"I don't suppose you recorded the interviews."

"I videotaped them with the Sony camcorder I brought along to document my vacation."

"They didn't mind?"

"Not at all. They were quite accustomed to being on camera."

"Great job, Thanks-Dad. You're really getting the hang of it. Don't forget what street reporting is all about when you land the big job in the corner office."

"I won't."

"After you write this up, let me look it over before you give it to Lomax, okay?"

"You can have it tomorrow. It's already written; I finished it on the plane."

"Good."

"Double byline, right?"

"Hell, no," I said. "Why share the credit when you did all the work?"

"There wouldn't have been a story if you hadn't pointed me in the right direction," he said. "I think your name should be on it."

"You don't have to do that."

"I want to."

"Up to you," I said. "Lomax will want to

hold the story for Sunday and strip it across page one. It's gonna make a hell of a splash."

But first, I owed a couple of people a heads-up.

46

The maid answered the bell and ushered me into the library, where Sal Maniella was waiting for me. I found him seated on the couch, admiring the autograph on the title page of Ian Fleming's *Moonraker.* Copies of *Casino Royale, From Russia with Love,* and *On Her Majesty's Secret Service* were fanned out on the coffee table.

"From the Swann Galleries auction?" I asked.

"Yes."

I'd looked up the auction results online. The signed first edition of *Moonraker* had sold for more than fifty thousand dollars.

I sat beside him and placed both volumes of the Grant biography on the coffee table. "Thanks for letting me borrow them," I said.

"You're most welcome. Let me know if there's anything else you want to read. After all, what good are books if you can't share them?"

"I never got around to reading *Moonraker,*" I said, "but if I ever find the time, I'll buy a used paperback. I'd be afraid to even breathe on this copy."

"Don't be," he said, and placed it in my hands. "You can read it here if you like; it shouldn't take more than a couple of hours. But I'm sure you understand why I'd prefer it didn't leave the premises."

"Of course."

"By the way," he said, "I've been meaning to talk to you about your collection of pulp detective magazines."

"The magazines that were in the boxes you don't know anything about?"

"Those would be the ones."

"What about them?"

"Take special care with the June 1935 edition of *Black Mask.* It contains the first printing of a story by Raymond Chandler, and except for the tiny coffee stain on the spine, it's in remarkable condition."

"I suppose it is."

"If you ever decide to sell it, let me know. The last one that sold at auction brought five hundred dollars."

"You'll be the first one I call," I said. I could sure use the money, but I hated the idea of parting with it.

"So," he said, "why did you want to see me?"

I told him.

He picked up the crystal decanter, poured himself a shot of Scotch, and offered me one. I shook my head.

"Well," he said, "this will certainly cause some trouble for the governor."

"For you, too, I imagine."

"No, not really. Yolanda will plead me guilty to violating the state campaign finance law, and I'll have to pay a four-figure fine. But of course the governor's campaign committee will have to return the money, so I'll use that to pay the fine and be well ahead of the game."

"They'll return the money to the porn actors, not to you," I said. "I doubt you'll ever see any of it."

"Excellent point," he said.

"When the story breaks, there'll be a lot of pressure on the governor and the legislature to outlaw prostitution," I said.

"I imagine so."

"If they do, it will ruin Vanessa's brothel business."

"I very much doubt that."

"Really?"

"Really."

"How come?"

"I'd rather not say."

"The story's going to run Sunday, page one," I said. "We need some kind of quote from you and Vanessa."

"Just put us down for a 'No comment.' "

I walked into Hopes expecting to find Fiona at her usual table. Instead she was holding down a stool at the far end of the bar.

"You look exhausted," I said.

"I am. I spent last night trying to comfort Daniel and Carla Arruda."

"The parents of the kidnapped Pawtucket girl?"

"Yeah."

"How are they holding up?"

"Carla can't stop crying and begging God to send her little girl home. Daniel has already given his daughter up for dead and wants to shed blood; but he doesn't know who to kill, and it's driving him fucking crazy."

I didn't have anything to say to that, so I stared at the bar top for a moment.

"I bet you could use some good news," I said.

"You got any?"

"I do," I said, and then I told her.

"That's fantastic," she said. "How'd you

find out?"

"I didn't," I said. "It was Thanks-Dad." And then I told her how he'd done it.

"Pretty slick," she said.

"I think so, too."

"Of course, they'll all wriggle off the hook," she said. "Maniella will get fined and can grab enough cash to cover it by looking under his sofa cushions. The governor and the two committee chairmen will be *shocked, shocked,* about where the campaign contributions came from, and they'll give the money back. But the bastards won't dare to hold up my antiprostitution bill now. If they do, I'll make it look like they were all bought and paid for."

"Which they were," I said. "You were right all along."

"Have a drink with me," Fiona said.

"My doctor has advised against it."

"Would a little wine hurt? Come on, Mulligan. I've got a couple of things to celebrate."

"A couple? What's the other one?"

"Rome finally weighed in on my, uh, situation."

"And?"

"And it's politics or the church. I've been given a week to decide."

"Aw, crap."

"I couldn't have put it better," she said, and then she threw her head back and laughed.

"What are you going to do?"

Fiona drained her can of Bud and placed it on the bar. She slipped the gold band from her finger and held it before her eyes for a moment. Then she dropped the ring into the empty. She picked up the can and shook it, the ring clattering inside, and suddenly the mischievous smile I remembered from two decades ago was back. "So whaddaya say, Mulligan? Wanna fuck?"

"Uh . . . what?"

"Don't look so scared," she said. "I'm just kidding. Besides, you're not my type."

"I'm not?"

"No."

"Why is that?"

"Can you turn the governor into a pillar of salt?"

"Guess not."

"Bring a rain of burning sulfur down on the state house?"

"Only metaphorically."

"Well, there you go." She laughed hard and long, the sound mirthful but with a hint of hysteria around the edges.

"Going to hold a press conference?" I said.

"No. I thought I'd just give you the scoop.

Pull your pad out and I'll answer all your questions."

So I did. But I already had my lead: the clink of a gold wedding ring hitting the bottom of an empty beer can.

47

The "Who Are You?" ringtone interrupted my breakfast.

"I'm only going to say this once," the caller said, "so listen up." The voice was muffled — a man trying to disguise his voice. The gravel in it again reminded me of Joseph, but I still couldn't be sure.

"You again," I said.

"Shut up and write down this address: 8 Harwich Street. That's H-a-r-w-i-c-h. Got it?"

"Off Blackstone Boulevard?"

"Yeah."

"Then you must mean Harwich Road."

"Yeah, yeah, Harwich *Road.*"

"Nice neighborhood," I said.

"Fuckin' posh."

Would Joseph say "posh"? Would he even know what it meant?

"Do a little redecorating there, did you?" I asked.

"You'll find out when you show up. Another big story in it for you, so move your ass."

So that's what I did. I'd just pulled Secretariat out of the Mobowned parking lot across from the newspaper when the cell started playing "Who Let the Dogs Out?"

"Hi, Peggi."

"Something's wrong at Dr. Wayne's house," she said.

"What do you mean?"

"He didn't come to work this morning. Blew off an eight o'clock appointment with a big donor, which isn't like him at all. I tried his cell phone and it went to voice mail, so I called the house and a policeman answered the phone."

"A policeman?"

"Yes."

"What did he say?"

"That Dr. Wayne couldn't come to the phone right now. Then he asked me who I was and why I was calling."

"Did you get his name?"

"Parisi. Captain Parisi of the Rhode Island State Police."

"Where does Dr. Wayne live, Peggi?"

"Eight Harwich Road."

Dr. Charles Bruce Wayne's place was a two-story red-brick colonial with thick hedges on three sides and a wrought iron fence across the front. Three unmarked Crown Vics, two Providence PD squad cars, and the state medical examiner's wagon were parked at the curb out front. An ambulance waited in the driveway, nose out but in no apparent hurry. Three stay-at-home moms and their preschool toddlers gawked from the sidewalk across the street. I parked Secretariat behind one of the squad cars, and as I climbed out, Patrolman O'Banion of the Providence PD waddled in my direction. He didn't look happy to see me.

"Top of the mornin' to ya, Officer."

"Get back in your piece-of-shit Bronco and get the fuck out of here," he said, "or I'll arrest you and call for a tow." My story about him filching joints from the Providence PD evidence locker was six years old now, but we Irish know how to nurse a grudge.

"While you're doing all that," I said, "please let my friend Steve Parisi know that I'm here with information pertinent to this case."

"And what information would that be?"

"After I give it to Parisi, you can ask him."

O'Banion folded his arms, rested them on the top shelf of his potbelly, and gave me a hard look. I shrugged, took out my cell, and hit speed dial.

"Parisi."

"Morning, Captain."

"Sorry, but I'm a little busy right now."

"I know. I'm right outside."

"Aw, hell. Who tipped you this time?"

"An anonymous caller."

That made him pause. "Not the same one who tipped you off about the Chad Brown murders," he said.

"Sure sounded like him."

"Well, then stay right there until I can get to you, okay?"

"If I do, Officer O'Banion is going to arrest me and have my car towed."

"Let me talk to him."

O'Banion raised an eyebrow as I handed him the cell. He put it to his ear, said, "Yes, sir," a couple of times, and clicked off. Then he glared at me, swung his arm back as if he thought he was Josh Beckett, and hurled the phone across the street. I walked over, picked it up, and brushed the snow from it. It still worked.

I got behind the wheel of the Bronco, eased the seat halfway back, cracked the window, and set fire to a Cohiba. I'd finished the cigar and was a third of the way through my prostitution playlist when two

EMTs rolled a shiny black body bag out of the house and loaded it into the ambulance. The driver was in no hurry. He took a few moments to savor his cigarette before tossing it aside, climbing behind the wheel, and driving away. Fifteen minutes later, a crime scene investigator from Tedesco's office came out of the house, spotted the cigarette butt, picked it up with tweezers, and deposited it in a clear plastic evidence bag.

It was well past noon when Parisi exited the house. I slid down the passenger-side window as he headed my way.

"Hungry?" he asked.

"Yeah."

"I'm buying," he said. He opened the car door, swept some newspapers and empty coffee cups off the passenger seat, and got in. "Head downtown and find a parking spot near city hall."

Parisi's idea of springing for lunch turned out to be hot dogs and Cokes at Haven Brothers, one of the oldest lunch wagons in America. An immigrant woman named Anne Philomena Haven founded it in 1893 with money from her late husband's insurance policy. Originally it was a horse-drawn wagon, but it reluctantly joined the internal combustion age about ninety years ago. For longer than anyone could remember, Haven

Brothers has been a fixture on the street just outside the entrance to city hall. For a time, it is said, the lunch wagon drew its electricity by illegally tapping into the government building's power line. Every now and then, the city fathers denounce the place as an eyesore and drug addict hangout and try to close it down. Each time they do, loyal customers including drug addicts, Brown students, bikers, cops, hookers, reporters, and former mayor Vincent A. "Buddy" Cianci Jr. ride to the rescue. Buddy recommends the beans, one of the things he missed during his four years in federal prison on a racketeering conviction.

Haven Brothers has no seats, but it does offer a choice of dining accommodations. You can inhale grease-flecked air while eating standing up in a cramped and gritty indoor space near the grill, or you can take your food outside and join the pigeons by the equestrian statue of Civil War general Ambrose Burnside in the little park that bears his name. Most people prefer the park, even when it rains. Parisi and I walked through what remained of the snow and sat on the concrete base of the statue.

"Tell me about the call," he said.

"It was pretty much the same as the first one — a muffled voice giving me the address and saying there was a big story in it if I got there first."

"But this time you didn't."

"No."

"Put the phone on speaker and hit redial."

It rang eight times and went to a recorded message saying the voice mail mailbox had not been set up. Same as the last time.

"How'd you beat me to the scene?" I asked.

Parisi took five seconds to compose his response. "The good doctor's wife was out of town visiting family. She called the home phone and her husband's cell several times, got no answer, and became concerned. About six this morning, she called the Providence police and asked them to check on him."

"And they *did?*"

"Yeah. It's the kind of call they would normally blow off, but Wayne's an important guy, and the family has been a big donor to police charities; so they sent a two-man patrol car to the house. The officers found the back door jimmied, called for backup, went inside before it arrived, and found Wayne slumped in his desk chair in the den. He'd been shot once in the back of the head."

"Was there a computer in the den?"

"A desktop, yeah."

"Anything interesting on it?"

"Besides Wayne's blood and brains, you mean?"

"Yeah, besides that."

"No note left on it for you, if that's what you're asking."

"Anything on the screen?"

"It was dark. I didn't want to mess with it until the crime scene guys finished their evidence collection, but they should be done about now."

"Mind if I tag along?"

The medical examiner's wagon, two of the state police Crown Vics, and one of the city squad cars were still parked outside the house, but there were no TV vans in sight. Our crack local TV reporters hadn't gotten wind of the story yet.

Parisi led me around back, and we entered through the rear door, its jamb splintered where a pry bar had done its work. We walked down a short hallway and passed through open French doors to a large sunny den that smelled like the Chad Brown death house. I'd been at enough murder scenes to know that dead bodies often smell of expelled body fluids, but here the acrid smell of urine seemed unusually strong.

To our left, floor-to-ceiling mahogany bookcases were filled with thick medical books, a couple of them with Wayne's name on the spines. Straight ahead, hanging plants, most of them in bloom, dangled from the ceiling in front of a bank of jalousie windows. To the right, a lab tech wiped a swab across the splattered screen of Wayne's desktop computer.

"You about done here?" Parisi asked.

"With the evidence collection, yeah," the tech said, "but I've gotta disconnect the computer and take it back to the lab so the nerds can look it over, see what's on it."

"Okay if I take a look at it first?"

"Long as you glove up."

Parisi tugged on a pair of latex gloves and touched the space bar on the keyboard. The computer screen lit up, displaying a paused video that was partially visible through the bloody mess. We looked at each other and both said the same thing: "Aw, fuck." Then he moved the cursor to the play button and left-clicked.

48

"Jack Daniel's, rocks," Parisi said.

"Yes, it does," the waitress said.

"And make it a double."

"Killian's for me," I said. I needed whiskey, too, and my stomach seemed to be getting better; but I didn't dare risk the hard stuff yet.

We had reconvened at Hopes after he'd finished up at the crime scene and I'd filed my story, and we were sitting together now at a table in back. It was nearly nine o'clock, and the Celtics-Knicks game I'd placed a small bet on was playing on the TV behind the bar. An off-duty fireman whose nickname, Hose Hogan, had nothing to do with his occupation, slipped some coins in the jukebox, and B. B. King's Lucille cried out with the opening licks of "There Must Be a Better World Somewhere."

We stared at our hands and waited silently for the waitress to return with our order. I studied the ropy scars on the middle and index fingers of my left hand, reminders of compound fractures from a time when the only villains in my life were the kids who played hoops for Syracuse and Georgetown. Then I slid my gaze to Parisi's thick, knife-scarred fingers and saw that his knuckles were red and swollen, as if he'd recently punched something. Neither of us looked up as the waitress placed our drinks on the table, but we both turned to watch her ass switch as she traipsed away. Some habits are hard to break.

We were natural enemies, reporter and cop, but we'd been getting along pretty well lately. Now we were trying to decide how much of ourselves to share. We reached for our glasses and drank deeply. Then we looked over the rims and caught each other's eyes. I wondered if I looked as haunted as he did.

"Recognize the girl?" he asked.

"It was Julia Arruda."

"Did you put her name in the story?"

"Hell, no," I said. I took another pull from my beer. "You gonna tell her parents about this?"

"Not on your life."

"At least they didn't kill her," I said.

"Maybe they're saving that for later."

We drained our glasses, and I signaled the waitress for two more.

"Captain?"

"Um?"

"You look like shit."

"You too."

Something buzzed in his breast pocket. He reached in and drew out a smartphone.

"Parisi," he said, and then listened hard. "Aw, hell. Well, keep working on it, and call me back immediately if you get anywhere."

"Bad news?" I asked.

"We fucked up. Wayne's computer is password protected. The crime scene tech unplugged it and took it back to the lab, and when he turned it back on, he couldn't get past the screen saver."

"Call him back," I said, "and tell him the password is Dark Knight."

"How in *hell* do you know that?"

"Reporters know all kinds of stuff."

He stared at me hard, then made the call. "Conner? It's Parisi. The password is Dark Knight. . . . Never mind how I know. Just type it in. . . . Great. Call me as soon as you figure out what else is on it."

He clicked off, downed his whiskey, noticed my glass was nearly empty, and signaled the waitress for another round.

"You're gonna have to tell me how you

knew that," he said.

"Confidential source," I said, "but let me see if she'll talk to you."

Peggi picked up on the third ring.

"Hi. It's Mulligan."

"Is it true? Is Dr. Wayne really dead?"

"Where'd you hear that?"

"There was something on the TV news at six."

"It's true."

"Somebody *shot* him?"

"Yes, somebody did."

"Do they know who?"

"Not yet, no."

"Does this have something to do with the bad stuff you said he might be into?"

"I think so."

"Oh, my God!"

"Yeah."

"I never knew anybody who got *shot* before."

"Are you okay?"

"A little shaky, but yeah. I'm all right."

"Have the police talked to you yet?"

"No."

"They're going to be talking to people who knew him, and you'll be near the top of the list."

"Okay."

"I'm with Captain Parisi of the state police

right now."

"The one that answered the phone when I called the house?"

"That's right. He wants to know how I learned the password to Dr. Wayne's computer, but I didn't want to involve you without your permission. Do you think you could tell him about it?"

"Will it get me in trouble?"

"No, I don't think so."

"Okay, then," she said, so I handed Parisi the phone. He listened for a few moments, asked a couple of questions, and then clicked off.

"We square now?" I asked.

"Not quite."

"How come?"

"She said you told her Wayne might have been involved in some bad stuff."

"I did."

"So where did you hear *that?*"

"Can't tell you."

"Another confidential source?"

"Yeah."

I held his stare for about ten seconds, then picked up the phone, called McCracken's cell, and listened to it ring five times before going to voice mail.

"He's not answering," I said. "I'll try again tomorrow, see if he's willing to talk to you."

"Think he will be?"

"I think so, yeah."

We leaned back in our chairs and finished our drinks.

"Another, Captain?"

"Better not. I've got to drive back to headquarters."

He dropped a twenty on the table and was about to get to his feet when his cell buzzed again.

"Parisi. . . . That right? How many? . . . Anything else? . . . Well, keep looking," he said, and clicked off.

"Developments?" I asked.

"You could say that. The techs found over two hundred child porn videos on Wayne's computer."

"Any of them snuff films?"

"Don't know yet. The techs are still looking at them, the poor bastards."

We fell silent and stared into our empty glasses.

"Captain?"

"What?"

"Got somebody you can talk to about all this?"

"Been talkin' to you, haven't I?"

"Not really, no."

His shoulders slumped. Suddenly, he looked smaller.

"I'm not much of a talker," he said.

"Me either."

"Guess I could talk to the department shrink if I really need to."

"Couldn't hurt," I said.

"What about you, Mulligan? You got somebody you can talk to?"

"Matter of fact, I do."

I dropped a few bills on top of his, and we walked out of the bar into a bitterly cold night. He got into his Crown Vic and headed for state police headquarters, his work only begun. I got into Secretariat and drove to Swan Point Cemetery to talk things over with Rosie.

49

Friday morning, Lomax plucked a Mc-
Donald's breakfast sandwich wrapper and
an empty coffee cup from the corner of my
desk, dropped them in my wastebasket, sat
on the freshly cleared space, and read from
a printout of the obituary I'd just filed.

Raymond "Pisser" Massey, 46, of 102
Plainfield Street, a reckless daredevil and
rabid "Jackass" fan, died suddenly
Wednesday evening after living longer
than he had expected and twice as long
as he deserved. His last words were,
"Hey, Shirley! Watch this!"

"Pretty good, huh?" I said.
"No, it isn't," Lomax said.
"No?"
"It's inappropriate."
"I think I've captured him to perfection.
This is the way Pisser would want to be

remembered," I said, pronouncing his name the Rhode Island way: "Pissah."

"But is it the way his family would want to remember him?"

"I gotta think it is. I got most of the details from his mother and sisters."

"Really?"

"Yeah."

"Huh."

"So we can go with it?"

Lomax scowled, removed his glasses, wiped the lenses with his shirttail, put them back on, and silently read the obituary through from beginning to end.

"All right," he said. "Let's do this. Take out the part about him living twice as long as he deserved. It's too judgmental."

"Fine."

"And remove the nickname. No way I'm printing 'Pisser.' "

"Will do."

"And take out all the references to public urination."

"You sure? Pisser took great pride in his ability to piss twenty feet in the air."

"I don't care. Take it out."

"Okay. You're the boss."

He gave me a curt nod and shuffled off, leaving me pleased that my campaign to make the obituary page more interesting was making a little headway. It was past noon before I finished the day's obituaries and pointed Secretariat toward the little bayfront town of Warren.

"So who shot him?" McCracken said.

"Wasn't you, was it?" I asked him.

"No," the private investigator said, "but I don't plan on sending flowers to the funeral."

"Then it's gotta be the same people who hit the Chad Brown snuff film factory."

"And its customers in Wisconsin and New Jersey?" he asked.

"I think so, yeah."

"State cops got any idea who the shooters are?"

"Not a clue."

"How about you?" he asked.

"I'm beginning to get an inkling."

"Want to share?"

"Not yet."

"I wonder how the shooters knew what Wayne was mixed up in," McCracken said.

"I've been wondering that, too. Did you mention your suspicions to anybody else?"

"No. You?"

"Not a soul," I lied.

McCracken swiveled his office chair and studied the framed photos of the PC basketball stars on his office wall. Then he turned back to me and changed the subject. "Have you given any more thought to coming to work with me?"

"I've been considering it, yeah."

He checked his watch. "Come on. I'll buy you lunch, and we'll talk about it." So we walked to Jack's on Child Street and kicked the idea around over clam chowder and littlenecks.

"Way things are going, you'll probably clear eighty grand the first year," McCracken said.

"That much?"

"Uh-huh."

"More than I'm making now," I said.

"Yeah, I heard the paper cut everybody down to a four-day week."

"More than I was making before that," I said.

"Really?"

"By a lot."

"Ouch."

"So what's your medical plan?" I asked.

"Don't get shot."

"Dental?"

"Don't get shot in the mouth."

"Retirement?"

"Buy lottery tickets."

"Good plans. What about parental leave

policy?"

"Don't have kids."

"I guess that about covers it," I said.

"So how about it?"

"I love being a reporter," I said.

"I know you do."

"But the paper is failing."

"So I keep hearing."

"I can't see myself working in TV."

" 'Course not. You're not pretty enough."

"Not dumb enough, either," I said.

"Maybe you could start a blog or something."

"Know anybody who makes a living doing that?"

"No."

"Me either."

"Tell me again what you like about reporting," he said.

"I like sticking my nose in other people's business," I said. "And then I like telling everybody in the state what I find out."

"As a P.I.," he said, "you'd still be sticking your nose in other people's business, but you'd have to keep your mouth shut about it."

"Half the satisfaction for twice the money," I said. "Not a bad trade-off, I guess."

"Want to stick it out at the *Dispatch* a

while longer?"

"I think so."

"Then let's revisit this in a few months," he said. "There's no rush."

"Thanks," I said. Before I left, I remembered to ask him if he'd talk to Parisi. He said he would.

It was after three by the time I hit the road for Providence. I'd just pulled onto the Wampanoag Trail when "Bitch" started playing on my cell phone. I let it go to voice mail, but she called three more times in two minutes, so I pulled to the side of the road and dug the phone out of my pants pocket.

"Mulligan."

"Hi. It's Dorcas."

"I know who it is."

"How are you?"

"I'm fine."

"You sure? I've been reading your stories about all the murders. It must be horrible for you."

Dorcas being civil? This was new.

"Hey," I said, "it keeps me on the front page."

"Well, that's something, I guess."

"It is."

"Well . . . uh, I've got something to tell you."

"Yes?"

393

"I've been seeing somebody."

Seeing somebody? Must mean she finally went to a psychiatrist. To be this nice to me, she had to be on some heavy meds.

"Who?" I asked.

"His name is Doug, and he's really sweet. Treats me like a queen."

Oh. "How nice for you."

"He's an older guy, owns his own construction business."

"I see."

"Are you okay with this? I was afraid you might take it hard."

"I'm happy for you, Dorcas."

"You are?"

"Yeah, sure."

"Mulligan?"

"What?"

"He's asked me to marry him."

"Congratulations."

"Doug's doing real well, so I won't be needing alimony after all."

"That's good to hear."

"So I was kind of hoping you'd be willing to expedite the divorce."

"Sure thing."

"You can have the house if you want it."

"I don't," I said. "I wouldn't be able to make the payments."

"You could sell it."

"The housing market has collapsed, Dorcas. Selling it could take a long time, and it probably would go for less than we owe on it."

"You want me to keep it, then?"

"Yes, I do."

"Okay. I'll have my lawyer draw up the papers."

"Good."

"You think you could sign them right away? We want to get married next month."

"I can do that."

"Thank you."

"You bet."

"You're sure you're okay with this?"

"I'll survive."

"Well, okay, then. Good-bye."

"Good-bye, Dorcas."

As I clicked off, I had the fleeting thought that I should warn poor deluded Doug; but I stifled it. I pulled back onto the road, cranked the prostitution playlist up loud, and sang along with the music. At one point I think I may have shouted, "Yippie!" But as I crossed the bridge over the Providence River, I felt suddenly deflated.

The witch was getting married again. How come I didn't have somebody?

50

Lomax stripped Mason's story across page
one on Sunday, and it caused an immediate
sensation. Preachers denounced the governor and the state legislature from the pulpit.
The governor, in turn, denounced the paper
for spreading the lie that he'd taken money
from a pornographer — and then promised
to return it. The Sword of God, assault rifles
at port arms, picketed the governor's Mc-
Mansion in Warwick, chanting, "Little
Rhody is not for sale" — a slogan that
couldn't have been more inaccurate. Fiona
announced a criminal investigation and
demanded immediate passage of her bill
outlawing prostitution. All the national TV
networks trumpeted the story. CNN embel-
lished its coverage with a hastily prepared
feature on Rhode Island corruption through
the ages, complete with video of a dozen
mayors, judges, and state legislators being
led away in handcuffs. FOX News dressed

up its report with spy camera video of half-naked hookers cavorting inside the Tongue and Groove. And a good time was had by all.

On Tuesday, the judiciary committees sent Fiona's bill to the floors of the house and senate. Wednesday morning, the house passed it by a vote of 72–2 with one abstention, and that afternoon, the senate approved it by a vote of 38–0. Thursday morning, the governor signed it into law. And that evening, Fiona went on television to crow that "the shameful era of legalized prostitution in Rhode Island is over" and to hint that she was considering a run for governor. I had to squint to be sure, but I think she was wearing makeup.

Next morning, the *Dispatch*'s editors huddled to discuss whether the newspaper should continue to refer to Fiona as "Attila the Nun." Lomax was in favor, calling the appellation colorful and instantly recognizable. The fuddy-duddy copydesk chief was opposed, saying it was now technically inaccurate. As the debate heated up, I could hear their raised voices through the closed conference room door.

The new law made prostitution a misdemeanor punishable by six months in prison, a one-thousand-dollar fine, or both, and it applied equally to hookers and their johns. The strip clubs were given just a week to clean up their act, and Mayor Carroza vowed that the Providence Police Department would be vigilant in enforcing it. So the night the law went live, I decided to check it out.

There were only a dozen cars in the parking lot at the Tongue and Groove. Inside, I found Joseph DeLucca chugging a beer at the bar. He wiped the foam from his upper lip with the tail of his Hawaiian shirt as I sat beside him.

"What are you doing here?" I asked. "I thought you got promoted."

"That's only for when the ex-SEALs are out of town."

"Oh. Too bad."

"Not really. I like this job better."

"How come?"

"Free beer and pussy."

As my eyes adjusted to the dark, I spotted several bullet holes from slugs that had gone wide of King Felix's nervous triggerman. I looked around and saw only six girls and a handful of customers in the place.

"Slow night?" I said.

"Thank God," he said. "I need the breather."

"How do you mean?"

"It's been fuckin' nuts in here the last week. Guys in a panic about the new law showed up in droves. All the regulars, half the student bodies of URI and PC, busloads of horny bastards from Boston, Hartford, and Worcester. All of 'em desperate to legally screw a hooker one last time. And don't even ask me about last night. It was *un-fuckin'-believable!*"

"Tell me more."

"By nine o'clock I counted four hundred guys in here, which is fifty over the legal limit, and there were more outside trying to force their way in. I put the other bouncer on the door, told him not to let anyone else in until somebody came out. That left me alone on the inside, and it wasn't pretty."

"How so?"

"Four hundred horny guys and forty hookers? You do the fuckin' math."

"Fistfights?"

"A couple, yeah. And a whole lot of pushin' and shovin'."

"That how you got the shiner?"

"Uh-huh."

"You got only ten private rooms here, right?"

"Right."

"How'd that work out?"

"Would have had a fuckin' riot, we hadn't

let the girls straddle guys reverse cowgirl at the cocktail tables. Shoulda been here, Mulligan. It was one hell of a party."

"But it's all over now," I said.

"No, not really."

"How do you mean?"

"Business will pick up again once word gets around."

"What word?" I asked.

"Hang around for a while and you'll see for yourself." He waved the bartender over and asked him to bring us a couple of Buds.

"How's the leg?" I asked.

"Healed up good as new."

We were watching a Hispanic girl with a strawberry birthmark on her ass hump a stripper pole when a tall brunette in a G-string and nothing else pranced up and rubbed her palm against the front of my jeans.

"I'm Caramel. What's your name?"

"They call me Mulligan."

"Want to have some fun with Caramel tonight, Mulligan?"

What I thought was that Marical would be even more fun, but what I said was: "I heard all the fun ended last night."

"You heard wrong."

"Yeah?"

"Why don't we find a dark corner where I

can suck your cock? Or if you want, we can get a private room, and you can fuck me."

The complimentary card for a trip around the world was still in my wallet. I wondered if I was the only one who heard it singing. It crooned the chorus to "Bad Girl" and segued into the opening verse of "Honky Tonk Women."

I met a gin-soaked barroom queen in Memphis . . .

"Sorry, Caramel. I think I'll just sit here and watch the show."

"You sure?"

"I am."

"If you change your mind, just call out my name, okay?"

"Sure thing," I said.

She spun on her stilettos and was gone.

"What's up with that?" I asked Joseph.

"Just business as usual."

"What about the law?"

"What about it?"

I thought about it for half a second. "When the governor and the state legislators stop taking your money," I said, "you pay off the cops."

"Mulligan," he said, "you never heard that from me."

51

Maybe it was because I'd gone so long without sex, but today Vanessa Maniella looked especially enticing in a tight cashmere sweater that showed off the swell of her breasts and a short gray skirt that displayed a fine pair of legs.

"Thanks for agreeing to meet me," she said.

"You're welcome."

"I thought it was time we got to know each other better."

"Of course you did. My boyish charm is hard to resist."

"I didn't mean it that way."

"No?"

"I'm not into men."

"Oh."

"Sorry to disappoint."

"Don't tell my achy breaky heart."

"Billy Ray Cyrus?"

"Yeah, but he wrote it about me."

We were seated at a table for two in the Cheesecake Factory at the Providence Place Mall. Outside the plate glass window, I could see Black Shirt, or maybe it was Gray Shirt, keeping an eye on us from a Hummer that was parked illegally on the street.

Before I could ask Vanessa what she really wanted, the waiter arrived to take our drink orders, a pineapple mojito for her and a club soda for me.

"On the wagon? I thought you'd be celebrating."

"And why would I be doing that?"

"Your story about our campaign contributions is getting a lot of attention," she said.

"It is, but my sidekick, Mason, did most of the work."

"Bet the two of you are heroes at the *Dispatch* these days."

"Oh, yeah. They're erecting a statue of us in the lobby."

"Probably win one of those big journalism prizes, too," she said.

"No way. They always go to long, boring five-part series that no one ever reads — except, of course, for the poor bastards who have to edit them. Dave Barry, the humor columnist, says newspapers should stop publishing them — that they should just write them up and submit them for prizes.

He figures that would save enough trees for a new national park."

"Maybe they could call it the Pulitzer Forest," Vanessa said.

"That's just what Dave Barry said."

"Well, your story certainly impressed me," she said. "I thought we'd done a pretty good job of covering our tracks."

"You had."

"That's why my father and I want you to come to work for us. We need someone with your abilities."

"And how would I be using them, exactly?"

"To find other people who are good at covering their tracks."

"What people?"

"We can't get into that until you agree to take the job."

"Pig in a poke," I said.

"You'd be digging up dirt on some bad people, Mulligan. And we can pay you a hundred K to start."

"Would I have to wear a tie?"

"Wear whatever you want."

No way I would ever work for the Maniellas, but I allowed myself a moment to dream on what a hundred grand a year would buy. More vintage blues records. A better sound system to play them on. An apartment with no cracks in the plaster. A Ford Mustang to replace Secretariat. Name it Citation, maybe. Or better yet, Seabiscuit.

"So what do you say?" she said.

"I'm thinking about it." I wondered if the new Mustang came in yellow.

"I think you'd like the fringe benefits," she said.

"Dental?"

"No, but the women at my clubs would be available to you whenever you wanted them."

"Ah."

"One of the girls at Shakehouse looks a lot like Yolanda," she said. And then she winked.

"Yum," I said.

"Use that complimentary card I sent you?"

"I haven't."

"Really?" she said, her eyes widening in surprise.

"Really."

"Why not?"

"I don't know. Maybe I've got some scruples I didn't realize I still had."

"Need some more time to think about the job?"

"I do," I said, hoping I could learn more by stringing her on.

"Okay, but don't take too long. Our offer won't last forever."

The waiter arrived to replenish our drinks, rattle off the specials, and take our orders. She asked for the Chinese chicken salad. I ordered the club sandwich.

"So, Mulligan," she said, "how long before the *Dispatch* goes out of business?"

"Don't know. A couple of years, maybe."

"Dad's been reading your stuff online. He says you don't write well enough to hook on with a slick magazine or make a living writing books."

"I'm afraid he's right about that."

"What will you do if you don't take our offer?"

"No idea."

"Public relations?"

"Christ, I hope not. I'd rather dig graves than write press releases for Textron or flack for the governor."

Vanessa shook her blond tresses and giggled. "Scruples suck, don't they?"

"They do. I've tried to run them off, but they keep crawling back."

The entrées arrived, and we both dug in.

"You said you wanted us to get to know each other," I said. "Is that a two-way street?"

"Got some questions about me, do you?"

"I do."

"So ask them."

"How come you live with your parents?"

"I didn't always. In my twenties, I was married for a couple of years, but that didn't work out. For obvious reasons. I moved back home, and I've been living there ever since."

"Doesn't cramp your style?"

"I've got my own entrance. My lifestyle isn't an issue with Mom and Dad. And our main office is in the house, so my daily commute is a ten-second walk down the stairs."

"What's it like being a woman who runs a business that exploits women?"

"It doesn't."

"Come again?"

"I know you've been in our clubs, Mulligan. Have you watched the girls interact with the customers?"

"Sure."

"The way they flirt to get the men to spend money on them?"

"I've watched them grind on laps and stick boobs in faces. Had it done to me once or twice, too, but it didn't occur to me to call it 'flirting.' "

"And who do you think is being exploited in these situations?"

"Ah," I said. "I see what you mean."

"There's always gonna be prostitution, Mulligan. As long as men have cash and women have pussies. Some of the girls do it because it's easier than working for a living. Some do it because it's the only way they *have* of making a living. We give them a safe, clean place to work. They get free medical checkups once a month. And we protect them from street pimps who would abuse them, hook them on heroin, and take most of their money."

"You make it sound like a public service."

Vanessa sighed and ran her finger around the rim of her empty cocktail glass.

"Dad and I talked about closing the clubs after Attila the Nun's bill passed," she said. "The money they bring in really isn't worth the hassle. But then we thought about what would happen to the girls if we closed up shop."

"King Felix would happen," I said.

"And a dozen more like him, yeah. So we decided to stay open."

"By paying off the cops," I said.

"Can you prove that?"

"Not yet, but I bet I could if I tried."

"Then don't try," she said.

"What about the pornography business?" I said. "Nobody being exploited there, either?"

"It's pretty much the same as with the clubs, except for one thing."

"What's that?"

"With porn, the men aren't exploited, either. They get laid *and* paid."

"A perfect world," I said.

"Smart-ass."

"I can't help it. It's genetic."

"Then I'll try to make allowances."

"So how does child porn fit into this perfect world?"

"It doesn't."

"Never dabbled in that?"

"Of course not. It's an abomination."

"Never cut up any little kids and fed them to Cosmo Scalici's pigs?"

"And we were having such a nice conversation up till now, Mulligan. I can't believe you would ask me that."

The waiter cleared away our plates and took our dessert orders. Vanessa ordered the chocolate tower truffle cake. I asked for another club soda.

"While you're mulling our job offer," Vanessa said, "do you think you could refrain from poking into my family's business?"

"Hard to say."

"I could have the ex-SEALs pay you another visit."

"Wouldn't do any good," I said.

"Yeah," she said. "I kinda figured that."

52

"The Maniellas offered me a job," I said.

"Doing what?" Lomax said.

"They were a little vague about that."

"I've seen you in the shower at the Y, so it can't be on-camera work."

"Fuck you."

"What's it pay?"

"A hundred grand to start."

"Then if you don't want it, I'll take it."

"This could be our chance to find out what the hell is going on," I said.

"How do you mean?"

"I take the job undercover, see what I can learn from the inside."

"No way."

"Why not?"

"Because we don't do things that way. You know that."

"Maybe we should reconsider."

"Uh-uh. These things always go badly. ABC's undercover investigation of the Food

411

Lion grocery chain ended up costing them a fortune in legal bills. We don't tell lies in order to report the truth, Mulligan."

53

A mystery that began with a single murder more than five months ago now had tentacles that stretched from Newport's scenic Cliff Walk to a bloody bedroom in the Chad Brown housing project, from a Pascoag pig farm to a bullet-riddled strip club in Providence. It had taken the lives of an ex–navy SEAL, three snuff film producers, a Brown University dean, a New Jersey child porn aficionado, and a pedophile priest in Michigan. I didn't give a shit about any of them, but it had also snuffed out an uncertain number of children.

I'd gotten some page one stories out of it, but I still didn't know what the hell was going on. I decided to take another stab in the dark.

A half hour on Google turned up several dozen charities dedicated to finding missing children and protecting them from sexual predators: the Polly Klaas, Amber Watch,

Bring Sean Home, Child Alert, Tommy, and Molly Bish Foundations, the National Child Safety Council, and a bunch more. Most were organized as 501(c)(3) charities. That meant the names of their benefactors were a matter of public record.

As it turned out, Sal Maniella had donated money to five of them — more than three million dollars over the last ten years. His daughter, Vanessa, had contributed another quarter of a million. I wondered why. I figured the easiest way to find out would be to ask them, so I called the lake house and got them both on speaker.

"Your numbers are correct," Sal said, "but is it necessary to put this in the paper? We understand that it's public information, but we prefer to keep a low profile."

"That's right," Vanessa said. "We don't want every bleeding heart on the planet hitting us up for a donation."

"I understand that," I said, "but can't help wondering why you are so generous with this particular cause."

"Because it's a worthy one," Sal said.

"Well, sure, but so are the Jimmy Fund and the American Red Cross. Is there some personal motivation behind these donations?"

"Personal reasons are, by definition,

personal," Vanessa said.

"Were either of you abducted or molested as children?"

"Absolutely not," Sal said.

"Any members of your family?"

"No."

"So I'm supposed to believe that the state's top madam and one of the country's biggest smut peddlers just happen to have a soft spot for kids?"

"There's no need to insult us, Mulligan," Maniella said. "Haven't I always treated you with respect?"

"You have," I said. "I apologize for my choice of words. I would defend their accuracy, but perhaps they were unnecessarily indelicate."

"I accept your apology," Sal said.

But Vanessa had the last word: "Go fuck yourself, Mulligan."

Wednesday afternoon, I pointed Secretariat north toward the Bryant University campus in the bedroom community of Smithfield. Back in 1966, when the school granted Sal Maniella his business degree, it was called Bryant College and operated out of a handful of antiquated buildings in Providence. I found the 1966 yearbook in the library's reference room and flipped through the pages of sports and club pictures in the back, scanning the captions.

Sal showed up in two action shots of the basketball team. In the first one he was in the background, sitting on the bench as the team's star forward let a jump shot fly. In the second one he was leaping in the air, celebrating the final win of the team's undefeated season under coach Tom Duffy. The Bryant Indians — later renamed the Bulldogs in a bow to political correctness — won the NAIA national championship that year. I'd had no idea Sal had been on the team.

I flipped to the page with the formal team group photo and got another surprise. Dante Puglisi, Sal's dearly departed double, was in it, his arm draped over Sal's shoulder. I hadn't realized the two went that far back. I copied down the names of all seventeen players, returned the yearbook to its shelf, and asked the reference librarian for directions to the alumni office.

"I don't understand," Paloma McGregor, the alumni director, said. "Why are you interested in the 1966 men's basketball team?"

"Because they won the NAIA national championship."

"What's the NAIA?"

"Sort of like the NCAA, but for really small colleges."

"We're in the NCAA now, Division Two," she said.

"I know."

"Nineteen sixty-six was a long time ago," she said.

"Forty-four years."

"Before my time," she said, but I already knew that. I put her at thirty, with a trim body and a wild mane of black hair that a few guys were probably still lost in. A dancer's legs flashed beneath the hem of her black pencil skirt.

"Before my time, too," I said.

"You're a *news* reporter," she said. "Why do you care about ancient history?"

"Next year marks the forty-fifth anniversary of the only national championship in Bryant history. I thought it would be a good idea to contact the members of the team and write a tribute for the *Dispatch*."

"Oh, that *is* a good idea," she said. "And you want my help with contact information?"

"I do."

She turned to her computer and tapped on the keyboard, red talons flashing.

"Ronald Amarillo and Dante Puglisi are

deceased," she said. "Of the remaining fifteen, I have addresses for eleven and telephone numbers for six, but I can't be sure how much of this is current."

She clicked her mouse, and a laser printer hummed and spit out a sheet of white paper. She folded it in threes, slipped it into a white business envelope with the Bryant logo on it, and handed it across the desk to me.

"If there's anything else I can help you with, don't hesitate to call," she said, flashing a smile that made me want to know her better. She was so pleasant and helpful that I felt guilty about deceiving her. Maybe I'd have to write a story about the team after all.

That afternoon and all the next morning, I worked the phones. I learned that the team's star forward had suffered a stroke and was living in a nursing home in Pawtucket. But the starting center and shooting guard were both well and living in Rhode Island, and they were still the best of friends. They remembered Maniella as a slow-footed forward who was a tiger on the boards; but, no, they'd never hung out with him, and they never got to know him well. The phone numbers and addresses for a couple of bench players turned out to be no good, and I couldn't find any listings for them in the Internet telephone directories. It was nearly noon when I called the Brockton, Massachusetts, telephone number for Joseph Pavao, who had been the team's starting point guard.

"Of course I remember Sal," he said. "He, Dante Puglisi, and I roomed together. We were darn near inseparable back in the day — working out, drinking, chasing skirts. Even cracked a book or two every now and then."

"Did you hear what happened to Dante?"

"Yeah. A damn shame. Cops catch the guy who did it?"

"Not yet, but they're still looking."

He agreed to meet me at nine the next morning at a Brockton coffee shop creatively named Tea House of the Almighty. He was already there, pouring a whole lot of sugar into his mug of black coffee, when I walked in and sat down across from him.

"Nice place," I said.

"I like it."

"The Almighty ever show up to check the till?"

"He never shows his face, but I sense his presence every day."

I put him at five feet ten, with stringy

arms, a sunken chest, and a bowling ball–size potbelly. He wore a red plaid work shirt with a gold cross showing at the neck and a green baseball cap with the words "World's Best Grandpa" above the bill. It was hard to imagine him as an athlete.

"Tell me more about you, Sal, and Dante," I said.

"The three of us were wicked sinners. Drunk out of our skulls or high on marijuana most of the time, 'cept on game days, and copulating with every girl what would let us. Being as we were big men on campus, a lot of 'em did."

"Good times," I said.

"Sure thing, if hell's what you're aiming for. After college I found Jesus and got over the wildness. I guess Sal and Dante never did."

"The way I heard it, Sal got his start in the pornography business when he was still at Bryant."

"You heard right," he said. "Sal shot most of the pictures for his skin magazine in our dorm room. He'd smoke a little weed with a girl and then get her to pose naked on his bed. Sometimes he'd bring in two or three at the same time and talk 'em into pleasuring each other, if you know what I mean."

"I do."

420

"Sal let Dante and me help out with the lighting, not that he needed the help. It was just an excuse so's we could watch. Afterward, we'd all get to drinking, and sometimes the girl would sleep with one of us. Couple of 'em took on all three of us, God forgive me."

"Were any of the girls underage?"

"I don't believe so. Sal was real careful about that, always checking ID to make sure they were at least eighteen. He got real righteous about it after what happened to Dante's little sister."

"Tell me about that."

"Awful thing. She was just eight years old when it happened."

"When was this?"

"Our junior year. Dante turned white as a sheet when he got the news over the telephone. He put down the receiver, curled up in his bed, and cried like a baby. Sal got down on his knees at the bedside and held on to him until Dante stopped blubbering and told us what was wrong."

"Which was what, exactly?"

"Some animal grabbed her off the playground near her house. The cops found her tied to a tree the next day, raped and beaten, but still breathing, thank the Lord."

"Where was this?"

"In New Haven, Dante's hometown."

"The cops catch the guy?"

"They figured out who did it all right, but they didn't have enough evidence to charge him. Left his DNA all over her, I imagine, but they didn't know about that stuff back then."

"Dante must have been pretty angry about it."

"All three of us were."

"You do anything about it?"

"I probably shouldn't talk about that."

"Dante's sister. What was her name?"

"Rachel," he said. "Rachel Elizabeth Puglisi."

"Know where she is now?"

"Dead."

"What happened?"

"Way I heard it, she seemed to recover from the attack; but sometime after she turned thirteen, she found the tree she'd been tied to and hanged herself from it, God rest her soul."

54

The *New Haven Register*'s Web site didn't include archives, so I called the paper and was told that its news library had never digitized them. Still worse, all its paper clippings from the 1960s and 1970s had been discarded. Fortunately, the city's public library had all of the old newspapers on microfiche.

Friday, the deputy sports editor called in sick so he could interview with ESPN, and I got stuck editing basketball game stories and laying out sports pages all day. It was Saturday before I could saddle up Secretariat and make the two-hour drive to New Haven. When Secretariat was younger, he could have done it in an hour and a half.

An attendant in the public library's reading room set me up with a microfiche reader. "It's not often that somebody asks for these old newspaper files," she said, "but you're the second one in the last few weeks."

"Who was the other one?"

"I didn't get her name."

"What did she look like?"

She frowned and shook her head. "I'm sorry," she said, "but I can't help you with that. We respect people's privacy here."

I started with the September 1, 1966, edition of the *Register,* began scrolling, and immediately got caught up in it.

Red Guards were on the rampage in China.

Senator Charles Percy's twenty-one-year-old daughter was found stabbed and bludgeoned in the family mansion on Chicago's North Shore.

A new TV show called *Star Trek,* starring a former Shakespearean actor named William Shatner, debuted on NBC.

Scotland Yard arrested Buster Edwards and charged him with masterminding the Great Train Robbery.

President Lyndon Johnson visited American troops in Vietnam.

The Baltimore Orioles swept the Los Angeles Dodgers to win their first World Series ever.

Edward Brooke of Massachusetts became the first black U.S. senator since Reconstruction.

A B-movie actor named Ronald Reagan

was elected governor of California.

Dr. Sam Sheppard, on trial for murdering his pregnant wife, was acquitted.

The Beatles went into seclusion to record a new album; according to record industry gossip, the working title was *Sergeant Pepper's Lonely Hearts Club Band.*

Stop it, I told myself. *If you keep this up, you'll be sitting here for a month.*

Ninety minutes after I started, I spotted a one-column headline at the bottom of page one in the October 30 edition:

Girl, 8, Raped and Left Tied to Tree

New Haven — An 8-year-old city girl who was abducted from a playground near her home 12 hours earlier was found tied to a tree about a hundred yards from the Pardee Rose Garden in East Rock Park yesterday morning, New Haven police said.

Police said she was rushed to Yale–New Haven Hospital, where she was listed in fair condition with a broken nose, a fractured left arm, and multiple abrasions and contusions. A hospital examination determined that the girl had been raped, police said.

Police detectives were still in the park

late yesterday afternoon collecting evidence.

Out of consideration for the family, the story didn't mention her name.

I kept scrolling. Over the next few months, occasional updates appeared on inside pages:

Police Vow to Find Girl's Attacker
Hamden Man Questioned in Child Rape
Police Arrest Child-Rape Suspect
Child-Rape Suspect Released, Police Cite Lack of Evidence
Child Rape Case Still Open

Then nothing until April 3, when the following appeared:

Child Molester Beaten

New Haven — Alfred V. Furtado, 44, of 62 Evergeen Ave., Hamden, a convicted child molester, was found naked and tied to a tree in East Rock Park yesterday afternoon. Police said he had been savagely beaten.

He was taken to Yale–New Haven Hospital, where he was reported in serious condition with a fractured skull.

Police said he also suffered two fractured kneecaps and a broken eye socket. His nose, left clavicle, and five of his fingers were also reported broken, and his sex organs had been mutilated with a sharp object, police said. A baseball bat and a hunting knife recovered beside the tree may have been used in the attack, police said.

Furtado was found tied to the same tree that had been used to bind an 8-year-old New Haven girl after she was beaten and raped last October, police said. They added they are exploring the possibility that the two crimes are linked.

Furtado was initially arrested in connection with the attack on the girl, but he was subsequently released for lack of evidence. Police said he has a criminal record that includes public lewdness and molestation, and that he served 7 years of his 15-year sentence for the violent rape of a 10-year-old East Haven girl in 1957.

When I walked out of the library, it was after seven P.M. and raining. I dashed to Secretariat and drove home in the dark. I parked illegally on the street outside near my apartment, trudged up the stairs, shrugged off my damp clothes, and stepped into the shower. I stood under the hot water for a long time. It took the chill off but didn't do much to wash away the day. Maybe talking about it would help.

"Hi, Yolanda. It's Mulligan."

"Hi, baby. You okay? You sound weary."

"That I am."

"Tough day?"

"Tough year. Uh . . . listen, I know it's on the late side, but I wonder if you'd like to have a nightcap. Maybe grab a little something to eat somewhere."

"Sorry, but I can't."

"No?"

"No."

"Okay, then."

"Mulligan?"

"Yeah?"

"I've started seeing somebody."

"Oh."

"He teaches chemistry at Brown, and he's a really great guy."

"What's he got that I don't?"

"You know."

"Oh, that."

"Can't say I didn't warn you."

"No, I can't. . . . He's there now, isn't he?"

"Uh-huh."

"Well, I better let you go, then."

"Still friends?"

"Always," I said.

" 'Night, Mulligan."

"Good night, Yolanda."

So what. I'd been shot down by women before. Short ones and tall ones. Plump and skinny. Blondes, brunettes, and redheads. White, black, and yellow. Schoolteachers, barmaids, reporters, secretaries, and college professors. Most times, I'd shaken it off with a shot of Bushmills and a good night's sleep. This was one of those other times. This time, I felt blue drop over me like a shroud.

I pulled on jeans and a sweatshirt, zipped a windbreaker over it, tromped down the stairs, and stepped out into the rain. It was coming down harder now, but I didn't care. Like a batter who'd been drilled in the ribs with a fastball, I needed to walk it off. I sloshed two blocks north on America Street and turned right. The bars and restaurants on Atwells Avenue beckoned, but I wasn't in the mood for food, light, or company that wasn't Yolanda. I walked east to DePasquale, turned right, and trudged past a long row of triple-deckers and rooming houses all the way to Broadway. There I turned right, walked to the corner of America Street, and turned back toward home.

Outside my apartment, Secretariat shivered in the rain. I climbed in, wrung the wet from my hair, and fired the engine. The drive to Swan Point Cemetery took fifteen minutes. I thought about leaving the Manny Ramirez jersey in the car, not wanting to get it wet, but on a night like this, Rosie would welcome what little warmth it could provide. I draped it over the shoulders of her gravestone, sat in the mud, and rested my back against the cold granite.

"Evening, Rosie. How are you tonight?"

The same. Rosie was always the same now.

"Me? I've been better. . . . Yeah, it's about that lawyer I've been seeing. Remember me telling you that as long as she didn't say, 'Let's just be friends,' I still had a chance?"

Rosie always remembered everything.

"Well, tonight, she finally said it."

55

"I'm confused."

"What about?" Fiona asked.

"Sex and religion."

"Oh, that."

"Yeah."

"Welcome to the club."

"You too?" I asked.

"About religion, sure. Sex? Not so much."

We were sitting at opposite ends of a brown leather couch in her parlor, she with a calico cat in her lap and I with a rolled-up copy of the *Dispatch* in my left hand. An autographed photo of Fiona getting a peck on the cheek from Barack Obama stood on the mantel in the spot where a photo of Joseph Ratzinger in his white-mitered, post–Hitler Youth incarnation used to be. The log fire she'd lit when we came in from the cold had burned low. The red coals hissed and popped.

"Vanessa Maniella gave me the 'oldest

profession' speech," I said.

"Let me guess," Fiona said. "She claims prostitution is older than the Bible, that women have a right to sell their bodies, and that all she's been doing is providing them with a clean, safe place to do it."

"Pretty much," I said, "although somehow she made it seem a little more convincing."

"Taking your moral guidance from a madam now?"

"Better her than Reverend Crenson. Besides, my old confessor Father Donovan is no longer handy. The bishop shipped his pedophile ass off to Woonsocket."

"There are other priests."

"I prefer a lifelong friend to a stranger in a white collar."

She took a deep breath and let it out in a long sigh. "There's no denying that prostitution is as old as mankind," she said, "but so are stealing, abortion, and murder."

I didn't want to get sidetracked by the abortion argument, so what I said was, "I see your point."

"I've seen how troubled you are by the child porn you've been exposed to," she said.

"What's that have to do with prostitution? Men who lust after children have no interest in grown women."

"It all flows from the same sewer," she said. "The commercialization of sex debases and dehumanizes us all. It leads people to think of one another as pieces of meat instead of creatures with immortal souls."

I must have looked doubtful because she added, "And if you don't believe that, there's always 'Thou shalt not commit adultery.' "

"Says who?"

"I can't believe you just said that."

"As I understand it," I said, "those words were written three thousand years ago by the Hebrew elder of a tribe that treated women as property."

She shook her head sadly and fell silent for a moment. When she spoke again, it was in a whisper.

"I don't deny that my faith in the church has been shaken," she said. "The doctrine of papal infallibility is tyrannical bullshit. The church's medieval views on AIDS and contraception have gotten thousands of people killed. The bishops who protected pedophile priests for decades are fucking criminals. If I had the balls, I'd indict the sons of bitches. But I've never turned away from the Word of God."

"Good for you, Fiona," I said. "Good for you."

56

"The publisher specifically requested you, Mulligan," Lomax said.

"How come?"

"Apparently he liked the way you handled the Derby Ball story last September. Besides, this soiree is right up your alley."

"How so?"

"It's a fund-raiser for the Milk Carton Crusade."

"What the hell's that?"

"Another one of those groups dedicated to finding missing children."

"What's the publisher's interest?"

"I gather he's a contributor."

"Do I have to wear a monkey suit again?"

"You can put in for it."

"Hotel?"

"No. We need to keep expenses to a minimum. You can drive down and back the same night, or if you want you can stay at Mason's place. He already offered."

So Tuesday night after work, I found myself riding shotgun in Mason's restored 1967 E-Type Series 1 Jaguar as it zoomed over Narragansett Bay on the Jamestown Verrazzano Bridge, Providence a cold glance over our shoulders.

"Hungry?" he asked.

"I could eat something."

So he slipped down a few side streets and parked in front of the White Horse Tavern.

"It's on me," Mason said as we settled into a booth; so I ordered the prime tenderloin beef appetizer and the butter-poached New England lobster, the most expensive items on the menu. For Mason it was the White Horse clam chowder and the chanterelle mushroom risotto. He ordered wine; I wanted beer but figured it was safer to stick with water.

"Still no developments on the missing girl?" he asked.

"Julia Arruda?"

"Uh-huh."

"Not even a whisper."

"Think she's dead?"

"I don't know, Thanks-Dad."

"You've been looking down lately, Mulligan. Are you okay?"

"Never better."

"The fund-raiser doesn't start till eight

tomorrow night, so you can sleep in."

"That would be my plan."

"So what do you say we do the town tonight?"

"I'm not really in the mood."

"Come on, Mulligan. We can hit the Landing or the Boom Boom Room, have a few drinks, maybe get lucky with a couple of Salve Regina coeds out for a good time."

"I'm too damn old for coeds. I'd rather go to your place, watch *CSI: Miami,* and turn in early."

Mason still lived on the family estate off Ocean Drive, where he had his own apartment with a separate entrance. Once inside, he opened a couple of bottles of Orval, a Belgian beer I'd never heard of, and joined me on a black leather couch in front of a huge flatscreen. As the *CSI: Miami* theme began to play, I told my gut to shut up and took a sip.

"Why do you watch this show?" Mason said. "It sucks."

I pointed at the screen and said, "Because of this part right here."

David Caruso, aka Lieutenant Horatio Caine, stared at a naked, impossibly tanned young woman floating facedown in an impossibly blue swimming pool. He slowly raised both of his hands, gripped his sunglasses at the hinges, and ever so slowly slid them off his pasty, pocked face. He studied the girl some more and grimaced as only David Caruso can. Then he raised the sunglasses ever so slowly and, with the deliberation of a surgeon performing laparoscopic liver surgery, slid them on again.

We both laughed.

"He does the same thing every week," I said. "It's his signature move. I wonder if he realizes how ridiculous it looks."

We hung in there for *The Daily Show with Jon Stewart,* but when *The Colbert Report* came on I was ready to turn in. Mason graciously offered me his bed, but I took the couch. Shortly after the lights went out, the little girl with no arms made her nightly appearance. She didn't have anything to say tonight. She just stared down at me and sadly shook her head.

57

Mason drove leisurely down Bellevue Avenue past the fairy-tale castles that the robber barons had built. As we slid by Clarendon Court, I saw Officer Phelps parked in the entrance, keeping a sharp eye out for any reasonably priced, and therefore suspicious, automobiles. I was grateful to be riding in a Jag.

Mason joined the procession of supercharged European carriages heading toward Belcourt Castle, and when we reached its gilded gates, he pulled over to let me out.

"Just call when you want me to pick you up," he said.

"Will do, Thanks-Dad."

Inside the walled courtyard, the same Emperor Penguin was manning the mansion's oaken door. I handed him my invitation, and he checked it against the guest list.

"Things must be looking up," he said.

"You smell better, and you're using your real name."

The spread on the antique walnut trestle table in the vast first-floor dining room wasn't as lavish as the last time, the charity prudent with its donors' money; but the chicken-pecan finger sandwiches tasted good.

I jogged up the winding oak staircase to the vaulted ballroom, where a string ensemble was playing chamber music at a volume low enough to encourage conversation. About three hundred people, the men in black tie and the women in what I took to be this season's designer originals, stood in clusters and murmured.

Beside the huge hearth a larger group, perhaps a dozen people, had gathered around a slim figure with a lion's mane of pewtergray hair. A black pirate's patch covered his right eye. The face resembled one I'd seen on more than a dozen book jackets, but it was grayer and more deeply lined than I remembered, so I couldn't be sure.

Andrew Vachss was the author of a series of novels about a career criminal named Burke who specialized in hunting down pedophiles, ripping them off, and putting them in the ground. Vachss was also a lawyer known for suing child abusers on behalf of their victims with more than the customary courtroom vigor. A decade ago, when the defendant in one of his lawsuits was found dead at the bottom of a New Hampshire quarry, the authorities wondered if Vachss had put him there but they quickly dismissed the idea. The complete text of his statement to the police: "I hope his eyes were open all the way down."

He'd be a great interview for tonight's story — if this were actually him.

I strode over, stood next to the man, waited for a lull in the conversation, and stuck out my right hand. "I'm Mulligan, a reporter for the *Providence Dispatch.* Can I have a few words with you?"

His one good eye slid from my face down to my shoes and slowly back up again. Then he spun on the heels of his black wing tips and turned his back on me. Only then did I notice that Sal Maniella had been in the group around him.

"Was that Andrew Vachss?" I asked.

"If he'd wanted you to know his name," Maniella said, "he'd have told you."

Pressing him wouldn't have gotten me anywhere, so I changed the subject. "Why are you here? Come to make a contribution to the cause?"

"The Milk Carton Crusade was formed by two women from Pittsburgh whose daughters were murdered by the same pedophile two years ago," he said. "The organization doesn't have much of a track record yet, but I thought I'd listen to their pitch."

"Going to hang around and enjoy the Newport nightlife for a few days?"

"No, I don't think so. But before I head back tomorrow, I'm going to go over to the Cliff Walk, say a prayer for Dante, and toss a wreath into the water."

"Don't get too close to the edge," I said. "The rocks are pretty slippery there."

"Given any more thought to coming to work for me?"

"Some."

"Look, why don't you come along tomorrow and show me the spot where Dante was killed? Afterwards I'll buy you breakfast at the coffee house in Washington Square, and we can talk some more about my job offer."

So at nine thirty the next morning I was waiting at the end of Mason's long cobblestoned drive when a black Hummer rolled up and its back door swung open. I climbed in, sat beside Sal, and saw that Black Shirt, or maybe it was Gray Shirt, was behind the wheel. I'd never ridden in one of those monstrosities before. Just sitting in it felt ridiculous.

The ex-SEAL parked illegally near the entrance to the Cliff Walk, plucked a Rhode Island State Police "Official Business" pass from behind the visor, and dropped it on the dash. I didn't ask how he came by it; he probably bought it from the same counterfeiter who sold me mine.

We got out and strolled through the entrance to the Cliff Walk, the ex-SEAL lugging a funeral wreath of hydrangea, chrysanthemums, and gladioli. A light drizzle fell from the steel-gray sky. Below us, fog hugged the surface of the ocean, but I could hear the surf angrily slap the face of the cliff. The footing was treacherous, the wet schist slick beneath our feet. I turned north and led the way. We'd gone about thirty yards when I stopped and studied the rocks.

"This is where it happened," I said.

Sal just stood there for a moment, staring at where the ocean was supposed to be, but in this weather there was nothing to see. Then he bowed his head and prayed:

"God our Father, your power brings us to birth, your providence guides our lives, and by your command we return to —"

It was the kind of rain that muffles sound. I could barely hear the blasts from the

442

foghorn at Castle Hill. Even without the rain, I doubt I could have distinguished between the smacking of the waves and the soft slap of sneakers on wet rock. I didn't know he had come up behind us until I heard the first pop.

58

I spun toward the sound and saw a hand gripping a little nickel revolver. A thin brown finger squeezed the trigger, and the gun popped again.

Slugs fired from cheap little handguns are low-caliber and have a slow muzzle velocity. When they enter the back of a skull, they don't come out the front. They just bounce around inside.

Sal crumpled.

The ex-SEAL dropped the funeral wreath and reached inside the flap of his raincoat.

I grabbed for Sal and missed.

A Glock 17 appeared in the ex-SEAL's hand.

I reached for Sal again.

The Glock cracked, the muzzle flashing in the corner of my eye.

Sal toppled over the edge and vanished in the fog.

I reached for the .45 tucked in the small

of my back, but it wasn't there. It was miles away, hanging on my wall.

The Glock cracked again. The second shot blew the assassin off his feet, the little pistol sailing from his hand and clattering on the rocks. He landed in a broken heap at my feet, blood welling from a hole in his chest. A quarter of his skull was gone, but there was enough left for me to make the ID.

Dying hadn't changed him all that much. Marcus Washington, King Felix's sixteen-year-old gun hand, still had those flat, dead eyes.

The ex-SEAL tucked the Glock back inside his raincoat. "Dumb fuck," he said. "If he'd shot me first, he could have iced all three of us, no problem."

He kicked Marcus savagely with the toe of his boot. Then he unzipped his fly, straddled the corpse, and urinated on it.

I bent down, picked up the funeral wreath, and tossed it into the sea. I was reaching for my cell to dial 911 when the truth hit me with the force of a newspaper bundle heaved from the back of a delivery truck.

59

The Newport cops had some questions for me. Then Parisi wanted his turn. He drove me back to state police headquarters, tucked me away in an interrogation room, and kept me waiting for two hours before coming in to grill me. This time, he didn't confiscate my cell phone; so while I was waiting I called Lomax and fed him details about the murder. When Parisi finally got to me, I answered all of his questions.

But I didn't tell him everything.

By the time he finished with me, it was nearly midnight. I was famished and dead tired. The captain was kind enough to drive me home. I stepped inside my apartment, opened the refrigerator, and found a half quart of milk, two bottles of beer, and a block of cheddar cheese. The milk was sour, so I poured it down the sink. I couldn't remember when I bought the cheese, but it was still yellow and I didn't see anything growing on it. I gnawed the cheese standing up, washed it down with one of the beers, and took the second one into the bedroom. There, I stripped off my clothes and left them where they fell. Then I took my laptop and the beer to bed with me.

Could urine be tested for DNA? I didn't know. I fired up the laptop and started searching for the answer.

When I awoke the next morning, the laptop was still on my belly, the screen dark and the battery dead. Somewhere, Don Henley was singing "Dirty Laundry." For a moment, I thought it was coming from my neighbor's apartment. Then I shook off the cobwebs, got out of bed, picked my jeans off the floor, and plucked the cell from the pocket.

"Mulligan."

"Where the hell are you?" Lomax said. "It's nearly ten, for chrissake."

"I'm fine, thanks," I said. "And how are you?"

"I don't have time for pleasantries, Mulligan. Nice job last night, but I need you to get your ass in here to write Maniella's obit."

"I can do better than that," I said. "Plan on a page one start with a half-page jump inside."

Sunday morning, my long story was stripped across the top of page one:

Salvatore Alonso Maniella, 65, the reclusive Rhode Island pornographer who was murdered in Newport on Thursday, was more than he seemed.

Although he had no scruples about exploiting women for profit, he bore a deep antipathy toward anyone who sexually abused children, the result of a traumatic incident that occurred in his youth. For at least a decade, he secretly contributed millions of dollars to organizations that fought for missing and abused children and their families.

And there is mounting evidence that military-trained assassins in his employ routinely hunted down and killed pedophiles. Among their apparent victims: the three child pornographers who were shot to death in the Chad Brown housing project; a pedophile priest in Fon du Lac, Wis.; a child pornography collector in Edison, NJ; and Dr. Charles Bruce Wayne, the Brown University Medical School dean who had a similar taste in entertainment. All of those killings occurred in the last few months, but there could well have been others.

In a display of contempt, the killers often urinated on their victims, apparently unaware that urine contains traces of DNA that could be used to identify them. . . .

Twenty minutes after the paper hit the streets, Jimmy Cagney's voice screeched from my cell: "You'll never take me alive, copper!"

60

"What the *fuck?*"

"Morning, Captain."

"How the hell did you figure all this out?"

"Remember when Maniella's ex-SEALs trashed the Tongue and Groove ten years ago?"

"I heard about it, yeah."

"When they were done, they pissed on the stripper poles."

"Where'd you get that?"

"From a confidential source."

"Going to tell me who?"

"No."

"And the ex-SEAL who took out Maniella's murderer urinated on the body," he said.

"He did."

"Sounds like you're jumping to an awfully big conclusion."

"There's more."

"What?"

"The Chad Brown murder scene stunk of

urine," I said, "and so did Dr. Wayne's study."

"We figured the victims evacuated when they got shot."

"Maybe they did," I said, "but they weren't the only ones who pissed on your crime scenes."

"I've already ordered DNA testing of the victims' clothing," he said. "That should tell us if you're right."

"I am."

"Why didn't you tell me about this when I questioned you Thursday night?"

"Maybe I just figured it out," I said. "Or maybe it slipped my mind."

"Why didn't you give me a heads-up before the story hit the paper?"

"I guess that slipped my mind, too."

"You really fucked me on this."

"Bullshit. I solved the damn case for you."

"Yeah, but the ex-SEALs are in the wind."

"Maybe I'm okay with that," I said.

"Well, I'm not."

"What about King Felix?" I asked. "Can you put him away for Maniella's murder?"

A five-second delay. "I doubt it. He claims Marcus Washington acted on his own, and the only one who could say different is on a slab in the morgue."

"Think Felix was also behind Dante

Puglisi's murder?"

"I do," he said, "but there's no way to prove that, either."

61

First thing Monday morning, I was awakened again by the sound of Don Henley's thin tenor.

"Mulligan."

"I need you to come in early today," Lomax said.

"Check your schedule. It's my day off."

"You never take a day off."

"Well, I am today."

"It's important."

"Tough shit," I said, and clicked off.

Naturally, he called right back.

"I'll pay overtime."

"Not interested."

"Pieces of another kid have turned up at Scalici's farm," he said.

"Send somebody else."

"I don't have anybody else."

"Not my problem."

"Mulligan?"

"Yeah?"

"The cops think it's Julia Arruda."

The scene at the farm was all too familiar: a small lump under a blue tarp, detectives pawing through a pile of garbage, Parisi inside the farm house talking with Scalici. I took notes, going through the motions, but my heart wasn't in it.

That evening, Parisi called to say his detectives had found some bits of human skull in the garbage. They looked as if they'd been smashed into fragments with a hammer. So much for the mystery of what the child killers were doing with the heads.

62

That evening I found Fiona hunched at her usual table at Hopes, drinking beer with Anne Kotch, an assistant attorney general. I got myself a club soda from the bar, strolled over, and joined them.

"Would you mind giving Mulligan and me a few minutes?" Fiona said, so Anne got up and claimed a stool at the bar.

"I'm glad you showed," Fiona said. "I could use a friendly shoulder."

"How come?"

"I handled the Arruda notification myself."

"Why put yourself through that? The state cops could have done it."

"I owed it to the parents."

"Must have been awful."

"Worse than you know."

Fiona's lower lip quivered, and I noticed then she was wearing lipstick. Her shoulders shook, and she began to weep. I got up, stood behind her chair, wrapped her up in a hug, held her until the shaking stopped, and then sat down again across from her.

"That was one hell of a story yesterday morning," she said.

"Thanks."

"Probably earn you a big journalism prize you can hang on your wall."

"I don't much care about that."

"Well, you should. You earned it. You did a brilliant job figuring everything out."

"Not really," I said. "After all, you figured it out first."

"What are you talking about?"

"You know exactly what I'm talking about."

"Think you know the rest of it, do you?"

"I do."

"Tell me what you think you know."

"You did your own research on Sal weeks ago and learned he was a big donor to child protection groups."

"I might have."

"And you went to the New Haven Public Library, dug into Puglisi's past, and learned what happened to his sister."

"So what if I did?"

"Once you had all that, it wasn't much of a leap to guess Sal was the one behind the hits on the child pornographers."

"Go on."

"It was around that time that I told you my suspicions about Wayne."

"I remember."

"There were only two other people who knew Wayne might be dirty," I said. "One of them was the source I got it from, and I know for a fact he didn't tell anybody else. The other was Wayne's secretary, and she's way too naïve to have done anything with the information."

"So?"

"So after I told you my suspicions, you passed them on to Sal."

"Why would I do that?"

"Because you couldn't touch Wayne legally. You didn't have enough to get a warrant for his computers."

Fiona raised her beer to her lips and discovered the can was empty. I got up, walked to the bar, and fetched her another. She took it from my hand and drank deeply.

"Is Vanessa going to continue her father's crusade?" I asked.

"Let's say I have reason to believe she will."

"Going to hunt down the child pornographers who are still on the loose, is she?"

"And maybe the child porn fans we found

on the computers at Chad Brown," Fiona said.

"The four who haven't been shot yet, you mean."

"Those would be the ones."

"Wow," I said.

Fiona closed her eyes for a moment, and I saw her lips moving. Perhaps she was saying a prayer. When she was done, she rested her arms on the table, leaned forward, and looked into my eyes.

"We live in God's beautiful world," she said, "but there is evil abroad in it. Monsters are hunting our children. I don't seem to be very good at catching them, and neither are the state police. Maybe it's a good thing that there are others who hunt the hunters."

"And do God's murderous work?" I asked.

She didn't have anything to say to that.

"I can't fucking believe this," I said.

"Neither will anybody else, Mulligan. Besides, you can't prove any of it."

"If I worked at it, maybe I could."

"Might be worth it," she said. "It would give you something to hold over the head of the next governor if you ever happen to need a favor."

With that, I got up to go. At the door, I turned back for one last look. Her eyes were stone.

63

It was raining again when I stepped out of the bar and whistled for Secretariat. He didn't come. By the time I tracked him down at an expired meter by Burnside Park, my old Boston Bruins jersey, the one with hockey god Cam Neely's number 8 on it, was sopping. I slumped behind the wheel, tore the fucking thing off, and chucked it into the backseat. Then I cranked the ignition, let the engine idle for a few minutes, snapped the heater on, and felt a blast of cold air. I'd forgotten it had stopped working again three days ago.

I was sick to death of this rotten Rhode Island weather. I watched the rain fall and cursed John Ghiorse, Channel 10's septuagenarian weatherman. Then I cursed God. I stopped cursing when it occurred to me that neither of them had anything to do with it.

I just sat there and listened to the rain tap the roof, thinking about how journalism used to be fun. I remembered how I used to sit courtside at Providence College and Brown University basketball games, stuff my face with hot dogs, and fill my notebook with words that made no mention of severed arms or missing children. I remembered coming to work every day to a newsroom filled with dedicated professionals who were in love with their jobs and never wanted to be anywhere else. I remembered when nearly everyone in the state spent at least a half hour every day reading the paper.

But that was a quarter of a lifetime ago, and those days were never coming back.

I was sick to death of layoffs, buyouts, and forced retirements. I was sick of Fiona's crocodile tears, the pop of small-caliber handguns, and the candied stench of corpses. I was sick of decaf and club soda, of the gnawing in my gut that never completely went away, and of the child with no arms who still haunted my dreams. I was sick of people who found a way to justify murder, and of the undeniable fact that one of those people was me.

I was sick of feeling alone. I needed to wrap myself around somebody. I took out my cell and started to call Yolanda, but she was wrapped around somebody else.

I put the Bronco in gear and drove. I

meant to go home. I really did. But on this night, Secretariat had a will of his own. As he rolled past the Cathedral of Saints Peter and Paul, its brick edifice dark and brooding, I thought about going inside. But I didn't.

A passage from the Book of Job flashed through my mind: "When I looked for light, then came darkness."

Before I knew it, the red-and-blue neon sign on the roof of the Tongue and Groove winked through the drops on my rain-splattered windshield. I pulled into the lot and parked. Joseph had been right. Word had gotten around. The lot was nearly full.

I pulled my wallet from my hip pocket and slid out the card for a complimentary trip around the world. It had been a long time since I'd gone on any kind of trip. I turned on the overhead light and studied Marical's picture. Her tobacco-colored skin was flawless. Her small breasts were enticing. And no hair concealed the paradise between her legs.

The rain fell harder now. It pounded the roof, turning the Bronco's passenger compartment into the inside of a drum. Yet somehow, I could still hear Marical's musical voice.

I show you a good time, beebe. Eef you get

461

wit me, I make you world go round like cray-
see.

I sat there and listened to her say the words over and over for a long, long time.

ACKNOWLEDGMENTS

Susanna Einstein is more than a great agent; she is also a superb story doctor whose suggestions significantly improved this novel. My wife, Patricia Smith, one of our finest poets, edited every line on every page. And thank you, baby, for allowing me to excerpt your poem "Map Rappin'." I also owe a debt of gratitude to the hardworking folks at Forge, including Eric Raab for his skillful edit of the manuscript.